The Tale of Cloran Hastings

Brandon M. Dennis

For Mom.

CONTENTS

PROLOGUE

"Lower the sails!" cried Captain Reuben over the sound of the roaring wind. *Wavegrazer* thrashed violently in the gale as the crew scrambled to lower the sails. The storm had appeared instantly on what was once a calm sea and took the sailors by surprise. The ropes creaked and groaned and a few snapped, and the men struggled frantically. The wind filled the sails, wrenching the ship back and forth. The sea surged onto the deck, knocking a few of them out of the riggings. At last, the main sail was loosed and it fluttered, releasing its wind.

"What did you do to anger the sea?" called Percy to his captain. Reuben held the large green wheel in his hands and strained every muscle, trying to keep it steady.

"She doesn't have to have a reason, boy," shouted Reuben over the din. "She's fickle and jealous and kills irrationally."

A swift moving wave rose suddenly over the bow and crashed down onto the deck, knocking all but Reuben over.

"Everyone get below!" ordered First Mate Cloran. "We can talk about it afterwards." Reuben motioned for Cloran to come. As the other sailors made their way to the door, Cloran struggled towards the wheel.

"This is no natural storm," said Reuben. "She wants me dead this time. I've eluded her for too long."

"Don't be foolish," said Cloran. "We've weathered far greater storms than this. As long as the captain stays at the wheel, we will come through!"

"Look," said Reuben. "The winds are dying down. She knows that she can't get me with the wind. Waves will come now, I know it."

"Cloran! Let's go!" called Len. Most of the men had gone below, but Len and Percy held open the hatch, waiting for their friend. Just then, the ship was lifted and the men felt their hearts sink into their stomachs. The sky crackled with lightning and rain began to pour at a sharp angle. From atop the rolling wave, Reuben could see the expanse of the ocean out before him. For a brief moment, he felt a familiar calm that only the sea-mist gave him, but a great fear soon replaced it. He could feel her anger in the air, and it was directed towards him.

The wave crested and *Wavegrazer* slid awkwardly down its back. Its nose dipped into the ocean and flooded the deck when it bobbed back up. It rocked to port and the men clung to the ship with all of their strength. Water came at them from every direction and Cloran coughed on the salty spray.

"Here she comes," said Reuben calmly, and he looked off towards the horizon. "I'll soon meet a sailor's end. Tonight I'll dine in Old Roper's court."

"Don't say that! What's wrong with you?" cried Cloran.

Suddenly the rain stopped and *Wavegrazer* leveled out. A dark shadow engulfed the ship and Cloran faced the prow. A pillar of water raced towards them. Percy and Len shrieked, but Cloran couldn't even move. The horrible sight paralyzed him, and as the pillar came nigh, he swore that it contorted into the shape of a clawed hand, clenching shut.

"Never tempt the sea," said Reuben in a dead voice.

Cloran faced his captain, whose fierce green eyes pierced his soul. Reuben's hawkish face was deathly pale but his eyes flashed violently. He grabbed Cloran by the collar and shouted into his face.

"Do you hear me Cloran? Never!" he cried, and then the water fell.

CHAPTER ONE

The Lonely King of Menigah

King Bozin lived in the grandest castle of Menigah. He was leader of the entire continent, and his days were peaceful. The years of war and strife between nations were over, and Bozin could rest at ease. His kingdom stretched from the northern shores of Menigah, far into the middle of the continent, and his people were happy.

But Bozin was not happy. He was normally a just and kind ruler, who gave generously to those in need and whose hands were open to all who asked. Recently, however, a dark mood had crept upon him, and he had grown short with his servants and sometimes harsh in his judgments. He found no joy in the daylight. The stars could not cheer him, and the moon soured his disposition. The cause of his melancholy was his loneliness. His wife was long gone, separated from him by her death during the terror years of the Noths. His daughter Celeste had left many months before, at the onset of spring, to visit her uncle Sakal who ruled the kingdom of Miotes, far away on a continent in the northern Sea of Dirges. Bozin loved his daughter dearly. She was bright and fair, and made him laugh with every word she spoke. The officials wearied him. Work choked him. He felt strangled and parched. Celeste's voice was like the trickling of a clear stream that bubbled over many stones, and only it could cure him. He needed some light.

He stood up from his throne with creaking limbs, taking leave of the officers and ambassadors. His guards escorted him to his chambers and then he bid them leave. Sitting in his favorite chair, he sighed, letting his body settle into the big, soft seat. After a moment, he pulled a nearby rope, and shortly thereafter, a servant appeared.

"Summon the Seneschal," he declared, and the servant went shuffling off. Soon the doors opened and in came Josak.

"Yes my king?" he asked, and Bozin smiled wearily.

"I'm tired, old friend, and I need to be cured." Josak and Bozin had always shared an unusual friendship. Josak alone among Bozin's old officers had stayed true to him during the Noth corruption years before, hiding himself away until Bozin took back his throne. "I miss my daughter," he explained with a weak voice. "How much longer will she be away?"

"We might have been able to send a ship to fetch your daughter a month ago, but with winter approaching it is probably best to wait for spring. The sea is too treacherous this late in the year to attempt any sort of extended voyage." At this news, Bozin's heart sunk heavily within him and he closed his eyes. At length a thought occurred to him and he sat up quickly.

"I certainly wouldn't want to place my daughter in any danger," he said, "but there must be someone who could complete the journey safely. Josak, who is the finest sailor in these parts?"

"There is no question," said Josak with a smile as the legends of warriors and heroes came to memory. "We have many fine sailors within the bounds of our seafaring nation, but none can compare with the might and skill of Cloran Hastings, who is the finest sailor in all the land. They say that he flayed the Giddendrach and slew the Horned Whale. They say he can speak with the waves and the waves respond, and that he is the master of all sea life and can captain any ship. As I recall, he should be arriving in port tomorrow morning after nine months at sea. He and his crew have been trading with the wealthy merchants of Rogvelt."

"Ah," said Bozin in his chair. His eyes cleared and he sat up, and as he did, all weariness seemed to fall from him. He leaned closer to Josak, with a peculiar glint in his eye. "Cloran Hastings is it? Yes, yes I have heard of him, he captains the ship *Wavegrazer*, very good. Arrange for a messenger to meet him tomorrow when he arrives in port. I need him to sail north to retrieve my lovely Celeste. I desire nothing more than to hear her voice once again. All is coarse and dull to me while she is away."

"My lord," said Josak slowly, "the waves are too rough this time of year. Don't you think it would be wiser, for your daughter's safety, to wait until spring when the seas calm down?"

"Normally," said the king leaning back in his chair, "but this man has considerable skill at sea, as you have said. A skilled sailor should be able to manage any weather."

"But Bozin, he and his men have been at sea for nine months and they are just getting back tomorrow. All they will want to do is go home to their wives and families and to rest after being absent so long from land. Winter is the time for rest."

"Surely he will not refuse this journey, Josak, especially if his king asks it of him."

"I doubt that he will refuse. He is a duty-bound man, but the seas will be perilous, especially in the icy regions where your brother resides. You must not ask him to go out so soon after just returning, into the dawn of winter."

"Didn't you just say that he is the best sailor in the world?"

"Yes, that is his reputation Bozin, but—"

"If the man can't sail north during winter, then he doesn't deserve to be called the best sailor in the world." Bozin stood and walked quickly to a nearby window, his back to Josak. When he turned, his face was sullen and he seemed distraught. "I don't think you understand, my friend. Being separated from my child is a pain that I have little strength left to endure."

"You have withstood greater hardships than this, Bozin," said Josak flatly. Bozin raised an eyebrow and nodded.

"Aye, I have been through my share of worries. I have battled great evils during my life and have had my share of sorrow. I have fought illness and corruption, treachery and rebellion. My body has been possessed and robbed from me, and yet I have endured and recovered it all. But…" He sighed and covered his face with his hand. "But I feel my years drawing to a close. Men weren't meant to live through so many troubles, and the past has taken its toll on me. I've earned the convenience of living the rest of my life in peace and happiness, but I can only be happy with Celeste close by. I need this Josak. I am a patient man and if this were anything else I could wait, but I feel my strength draining. I need to see my daughter."

Josak lowered his eyes. Josak was usually able to reason with Bozin, but there were certain times when the king stubbornly took hold of something and would not let go, and no amount of persuasion would change his mind. This was one of those times.

"If that is your decision, then so it will be. I will notify Cloran Hastings of your request when he arrives from Rogvelt."

Bozin nodded, closed his eyes, and then he smiled. It was a smile that Josak had not seen for many months. The lines in his face were deep and unmoving and his brow was still dark and furrowed, but Bozin looked relieved of at least one of his many burdens. He opened his eyes and exhaled.

"This is good, just as it should be. I will not have to wait long. I can now bear the hours of lonely work that await me. My daughter is coming home, and I will work patiently until she arrives." Bozin walked back towards his throne and his guards appeared out of nowhere to follow. His walk was stiff but his pace was quicker and he seemed confident enough to carry on for just a bit longer. Josak left the king's chambers and walked slowly down the long corridor to his offices.

"Forgive me, Cloran," he muttered.

CHAPTER TWO

The Long Awaited Homecoming

T he sun had just peered over the horizon and with it came a strong northern wind. Riding at the front of that wind came a ship that had not seen land in months. The ship's two sails were full, and it creaked and groaned as it eased into place beside the strong docks of Stren. When it came to a stop, the ship sighed, settling down for a long overdue rest. It rocked gently in the shallow waves. Barnacles covered its hull. Its boards were pitted and its sails had many tears. It looked like an ancient relic that had come from the depths of the sea itself to taste the scent of the air once again. It was old but strong, a noble ship that had seen many things. Carved across its bow was its name, painted white: *Wavegrazer*.

The harbor at which the ship arrived belonged to Stren, the capital of Menigah, and the kingdom's most populous city. The land was dusty and warm, but comfortable, cooled by a sharp breeze that came from the sea, which cheered the local inhabitants. The city was a tangled mesh of dirt and cobblestone roads that wove in-between brick and stone buildings, at times confusing even those who had lived in Stren their whole lives. Every morning, the sounds of businessmen, travelers and merchants pulling their carts, selling their wares and haggling with each other filled the streets. The northernmost point of the city opened up into a round harbor, where the buildings were all made of wood.

Long and sturdy docks shot out from the mainland across the sea, to which were moored ships of all shapes and sizes. Though craftsmen from a myriad of trades called Stren their home, more sailors and their families lived there than in any other city in Menigah, and maritime culture permeated the society.

A plank of wood shot from over the side of the ship, and the gangway was lowered onto the docks. Six weary sailors descended from the vessel, walking with wobbling sea legs. Lastly came a tall man wearing a wide hat and a long coat with big brass buttons. His face looked like it was chiseled from stone. His brow was dark and foreboding, but his gray eyes were kind and deep, as if the vastness of the sea existed within them. As he walked down the gangway, their colors surged like mighty waves.

Cloran Hastings had arrived home. He looked at the cloudy sky, closed his eyes and inhaled deeply. The dusty air was a welcome change after being so long at sea. The gulls cried above him and began to perch on his ship, but he didn't mind and neither did she. Both were ready to relax.

"We're home!" cried Cloran to his crew, and his sailors cheered. "After nine months, we are finally back. We've survived the harshest winds and the roughest waves, and if we've earned anything, it's rest. But I am sure you boys would rather spend some time at the Jade Unicorn polishing off a few rounds, so off with you! I will see you in the morning."

"It's time I find my Jessie!" said Mallory. Though exhausted from the long voyage, he ran off quickly with his short, sandy-red hair waving towards the heart of Stren to find his wife.

"Ah, a nap! That sounds good," said Darrell with a yawn. He stretched and reached for the sky before shivering and trotting off. He was the only one of the sailors to wear his long, curved sword at his side at all times, and he looked angry wherever he went with his crow-black hair and dark eyes.

"Ugh, I feel so salty," Turner complained, although in fact he was probably the cleanest of the bunch. He brushed the wrinkles out of his gray and white uniform, made sure his boots were tightly laced (with every loop the same length, mind you) and then brushed his blond hair back. "I think it's about time I took a nice, long bath," he said before walking off towards his home.

"It has been so long since I have seen Stren," said Jenkins, "that I think I will just wander around for a while. I wonder how many new shops have opened since we've been gone." Jenkins lightly walked into town and was the fastest to recover his land legs. His sandy hair wasn't particularly long or short, but he made sure to keep it out of his eyes. His eyes were bright and fierce, and it was often hard to look directly into them. No one could tell exactly what color they were, and if studied for any length of time, it would appear as if he were looking at something far away.

"I'm going to get some good food for a change," said Richards. "I'm surprised I survived on Greaves' cooking!" Richards ran off, laughing at Greaves who glared at him sharply.

He soon disappeared, his slender form vanishing amongst the townspeople as he dove into the busy street.

"If you don't like my cooking, you don't have to eat it!" yelled Greaves irritably, shaking his large fist. When upset he looked quite terrifying. His muscles flexed and the cords in his neck bulged out. His blue eyes shimmered, but he was always quick to forget his wrath, and even when he was angry, he wasn't *really* angry. He forgot all about Richards when he remembered that the merchants had just replenished their shops. "I wonder if I can find any spices from Rogvelt," he said, scratching his head through his short, brown hair, and he walked off to join Jenkins in reacquainting himself with the town.

Cloran grinned as he watched his boys go. He couldn't imagine a finer crew of sailors and was grateful that they had been with him for so long. He was reminded of his youth as a novice under Old Captain Reuben and wondered if Reuben had ever felt the same way towards his own crew.

Down from the ship came, last of all a tall, dark-haired fellow all in blue. He wore blue pants and a ratty blue shirt, and across his forehead was a blue bandanna. He walked down the gangway and stood next to his captain. He was First Mate Len, Cloran's right hand man and best friend. He too breathed in the harbor air, but coughed.

"It's not the best smelling air, but a welcome change I suppose," he said, and then he stretched his whole body with a groan. "Will we unload the ship tonight or tomorrow?"

"Tomorrow, I think. It has been a long journey and the lads need to stretch their legs. So do you, Len! No, I won't have you working much today, you need a break. Go get some rest."

"Fine!" said Len with a laugh, "but only if you insist. I think I'll go see if my room is still there. My landlord always tries to rent it while I'm away, even though I pay for a whole year in advance. I won't lose it if I can help it! What about you Cloran, what will you do?"

"I'm going to take a long nap. Tomorrow will be a busy day and I have some things I need to do tonight anyway."

"Are you going to see Adaire?"

Cloran was silent for a moment as he looked at the sky, and he smiled.

"Yes, that is what I will do tonight. I miss her terribly." The wind picked up, blowing Cloran's coat about, and he clutched it tight. Len eyed Cloran silently for a moment.

"It is hard on a woman to be in love with a sailor," he said at last. "The Sea can be jealous. She will not stand for another to love you. That is why I remain single. There is no room for a lady in my life, other than the Sea." Cloran didn't respond. Len gently grasped his shoulder. "You're going to have to make a decision sometime soon. It's not right to have two loves and two lives." Cloran sighed and looked at the planks beneath him, watching the water surge between the cracks.

"I know Len. I have a lot to think about. But I'll figure it out. I always do."

Cloran walked away slowly towards his house, leaving Len standing in the wind. After a moment, Len turned to the ship, stowed the gangway and then walked off into the heart of Stren to haggle with his greedy landlord.

Later that night, Cloran found himself winding his way through the many cluttered streets of Stren. The roadside merchants had packed up and gone home. Children out past their bedtime ran around in the dark, hiding in alleys and climbing onto roofs, spying on travelers as if no one could see them. The moon was full, but thin gray clouds sped past in the high winds, casting flickering shadows.

Cloran slowly meandered through the city until he arrived at the Jade Unicorn, a pub near the water. He opened the door and entered a room filled with clamorous singing, loud talking and men and women running about serving drinks and food. It was a familiar sight and one that he had long missed.

Cloran made his way to the counter where a busy little man stood polishing glasses and stacking trays. When the man finally looked up from his work, the sight of Cloran startled him.

"Cloran! I was wondering when you'd stop by. I expected you sooner!"

"Yes, well, I had to go home and see that things were as I left them. It is good to see you again, Tosh."

"And it's mighty fine to be seeing you as well! Business just isn't the same with you and your crew out of town. Usual table?"

"Sure. Is Adaire working today?" Tosh the barkeep's smile faded and he looked uncertainly at Cloran.

"Yes, she is working today. She works every day."

"Can I see her?"

"Cloran, you know I like you. But my Adaire has no place being with a sailor."

"I know. That's...partly why I want to see her. Can you send her by my table?" Tosh nodded and smiled.

"Sure Cloran. You know where to go. I have to get back to work. It's good to see you!"

Cloran left the counter and walked to his usual table in the back of the room. A woman with a long green dress and white apron was bustling around from table to table serving drinks and bringing food. Cloran watched as she worked. Her face was young and beautiful and her eyes were tired but kind. She had long, auburn hair and she wore a pleasant smile. After she served her drinks, she turned from the tables with a sigh and her smile faded, but she shook her head, stood erect and came swiftly to where Cloran sat. She did not look up, but set down a glass and adjusted her apron.

"Evenin', what can I—" she started, but when she looked up her eyes went wide and she dropped her empty tray. After a moment of astonishment, her face lit up with joy.

"Cloran! I didn't know you were coming in today!"

Cloran smiled and stood up and hugged her. Adaire threw her arms around his head and hugged him tightly.

"Took me long enough, eh? It sure has been a journey, but now I'm home, and hopefully for a good long while." Cloran sat back down and Adaire sat beside him.

"You will have to tell me everything! I am so glad to see you. I've thought about you every day."

"Can you join me tonight?" he asked. "I'd like to spend some time with you." Adaire nodded quickly.

"I have to finish my tables, but shouldn't be too much longer, and afterwards we can go off and talk all night. Do you want your usual while you wait?"

"Oh no, you're too busy. Just go and finish your work and I'll wait here."

"Nonsense! I am getting you something. Stay here and I'll bring you something good," she said, and she shuffled off before Cloran could argue with her.

After she was finished with her work, the two strolled off towards the water. They walked to the top of a small hill that overlooked the ocean and ended at a sheer cliff that reached the rocky shallows below. The couple sat on the cliff's edge and Adaire kicked her legs while Cloran told her all of what happened on his latest journey to Rogvelt and back, of the people he had met and the odd customs he had seen, the strange and wonderful smells, foods, alien attires and peculiarly wrought ships that were moored there. He gave her a little trinket he had picked up—a golden horse with silver hooves and mane. He told her of the many dangers he had faced and the strange creatures he had encountered on his travels.

"I love it when you tell me your stories. Sometimes I forget that there is a world outside of Stren and the Jade Unicorn."

"The sea is a hazardous place, full of peculiar creatures, strange peoples, and wonderful places. Many of the things I have seen I would never have believed had I not been there myself." They were both quiet for a time, embracing the cool night air and the smell of the sea below, watching the birds gather on nearby rocks and then fly off, across the sea to places they had never been but always remembered. She leaned against his shoulder and grasped his hand. She closed her eyes and buried her face in his arm. Clinging to him firmly, she fingered the calluses on his hands and the deep grooves in his knuckles. It was her arm now, not the Sea's. She had him back, and though she knew he might have to leave again someday, he was with her now, and she had a hold of him. The salty fragrance from his warm clothes filled her mind, triggering memory, and a sudden fright hit her as she realized how long ago it was since the first day she had held his arm. How much longer would it be this way? How many years would go by before she had him forever, and would never again have to share him with the Sea?

She stopped kicking her feet and turned towards the waves.

"I've been working at the Unicorn for eight years now," she said softly. "I'm tired, Cloran, and when you leave on these extended voyages it weighs heavily on me. I worry about you every time you step foot on that ship. I know you love me, and you know that I love you, but you can't string me along anymore. I have been faithful to you all these years, and I don't want anything more than to be your wife, but…"

She sighed and buried her face in his shirt again.

"You need to choose."

He knew fully well what she meant. The Sea was all he had ever known as long as he could remember. She had always been his companion and he had always been at her mercy. The thought of giving up the life of a sailor was a hard one to swallow. He put his arm around her, but didn't say anything.

"It's getting late," said Adaire. "I have to work again in the morning and I need my rest. Whatever it is you are trying to work out, please, do it soon." Adaire stood up and walked towards her home. The night went on, the sea sang, and Cloran waged a war within himself.

Morning arrived with the sound of gulls circling below. Cloran sat on the same cliff and had been there all night, but at last, his struggle was over. He came to his feet and looked out across the gray vastness before him. The early morning fog clung to his clothes like a blanket and his voice felt stifled, but he was not troubled. The sea surged in an angry rebellion. Waves clashed against the rocks below, and the great ocean seemed to be directing all of its hatred towards Cloran. She knew what he was about to do. Her protests, however, did not daunt Cloran. There was only room for one love in his life. He stepped to the very edge of the cliff and addressed the vastness called Sea:

"Many leagues have I crossed,
And great beasts have I slain.
Perils o'er tempest tossed,
I sailed the Deep Blue Plain.

To North Island have I been,
The Noth's Eye have I seen.
The Ballad Sea was mapped by me,
And every point between.

Mermaids cast their evil spells
And coo like earthly doves,
But no enchantment is as strong
As that which is called love.

The chains of love would make me drown
If I left my lover fair.
Farewell Deep Blue, my love of years,
I go home to Adaire!"

At this, the Sea ceased in her clamoring and the waves below went calm. The gulls perched upon the rocks and quit their screeching. All was still in the brooding silence that hung over the waters. Cloran knew that she was seething, but he didn't care. He had made his choice and was glad, and with a joy new to him, he turned and left the Sea to her anger.

He arrived at the harbor. Len and the crew were already unloading the ship. Merchants from all over Stren had sent their curriers to *Wavegrazer* to pick up the goods that they had commissioned Cloran to retrieve. The crowd was eager as the crew unloaded each item carefully, delivering it to its owner, and the merchants praised Cloran for his speedy delivery and careful handling of the cargo. Cloran climbed onto the deck and helped his crew unload.

"So I see she kept you out late, eh?" said Richards to his captain, and the crew laughed.

"That's to be expected after nine months, don't you think?" said Cloran with a wink. "I just ended up doing a lot of thinking last night."

"Oh sure, thinking, that's all," said Richards, nodding. "What about you Mallory? How was your evening with Jessie?" Mallory blushed and the whole crew chided and nudged him.

"I am afraid such stories are not carried with me onto the ship, you little scoundrels," he said, and the crew booed him.

"It's these merchants that are scoundrels," said Turner from the ramp. "They barely give me a chance to open the crates!" Turner faced the crowd of curriers. "Who here is from Mercos' Embroidery?" There were a few shouts of "Me! Me!" and some quarrels broke out and Turner laughed.

"Come now you cretins, you can't all be from Mercos' Embroidery. Luckily, I know Mercos' errand boy by sight, so the rest of you can bugger off! Peran, come here, take these." Peran climbed the ramp and took the garments, threads and cloths from Turner to take back to his master, then turned and harassed the other merchants for their greed.

"That's it! That's all I have! You all have what you paid for and you're getting no more, so off with you to your carts and stores and wagons!" The crowd dispersed and ran back to their masters to give them the highly expected merchandise.

Just then, a rider rode up to *Wavegrazer* and alighted.

"Captain Cloran Hastings!" called the rider. "I have a message for you!" Cloran peered over the side of his ship with a frown.

"A message? Who is it from?"

"King Bozin of Menigah!"

The crew was startled and Cloran most of all. He nodded and climbed down from the ropes to meet the messenger on the gangway.

"I hear you have been given a great honor sir," said the messenger as he handed a scroll to Cloran, "and let me just say that it is also an honor to meet you, the man who flayed the Giddendrach and slew the Horned Whale. We here in Stren hear so much about the mightiest sailor in the world!" Cloran cringed.

"I fear such stories are more tall tales than truth, really."

"Regardless, it's an honor all the same. But off I go—more messages to deliver!" The messenger turned and leapt upon his horse to go throughout Stren and finish his rounds.

Cloran stared at the scroll warily and then turned back to his crew.

"What is it? Read it!" they urged. Cloran shrugged and broke the high seal of King Bozin.

"Well it certainly is fancy," he said. "Let's see what the king wants of me." The crew gathered around Cloran and he cleared his throat.

> *"A message from our venerable*
> *King Bozin of Menigah;*
> *Just ruler of all the lands*
> *Between the northern shores of the continent*
> *Down to the river Spring Branch;*
> *Giver of gifts, keeper of wisdom,*
> *Defender of justice and all that is good;*
>
> *"To the celebrated Cloran Hastings,*
> *Acclaimed sailor of the realm,*
> *Flayer of the Giddendrach,*
> *Slayer of the Horned Whale,*
> *He who can speak with the waves*
> *And has named all manner of sea life—*

"Yes, O mighty Cloran!" interrupted Richards. "He who constructed the mountains and commands the rain!" Cloran winked and the men all laughed.

"'You have found favor in the eyes of your king. He has set aside a special task that only you can accomplish. You are hereby bidden to set sail as…soon as you can…'"

Cloran's voice trailed off and the crew held their breath in astonishment. Cloran blinked and re-read the sentence to himself to make sure he got it right before continuing.

"Um… *'you are hereby bidden to set sail as soon as you can to the land of Miotes and retrieve the king's daughter, the Princess Celeste of Menigah, who is visiting the kingdom of her uncle, King Sakal. In order to better complete this task, you will receive the finest provisions Menigah can provide, enough for every sailor on your ship to eat well for the entirety of the voyage. I will refurbish your ship to withstand the strongest winds and the harshest of winters. I shall give you all that you require for the journey, within reason, so that you might retrieve my dearest Celeste all the more swiftly. To better aid this swiftness, the king grants you authority over all the sea and the ships that ride it, now until your duty ends, to invoke the assistance of other vessels in your need, or to judge in matters of crime at sea so that justice and wisdom might accompany the reputation of such a servant of Menigah.*

"'Arrangements have already been made with the harbormaster and now only await your word to be set in motion. Go in all swiftness, favored sailor of the realm, and retrieve for the king his beloved daughter!'"

All were silent on the deck of *Wavegrazer* as he finished reading the scroll. Mallory hid his face, but no one else moved. Finally, Len spoke what they all were wondering.

"Doesn't the king know that we have just returned?"

"He can't seriously expect us to go out at the onset of winter, can he?" asked Jenkins.

"We've fought the sea for nine months," said Darrell, "and all men need rest after working for so long."

"Are there no other ships that the king could send?" asked Turner, and the whole crew voiced their thoughts from the deck of the ship for a good while. Cloran, however, remained silent. He just stared at the scroll, his brow furrowed and his eyes dark.

"Cap'n, tell us what you are thinking," said Greaves. Cloran's eyes were narrow slits and his mouth was taut. At length he met the faces of his crew and his look was fierce and miserable. No storm any of them had seen compared to the torrent that waged behind his eyes.

"This morning I said good-bye to the Sea," he said dryly, "and this is how she gets her revenge." He covered his face with his hand. The crew remained silent. They knew why he had made the choice. All knew Adaire and were fond of her, and could almost understand the torment he was under. Cloran shook his head and his face grew sullen and stern.

"Finish up here boys. I will be back shortly."

"But what will we do Cap'n?" asked Richards. "Are we going back out to sea?" Cloran turned and walked towards the gangway. He clenched his fists and the scroll crumbled in his hand.

"To duty we are bound and to it above all," he said over his shoulder. "As much as I am heartbroken to do so, I must obey my king. If the king feels that his need for his daughter's company is so important as to put us through all of this, then so be it. But I must talk with someone before I make my final decision." As Cloran walked down the ramp he could hear his crew whisper, "Adaire, he's going to Adaire." Richards leaned over the gunwale.

"What about us?" he called after Cloran but Len took him by the shoulder and turned him around.

"This is harder for him than any of us here, except maybe Mallory, who has Jessie to think of," he said. Mallory still would not show his face.

"He can simply say 'no' right?" asked Turner. "It isn't as if Bozin gave us a command. In fact I think the word he used was 'request'."

"A king never makes requests," said Jenkins dully. "He may call it one but it is always an order."

"Aye," said Len, "and I do not envy the decision Cloran has to make. He is basically deciding whether to do his king's bidding or to rebel against him, and rebellion rarely turns out for the best. If Cloran decides to do what Bozin asks, I will go with him. Surely no one here would desert his captain." The crew made no reply. At length Greaves dropped from the riggings.

"The captain has led us all over this great sea and treated us like sons. I will be the last to desert him. If the captain goes, I go."

"So will I," said Jenkins, and the whole crew said likewise. All except Mallory. He sat in the riggings with his face covered.

"What about you Mallory?" asked Richards. "Will you follow the captain or leave us?" At length Mallory showed his face, and he looked tired and drained.

"Tell me Len, you know the captain better than any of us. What will he decide?" Len looked at Mallory and was moved with pity.

"My friend, as much as it will pain him to do so, I fear he will in the end choose to do his king's will. He is a man bound by duty. There will be no rest for those who follow him." Mallory nodded, and leapt down from the riggings.

"Then I will follow him," he declared, much to the relief of the crew who did not want their company broken. "Yes, I will follow Cloran to the very edge of the ocean, where it cascades off the never ending falls, if that be his will. But today I will keep for myself, if Len gives me leave to." First Mate Len smiled.

"Go to your wife Mallory and spend as much time with her as you can. But do not tell her about your next voyage until the end of the day. Keep it as happy and unremorseful as possible." Mallory thanked Len and ran off into the city to find his wife.

"Why is it that he can go off when we need him?" asked Richards angrily, but the crew shook their heads and went back to work.

"Richards, have you ever been in love?" asked Len.

"Of course I have! Why, when I was younger I loved many girls in my town."

"But have you ever been *in* love? *Love*, Richards, which is completely different from infatuation. Has there ever been a person whom you loved so much that parting from her was like a blow to the chest?" Richards looked around skittishly and then lowered his gaze.

"Well no, I suppose not. I don't think I ever have been."

"Then there is no way you can understand. You have lived for yourself and for your comrades. Be content with that but also be aware of and compassionate with the emotions and trials of others."

"If you say so Len. If you say so."

Cloran stood before Adaire in her quarters at the Jade Unicorn. She sat on her bed with tears on her face and the crumpled scroll in her hands. The window was open and the wind picked up. A ribbon caught her hair back, but it blew freely over her shoulder. She dropped the scroll to the floor. She could hear the sea through the open window. It raged with laughter, and it laughed long.

"Do you have to accept?" Adaire asked, but she knew the answer. Cloran lowered his gaze and nodded.

"He is the king. And he is a good king, despite his stubborn moods. As much as I don't want to, I must do what my liege and lord requests. It is my duty."

"Is it worth it?" She looked up at him with her soft gaze and it almost moved him to tears. He knelt before her, took her hands in his, and kissed them.

"Nothing is worth being parted from you for any length of time. But when I come back from this last voyage, I will have the money I need to marry you and buy you a house and land, where we can raise children and where I can start a trade. If ever there was a voyage worth doing it would be this one, though anything that takes me away from you is hard to bear." He took her gaze. Her face was sad, but her eyes were alive and piercing. "Will you wait for me?" he asked, and at this her eyes welled up, but she brushed the tears away, bent forward and kissed his forehead.

"Of course I will wait for you. I have waited for you all these years and I will continue to wait for you." They stood, embraced, and remained so for a long time.

"My crew needs me. I must help get *Wavegrazer* ready."

"When will you leave?"

"The ship will be ready in a week, maybe less."

Adaire pulled away and caught his eyes.

"Tell me that you will come back."

"Come back? Adaire, you know I will be as careful as I possibly can, but—"

"I need to hear it."

Cloran couldn't recall ever making a promise that he couldn't keep. He made promises warily and rarely took oaths. His word was his bond and he was loath to commit to something he wasn't able fulfill. He couldn't promise that he would return. The sea was deadly and always an uncertainty, even for a sailor of his skill. There was no way he could know whether he would return from the voyage or not, even if he were sailing in the spring through calm waters on a journey close to home. He could not make such a promise.

"I promise," he said to her, and bent close to her ear. "I will come back."

CHAPTER THREE

A Nasty Scuff on the Port Side

The next week was a flurry of activity for *Wavegrazer* and her crew. Just as he promised, King Bozin spared no expense in getting *Wavegrazer* outfitted for the winter voyage. He had the ship hauled out of the water and scrubbed her belly clean of all the barnacles and sea creatures that had attached to it, which must have felt incredibly good. He pitched all the cracks and crevices in the hull. Her name was touched up with fresh paint and her railings were sanded smooth. He fortified her masts and washed the deck. He took down her sails and brought up new ones—sails without hole, rip or patch.

After she was fully scrubbed, cleaned, painted and made new, Bozin had her loaded with crates and barrels filled with provisions for the long voyage. Greaves received new cooking supplies, much to his delight, and he personally made sure that the larder was full to capacity with the foodstuffs he needed. All the beds were given new bedding and each sailor received a new blanket and pillow. Bozin had their gray and white uniforms cleaned and mended and they all got extra sets for the long voyage north.

At last, she was eased back into the water, but she did not moan and she did not creak. She rested proudly with her masts taller than ever, her prow standing nobly against the sky. Cloran, Len and the crew stood back and admired the ship.

"I haven't seen *Wavegrazer* this beautiful since that day long ago when I first saw her, Len, back when you and I sailed under Old Captain Reuben," said Cloran.

"I don't think she looked like this even then," Len replied.

The crew stood before the ship's prow admiring her new look, and not a few of them thought it wouldn't be so bad going out to sea again, manning such a fine looking vessel. Cloran smiled, and turned to his crew.

"Well boys, it has been a long week. Let's get some dinner! It's on me tonight." The crew cheered and the company walked towards the Jade Unicorn, which was not very far away. The Unicorn was not as busy as usual that night, but the sailors made sure to fix that. Tosh seated them at Cloran's table and the men immediately started laughing, talking loudly and making quite a scene, but the folk of Stren were used to such boisterous encounters and didn't mind.

"Order whatever you want, and be sure you get your fill," said Cloran. "I'll be back in a moment." Cloran went to find Adaire. As soon as he left, she scooted out of the kitchen with trays and glasses and ran around delivering orders to the people in the pub. Finally, she came up to where Len and the crew sat and laughed.

"Here for a final feast before you hit the waves, eh?" she asked and they all howled and hooted. "Well then, what do you want?"

"No, this isn't any good at all," said Greaves standing up. "You can't wait on us Adaire. I'd feel awful about it if you did. Come join us!"

"Hmm, I don't know," she answered, "I don't think Tosh over there would like that."

Greaves snorted.

"I'll go show him a thing or two!" he said standing up, and rolling up his sleeves he marched right over to Tosh the barkeep who was polishing glasses behind his counter.

"Hey there Tosh!" he said and Tosh looked up from his busy-work curiously.

"Hey there Greaves! What can I get you?"

"Well my good barkeep, all of us over at Cloran's table want Adaire to join us for dinner, but she's working see, and it's hard for her to work and eat dinner at the same time, don't you think? So we were wondering if you might set her loose for an hour or two so she can keep us company."

"That's all well and good for you now, but if I do that, then I won't have a waitress to serve the food! Where will I find another waitress, eh?" Greaves stood up strait and pointed his thumb at himself.

"Right here Toshy! I cook day in and day out for Cloran and the crew, and if I can do it for them, I can certainly do it a few hours for you. What do you say?"

"I have all the cooks I need in the back. What I need is a server, and a fast one. You don't look to be all that fast."

"I don't?" said Greaves, just a little hurt. "I can move as fast as Adaire whenever I want to, so hand me an apron and a tray, and let's see how fast I can serve some drinks!"

Tosh turned a skeptical eye at him and made a few grunting noises but in the end relented.

"You had better be just as swift!" he warned, and Greaves nodded and said he would be. "Oh, and Greaves?"

"Yeah?"

"Don't call me Toshy."

"Er, ah, will do boss."

Greaves marched over to the table where Adaire had just finished taking their order and he snatched the list from her hands.

"Sit down Adaire dear! Greaves is playing waitress tonight." The crew laughed and chided him and Richards told him to put on a dress, but Greaves just snorted and said, "Better be careful Richards, I'll be carrying your food! Anyhow Adaire, what do you want?"

"Oh, well, just a bowl of soup is fine."

"Just soup?" said Darrell. "Come now, get some solid food."

"All right, I'll have...some bread and meat, but keep it small."

"And what about to drink?" said Richards. "Get a nice tall glass of ale."

"No, none of that," she said, "but a glass of cider would be good."

"Cider?" said Mallory. "I didn't know you had that. I want one too!"

"And me!" said Jenkins, and then the whole crew wanted some. Greaves was scribbling fast on his paper and crossing out all the ales the men had ordered.

"Bah, you cretins quit changing your minds. I'll be back!" Greaves marched off to the back where the cooks were tossing food about. There was a bit of spilt ale on the table and Adaire quickly fetched a rag from her apron and started cleaning it up.

"Don't do that," said Jenkins. "You're a patron for the next few hours. Sit back and relax. We'll make Greaves clean it!"

"Sorry," she said and the crew chuckled. "Force of habit I guess. Where is Cloran?"

"He went to go get you I think."

"Maybe I should find him," she said, but just then, Cloran came down the stairs and walked to the table.

"There you are," he said.

"Yes, your crew kidnapped me and made me order some food," she said with a grin and the crew laughed.

"Good!" said Cloran, "and Darrell, I think you had best find another seat, because I'm sitting next to Adaire tonight!" Darrell scooted over and Cloran sat down, putting his arm around her. Just then, Greaves came up with a tray of glasses, looking awfully perplexed.

"It's harder getting around back there than I thought," he said, and he put down all the glasses. "Cloran, I forgot to get you one. What do you want?"

"Oh, whatever they're having."

"Cider it is then!" and with that he marched back to the kitchen.

"Hmm, I didn't know they had cider here."

Adaire began asking questions about all the things the crew had seen during their last trip and everyone had a great time bragging, exaggerating, and telling her of all the adventures they had been in. Cloran would pop in and change something if someone exaggerated too much (usually Richards). Greaves lumbered about the room with his sleeves rolled up, wearing an apron and with his big muscles looking terribly awkward, serving drinks and food to the other fellows in the pub. He made great entertainment for the crew who threw rags at him, which he of course had to pick up while under Tosh's scrutinous eye.

At that moment, the doors to the Unicorn opened and in came a slew of sailors. Cloran and crew didn't pay any attention to them at first, and Tosh seated the newcomers next to Cloran's table. Soon these new sailors were making as much noise as Cloran's boys. It was then that a tall fellow with keen eyes came in. He wore a wide brown hat, a long brown coat and sported scruffy black whiskers. He spoke with Tosh and laughed, then walked over to his sailors who hollered at him.

"Ho, Cap'n Percy!" called the newcomers, and the tall, keen-eyed fellow took a seat with his men. Cloran and Len, having seen this whole exchange, glanced at each other and stood up. They walked over to the table next to where Percy and his men sat and looked at the tall captain with big grins on their faces.

Percy at first didn't notice them, but he glanced up and his eyes went wide when they got closer.

"Cloran? Len?" he asked and they nodded as he stood up.

"Percy!" they both exclaimed and Percy laughed.

"Of all the barnacles that wash up here, I never thought I would see you two!" said Percy and they hugged and shook hands. Richards cleared his throat.

"Um, see, we're all sitting here wondering how you guys know each other. Want to fill us in?" he asked, and Cloran laughed.

"This is Percy, who Len and I knew way back when we sailed under my old captain. He was a fellow crewmate."

"And these," said Percy turning to his crew, "are my old friends Cloran and Len." Both crews looked at them in wonder. Their captains had told them old sailing stories about Reuben and his crew, and while stories may or may not be true, to see living characters from such stories makes them all the more real.

"Well then, let's make this party larger!" said Darrell. The sailors stood up, pushed the two tables together and gathered around it with Adaire in the middle. They compared stories about their captains' time as crewmen and surprisingly they all seemed to match nicely. Then they boasted about the adventures they had been on since then and it got quite competitive, but in the end, no winner was proclaimed and they laughed it up.

"So Cloran, do you still captain *Wavegrazer*?" asked Percy and Cloran nodded.

"Yes, and she is moored right here in Stren, if you want to see her."

"You bet I do! I haven't seen her in years, not since the captain died."

"Come then!" Cloran said, and Len, Cloran and Percy left the Unicorn and went to look at the ship. When they reached the docks, Percy stood before the prow of *Wavegrazer* with his mouth agape.

"Ah, just as I remember her," he finally said.

"We got her all fixed up this last week," said Len. "She was pretty worn out when we came into port."

"Can I board her? I'm being hit with a fit of nostalgia at the moment."

Len and Cloran laughed and lowered the gangway. The three men boarded the ship and Percy looked around quietly. Memories came flooding back, some good, some bad, and Percy was stricken with that feeling of loss that comes upon a man for no good reason when he visits a place he hasn't seen in years.

Percy pointed at the wide, round-tipped oars that were stacked neatly on the deck.

"Those are new. What do you use them for?"

"Tight places. They've come in handy on more than one occasion."

"You row the whole ship?"

"Sometimes."

"Your crew must have arms as big as tree trunks. Isn't it a little cramped on deck with those oars in the way?"

"Aye, it can be."

Percy chuckled and shook his head.

"You're hilarious Cloran. Only you, my friend, would think of something like that." Percy gazed towards the stern and raised an eyebrow.

"Is that the same wheel?" Cloran nodded and the three men went to examine it. It was a large green wheel that was rough and didn't look to be very comfortable to hold. Scattered at equal distances along the wheel were stones a little smaller than a fist, and they glimmered a deep but clear blue. Percy fingered the wheel affectionately.

"Tell me Cloran," said Percy lowly. "You've been captain of this ship for years now, and so perhaps you can answer a question that has been bothering me ever since my early years under Old Reuben. Does the wheel really have special properties? Does it really keep you from sinking?"

Cloran scratched his chin.

"Well, that's a hard question to answer. After all, she hasn't sunk yet, and whether that is due to an enchantment of the wheel or not I do not know. Reuben told me on many occasions that as long as the captain stands by this wheel, the ship will never sink, and I have no reason to believe that he was making it up."

"But do you feel anything within the wheel?" asked Percy earnestly.

Cloran nodded.

"Yes, actually. But only when I am far out to sea. If I grasp it with my bare hands I feel…well, it is hard to describe. I feel a sensation in my hands akin to the one you get right after your arm falls asleep and is just waking back up, only I also feel the coolness of cold running water. There is something special in this wheel, but I cannot name it. I tell you though; if ever in a storm, I will not move from this wheel. I won't risk the lives of my crew to chance."

"Amazing," said Percy as he fingered the wheel. He sighed and took off his hat to rub his brow.

"So are you two going out again?"

"Yes. We have to go to Miotes, on an errand for King Bozin," said Len. Percy cringed.

"Oh, that's no good. Miotes is a long ways away. You will arrive home in the dead of winter."

"We will, unless we hurry," said Cloran softly.

Percy gazed at the wheel again and nodded his head.

"It looks as if he at least outfitted you guys well enough. My boys and I arrived in port last night. Thankfully we don't have any pressing errands to do, so we should be able to wait the winter out." The three men stood gazing at the deck, the masts and the beautiful new sails, remembering the old adventures and misadventures that they had been in together under Old Captain Reuben.

"I know you are going out because you feel you have to," said Percy, "but do you think you can actually make it back? Bozin is taking a great risk. Even I hear rumor of your deeds around the world Cloran, but this is the Sea, and the Sea doesn't care about a man's reputation and will treat all ships that ride her indiscriminately. Can you really trust the Sea?"

Cloran sighed and looked at the tossing waves. Still they roared at him. *You can never escape me. I am the Sea.*

"No, I do not trust her, but I will master her and come home unscathed. I have to."

Percy nodded and motioned his two friends to follow.

"Come here, I want to show you my ship," he said. They disembarked from *Wavegrazer*, stowed away the gangway and then followed Percy a little further down the wharf to a larger ship that was moored there. It was taller than *Wavegrazer* and wider, had three masts and three big sails, but one of them, the largest, was dyed all blue, very bright so that it stood out boldly. The ship was long, had a wide stern and looked new.

"A fine looking ship!" said Cloran. "How did you manage to come across such a big brute?"

"Things have been going well for me since the war ended and I managed to come across this fellow. We call her *Blue Bane* and are fond of her. She takes a while to get moving and is slow to turn, but once she gains momentum she can move incredibly fast."

"I bet you can hold quite a bit in the hull," said Len. "You could probably stay at sea for a long while, eh?" Percy looked at his ship and smiled.

"We certainly can. I've been meaning to ask you, Cloran; how did you fare all those years during the Nurith Wars?"

"What do you mean Percy?"

"Well, before the war ended we had no contact with Rogvelt, and thus could not trade with them. I heard that many sailors lost their ships during those years and some even became impoverished. How did you pull through?"

"Ah," said Cloran nodding. "Yes, those times were difficult. Our consignments well-nigh vanished and I could hardly afford to keep her afloat. We managed to get enough business to pull through, though my poor sailors worked for next to nothing and we all lived on dried foods and very little water. We couldn't afford to properly outfit the ship, but every day we would do what work on her we could to keep her clean and in working order."

"How did you deal with piracy?" asked Percy, and at this, he became motionless and stared at Cloran intently. Cloran raised an eyebrow.

"It wasn't fun," said Cloran softly.

"We had to learn how to fight," added Len, "and we made a habit of carrying our arms with us at all times. Before the war I barely knew how to cut bread with a knife, but now…now I am very familiar with cutting." Percy nodded knowingly.

"Yes, we have had similar experiences. I suppose your reputation on the sea helped to quell the hearts of even the most stalwart marauders."

"Our reputation on the sea came about through our resistance to those stalwart marauders," said Cloran. "But what about you? How did you manage?"

"Well we—" said Percy, but he stopped short and laughed nervously. He tried to come up with something witty to say but failed, and with a sigh, he hung his head. "For me, those were some of the worst days of my life. Never before had I felt hunger so deeply, and my poor crew hardly had the energy to lift the sails. We fought as well, oh, how we had to fight…" his voice trailed off and for the first time Cloran noticed a curved blade sheathed at his side. Percy fingered the pommel absent-mindedly.

At length he shook his head and smiled wearily.

"Those days are over, and I pray they never return. I managed to keep my crew busy and our stomachs full. We are back in business, and business is good!"

"Enough reminiscing," said Cloran. "Come, let's join our crewmen! If we don't hurry, all the ale will be gone."

"You mean cider," said Len.

"Ah yes. Cider."

The three old friends entered the Unicorn again to the sound of clamorous laughing and table pounding.

"When the captain is away, the boys will play," said Percy and he grinned. Adaire was stuck between Darrell and Richards with a glass of cider in her hand, trying to keep it from spilling. She looked at Cloran with a look of "help me" written on her face. Cloran laughed.

"Move aside lads and be civil! Remember, there's a lady present. You be careful around her or I'll clobber you all!" He waded through the sea of boisterous sailors, nudged Darrell out of the way and scooted in next to Adaire, who leaned against his shoulder and sighed.

"Just think, when you guys leave I'll have no more excitement like this."

"Is that a good thing or a bad thing?"

Adaire laughed and kissed his cheek.

"Come home fast," she whispered into his ear, and then leaned against his shoulder.

Wavegrazer was fully prepared. The crew had boarded her and were busying themselves with getting ready for launch. Many of the residents of Stren, including the merchants that relied on Cloran's voyages to Rogvelt and back, had gathered around the ship to see her off. She was already a ship of legend, as was her captain and crew.

Len and the crew were making final sailing preparations, checking ropes for frays, doing inventory and the like. Just then, the ship rocked to the side violently and the sailors clung to the ropes. From the seaward side of the ship the sailors heard yelling and cursing. They peered over the gunwale and there sat another ship in the water, just a bit smaller than *Wavegrazer*—not as bulky but much longer. It had rammed up against *Wavegrazer*.

"Be careful!" called Len to the men on board the smaller ship. "We just got all cleaned up, so don't scuff us!"

"Get out of our berth!" cried the sailors on the other ship.

"Your berth?" shouted Richards angrily from the riggings. "We've been here for a week, and this is your berth? You can just sit there and be patient until were done with it!"

"We always tie up here," yelled what appeared to be the captain of the new ship, "and we will continue to do so. Now move!" The sailors on the ship ran to one edge so that it tipped and nudged *Wavegrazer*.

"Stop that!" said Len. "Be civil now; we won't be here long, and when we leave you can have your berth."

"Who do you think you are, telling us to wait? We won't be ordered around by the likes of you."

"My name is Len and this is *Wavegrazer*, and she will be leaving this afternoon. You can stop your bullying and play nice. Nothing you do will move us."

"Oh, so they think they can do whatever they want because they are Cloran's crew," chided the captain. "You are no big shots here and will not be treated like any, so mind your tongue and get out of our berth!" Greaves lost his temper at that point and ran to the side.

"You'd better watch yourselves you cretins or you'll get a bashing for your sharp words!" he threatened, and the men on the other ship rolled up their sleeves and reached for ropes to cast at *Wavegrazer*. Cloran's men dropped from the riggings and ran to the side to get ready for a fight, but Len yelled at them and held them back.

"Don't provoke them! We don't need a fight right now, not when we are about to set sail." He turned to the sailors on the new ship who were laughing and mocking them.

"You sailors obviously lack any knowledge of courtesy, but you will not pick a fight here today. We will leave shortly and then you can have the berth, but until then go somewhere else, or if you prefer, as I suppose you will, sit here and whine about it." Len left them cursing and yelling.

"Do they think they own the water?" murmured Jenkins.

"They probably just had a bad day at sea. If we leave them be they'll go off and bother someone else."

After a while they did. The ship bumped *Wavegrazer* a few more times, leaving a nasty scuff on her port side, then rowed around and berthed in the perfectly good spot that was just a few waves away. Len and the crew watched them as they walked onto the dock after tying up, swearing and making rude gestures at *Wavegrazer* and her crew.

"Behaving like that, you'd think they were marauders," said Greaves disgustedly.

"Maybe they are," said Mallory. "You've heard about the missing ships this past year. I think it's more than coincidence that they were all moored here. I bet they were taken out at sea rather than floundered."

"Who was it, Kern and his crew that came up missing the week we left?" asked Turner and Mallory nodded.

"Aye, and I have heard of three more ships that are late coming home since we arrived. I'd say we have some new marauders out there somewhere."

"That's not surprising, now that trade between Menigah and Rogvelt is increasing," said Jenkins as he climbed the riggings. "Those sailors who resorted to piracy during the Nurith Wars are probably loath to give up their new profession easily, now that trade has resumed." The crew eyed the newly arrived sailors with suspicion as they walked into town making a racket everywhere they went, but then they were gone and the crew got back to their duties, except Turner who looked over the side at the new scuff and fussed over it.

Cloran arrived at the ship with Adaire at his side. They didn't say much but held each other. The wind picked up and Adaire's dress blew about—a fine wind for sailing but not a good one for saying goodbye. At length Darrell peered over the side.

"We're all set to go Cap'n," he said. Cloran nodded and waved him off, then turned to Adaire.

"I'll be back as swiftly as I can. This will be my last voyage."

"Remember your promise to me," she said and looked him in the eyes. Cloran smiled and kissed her forehead.

"I won't forget. But now I have a ship to run and a crew that is waiting. I love you Adaire, and I will miss you! Don't work too hard, but work hard enough to keep your mind busy. Think of me, but don't worry." Adaire clutched his hand and squeezed it, but finally let go and Cloran leapt up the gangway and onto his ship. The crowd nearby cheered when they saw him, and the crew all waved to them and spouted words of boasting. Len came down from the ship and, saying goodbye, hugged Adaire.

"Don't worry, I'll keep an eye on him," he said and she smiled.

"Thanks Len, I know you will, you always have. Now don't keep him waiting!" Len boarded and brought up the gangway. The ropes were undone and cast aside and the sailors used the oars to push away from the dock. The men lifted the sails and the ship's nose turned north and, catching a sudden burst of wind, it took off at a great pace. Before long, *Wavegrazer* had become a mere spec on the sea, but still the crowd heard from a distance the sound of men singing, as the last masts disappeared over the horizon:

> *"To sea we go, to sea we go,*
> *We haven't reached our destiny yet.*
> *The sails are up, the sails are up,*
> *We haven't found the west-wind yet.*

No anchor to delay us now,
No sea-beast at our foremost bow.
We are the sea-trodders, we are the wave-masters,
Who ride amongst the whales.

Tarry no longer, work makes us stronger,
The sea is the fastest way home!"

The crowd dispersed and went back to their homes and bragged to their loved ones about how they saw Cloran Hastings, his crew and the legendary ship, and then made tall tales of how he looked, how mighty the ship appeared and how grim and fierce were the crew. But Adaire still stood on the dock as the sun crept higher into the sky. Her hair fluttered aimlessly in the wind and she stared out to sea until the singing no longer reached her ears. At length she shook herself and stood up strait. She bound her hair with a ribbon and dried her eyes with her sleeve. Proud and fair she seemed standing against the wind.

"Tarry no longer, work makes me stronger," she said, and she marched towards the Jade Unicorn to start her morning's duties.

CHAPTER FOUR

The Reef of Many Graves

They were six days out from Stren and the sailors were making good time. The wind had been at their backs all day and they had met with no adventures, which made Cloran glad. The gulls had long since disappeared from the sky, and as they sailed further across the sea, it became a deeper blue, its waves capped with silver. The sky had been clear ever since they left land, but on this day, clouds began to emerge. The sun still shone brightly, but through a mask of thin white clouds that came from the west. Further west could be seen darker clouds, but they were far away.

"Do you think those will reach us?" asked Mallory, pointing at the dark clouds.

"It's possible," said Cloran at the wheel. "If they are riding fast winds, they could reach us before nightfall."

"I hope they are riding slow winds," said Mallory shuddering. "I hate storms."

"What, scared of a bit of rain are you?" said Richards with a chuckle. "It's just water, it won't kill you."

"Still, I'd prefer to just skip it all together. A bit of rain can turn into a bit of storm fairly quickly."

"Hah, I'm not scared of a bit of storm. It would be a nice change of pace."

"I wouldn't mind a little rain myself," said Turner as he sat on his knees, scrubbing the deck. "It sure would wash away this soap before it had a chance to dry. The saltwater makes this deck so gritty! I fear it will never be clean."

"You wash that deck three times a day Turner," said Darrell. "I think we have the cleanest deck of any ship at sea."

"If I don't do it, no one will. You all would be living in filth if it weren't for me!"

"Actually, we'd probably get fed up with it after a while and clean up ourselves, but since you do it for us anyway, there's no need to worry about it."

Turner growled.

"Look there," said Cloran. In the distance, black jagged rocks came into view, and Cloran brought *Wavegrazer* towards them.

"It looks like a reef," said Greaves.

"Yes, this is the Reef of Many Graves," said Cloran, "the most notorious reef in all of Menigah. Many sailors have lost their lives to its jagged teeth."

"Can we get any closer?" asked Richards.

"I suppose, but I don't want to get too close."

"Most of us have never seen it," said Jenkins from atop the main mast.

"All right," said Cloran, "I'll swing by, but when we get close, man the oars so that we will have more control."

Wavegrazer swept towards the towering rocks and they quickly came into full view. The crew emptied the sails and furled them. The ship slowed and each sailor took an oar (except Jenkins who was atop the main mast) as Cloran eased her within a stone's cast of the reef. The men rowed slowly and Cloran sailed around its perimeter. There was little life on the reef, save a plant here and there and a few overbold crabs. Cloran did well to keep his distance from the numerous contorted rocks in gruesome shapes. But amid the dreary, jagged rocks, coral in hues of greens and blues sprawled throughout the reef.

"It's beautiful," said Jenkins from atop the tallest mast.

"Most deadly things are," said Cloran. Len opened the cabin door and came out onto the deck.

"Did you have a good sleep?" asked Jenkins, and Len yawned in response. He walked to the starboard railing and peered over the side.

"Ah, the Reef of Many Graves," he said. "Been a long time since I was last here. Quite a daunting place."

"Look there!" said Jenkins. He pointed to an outcropping of rock that had just come into sight.

"What is it? What do you see?" asked Richards.

"Wreckage."

Wavegrazer rounded a corner and came within sight of the outcropping. Immediately the men saw shards of wood and rope floating in the still waters. *Wavegrazer* drew as close to the wreckage as she could, but all they could see were bits and pieces, the shattered remains of a much larger vessel.

"This was recent," said Len. "The tide hasn't carried these bits away yet."

"I don't see anything but splinters," said Greaves leaning over the gunwale, oar in hand. "They must have smacked this reef pretty hard."

"I don't think they smacked it at all," said Jenkins. "Look."

As the ship slowly passed the rock outcropping, a small shallow cove came into view. There they found the bulk of what remained of the ship. Cloran eased *Wavegrazer* into the cove until the water became too shallow.

"It's burning," said Jenkins.

Cloran frowned and his brow wrinkled. He glanced over his shoulder for a moment and then turned back to the wreckage.

"This was no accident," he said. "I doubt that fire could set itself."

"Marauders?" asked Turner, and the crew exchanged glances. Cloran nodded grimly.

"Looks that way."

With a sudden lurch, the skeleton of the burning hull collapsed. Water doused most of the fires as it crumbled into the sea, but the reef was shallow and it did not fully submerge. It did, however, sink enough to expose a bare strand of smooth rock just behind it, and on it, eleven bodies lay.

"Bodies!" cried Jenkins from atop the mast. "Cloran, can we row any closer?"

"Not without running the ship aground."

"Jenkins make room, I'm coming up for a better look," said Darrell.

"No you're not! There's only room for one up here. Climb the ropes if you want, but don't climb too high!" The sailors set their oars on the deck and climbed the riggings to get a better view. From that altitude, they could see well over the smoldering ship carcass.

Eleven men lay on their backs, their drenched clothing clinging to them. The bodies rested side-by-side, one with its head facing north, the next with its head facing south. Their arms were folded on top of their chests, save those who were missing arms. At the foot of each body lay broken weapons; swords, hammers and spears. A bit of cloth—a cap or torn shirt—covered the face of each, and the corpses were just starting to stink.

"Ugh," said Turner, holding his nose. "They could have at least buried them."

"There's no sand to bury them in, just hard rock," said Darrell.

"Do you see anything of value?" asked Greaves, and the sailors scanned the area.

"Sails, masts, broken swords and bodies," said Len. "I see nothing of value. It looks as if they have been well plundered."

"It's odd that whoever did this caught the ship here at the reef," said Greaves. "What were they doing so close to it anyway?"

"This may not have been the place of the actual battle," said Jenkins looking down from his perch. "It very well could have taken place out on open waters, but after killing everyone on board, the marauders could have easily sailed both ships here and run the merchant vessel aground to make it look like an accident."

"Yes, but they could have just as easily sunk it in open waters, where we would have no evidence of it at all."

Jenkins scratched his chin.

"Hmm, I suppose that's true."

The crackling of the burning ship ceased as the sea extinguished the flames. All that remained of the vessel were ashes and black, smoking wood, but something in the water on the edge of his vision caught Jenkins' eye.

"There's a barrel in the water," he said, pointing north and behind them. "Actually, there is a trail of barrels. Someone is hauling away the spoils." The crew glanced at each other then turned to Cloran.

"Follow them!" yelled Richards excitedly.

"No, that isn't a good idea," said Mallory climbing down from the riggings quickly. "Whoever did this surely deserves to be punished, but we are not equipped to do so."

"We're all quite used to skirmishes," said Darrell. "I'm not afraid of these marauders. They will have a tough fight if they ever bump heads with us."

"True enough, but we don't even know if marauders did this. For all we know, this ship struck the reef by accident, and another that happened to pass by, like us, looted it. Even if it was the work of marauders, we are not the patrollers of the sea. We are sailors and we haul cargo. That is our job and we should stick to it. We don't have the time to run out and chase down a ship."

Richards grunted sharply and leapt onto the deck from the riggings.

"Leave it to Mallory to put forward the sole objection!" he said. "In everything we do, you alone act timid and unwilling to do the slightest thing that may be dangerous. That's just plain cowardice."

"I am no coward," said Mallory sternly. "I've never run from a fight, and never have I hid my face in battle. I've never feared the sea, and never in all my years as a sailor have I forsaken my shipmates. I am, however, prudent and conscious of my mortality, and in this case, I think it is unnecessary to go out of our way to seek strife that doesn't seek us, when we are pressed for time to begin with. If I didn't have someone at home waiting for me, perhaps I would be as reckless as you, Richards, but my life is not as important to me as it is to her and I must respect that and be careful with it, if only for her sake."

Mallory pulled his wedding band off his finger and held it up.

"What this symbolizes means more to me than anything, and I would be selfish to ignore prudence in the pursuit of some cheap thrill."

"Sure, bring up the wife and blame your cowardice on her, that's an easy way out of it," said Richards, but a sharp glance from Len silenced him. No one said anything for a moment as the sea chuckled to herself. Finally, Cloran shook his head and spoke.

"Mallory is right," he said. "We don't have the time. However, I bring to mind our duty, and duty is the only reason we are out here at this time of year to begin with. King Bozin gave us dominion of the waves, and as long as we continue on this journey, every ship that rides them is under our jurisdiction. So then, I suppose one could say that this merchant vessel met misfortune under our watch, and this I cannot abide. If we have the opportunity to rid the waters of a marauding vessel, I think it is our responsibility to do so, so that 'justice and wisdom' might accompany us, as I believe the king said in his letter. We will do what we can today and follow their trail until it becomes cold or we overtake them. Are we agreed?" The sailors nodded, even Mallory, and then quickly took to their work.

Len and the sailors took to the oars and rowed away from the reef, straining their bodies with each pull, and as they, rowed Cloran slowly turned *Wavegrazer* around in the small and shallow cove. The sailors unfurled the sails, pulled tight the riggings, and, catching a slow wind, Cloran eased away from the Reef of Many Graves and headed northwest, following the trail of discarded cargo. Jenkins was the only one who could clearly see the trail of barrels and crates from atop his mast, and he directed Cloran so that the ship stayed just within sight of it. The trail led *Wavegrazer* northwest, and then turned due west.

"Bring her starboard Cap'n," said Greaves. "Let's see if we can snag one of the barrels." The ship turned quickly, caught up by a strong wind, and Cloran brought her alongside a floating barrel. The crew cast ropes and hooks overboard and caught the barrel, hauling it aboard. It was not sealed and saltwater had found its way inside, but in the bottom of the barrel they found grain and rice.

"Spoiled," said Greaves examining it. He lifted up the barrel to see the word *'Ketubim'* stamped on its side. "It's from Rogvelt, from the island of Ketubim."

"The ship we found on the reef must have been heading back to Stren from trading in Rogvelt," said Cloran. "I wager they left Ketubim not long after we did, on our own way back."

"I see their ship!" shouted Jenkins from atop the main mast. "It is far away, but I can see the faint outline of a large sail against the pale sky."

"Back to your posts lads! Let's see if we can fill these sails." They pulled the halyards taught and wind filled the sails. Cloran chased after the shady ship as fast as *Wavegrazer* would go, but the dark clouds he had seen earlier were now overhead, and the waves grew rough. As the sun edged low on the horizon, rain began to fall, lightly at first but then hard and steady. The sailors went below to fetch their coats and then came back topside, buttoning up quickly. Jenkins strained his sight from the top of the mast and muttered under his breath.

"I can't see the ship any longer," he said finally. "It has vanished into the mist, and it will be mere chance to stumble upon them now."

Cloran nodded.

"Let's continue on our way then. Perhaps if we had stumbled upon the wreckage sooner we could have done something about it."

"It's a pity that we're leaving murderers free to whet their bloody appetite," said Richards. "With luck we might stumble upon them again, and then we can do away with the cretins."

"With luck!" said Darrell.

"With luck…" said Mallory.

Wavegrazer abandoned the chase and veered north. The rain continued to fall and drenched both crew and ship. The sun had set and the pink streaks of sky faded into a purple wash. Night arrived and sent a chill through the cold and wet men. Cloran stood at the wheel unmoving, but his lids were heavy.

"Go on below Cap'n, it's my turn at the wheel," said Len. Cloran nodded abruptly, pulled from his thought.

"What? Oh, right. Let's get some food in us and then start the evening shift. We will make up for lost time tomorrow!" The crew stretched and went below deck, where Greaves quickly prepared a meal of bread, butter, ale and dried strips of meat, but Cloran remained at the wheel. Greaves brought some up for

Cloran and Len and then went below to clean up. Len leaned against the main mast in the drizzling rain and ate his dinner while Cloran sailed on. He could tell Cloran wasn't quite ready to give up the wheel.

"What's on your mind?" Len asked. Cloran sighed, picked up his roll and took a bite.

"Suppose you are outside during the night and you stumble upon a cottage," he mumbled with a full mouth, "a well-lit cottage, with people inside feasting, dancing and telling stories. Who would have the better view; you, from the outside looking in, or they, from the inside looking out?"

"Well Cap'n, I think I would. After all, they are in a warm house, with many lights and much commotion to distract them. The window is just a small bit of darkness, an easily overlooked patch set against the firelight, intruding upon their bright, cozy house, and they would do well to ignore it. I, however, am standing in the cold and darkness, looking at the only bright thing near me—that one window—and all my thought and energy is focused upon it. I have a desire, Cap'n; a desire to go through that window and join in the warmth and merriment; a desire to get out of this cold and darkness and accompany the happy people inside. I will notice everything that goes on in that room since it is foremost on my mind, though the people inside won't give a second thought as to what may be outside their window." The wind picked up and the sails creaked and tugged at the masts, while the drizzling rain stung their faces as

Wavegrazer sped on through the night. Cloran gripped the wheel firmly and kept the ship in line.

"Here we stand, on an island in the midst of angry waters," Cloran said. "We have the lamps behind us, we have fires and soft bunks, but we are on the inside of the house, Len. We are on the inside, and the sea is that dark window. I can't help but wonder who might be watching from that window."

"You're thinking of the marauders," said Len and Cloran nodded.

"Not a week out from Stren and we stumble upon this wreckage. *Wavegrazer* is a merchant vessel and wasn't built for battle, though we'll do what we must. Whatever ship attacked those merchants is still out there. We know nothing about them. Suppose they have a better view of us than we do of them?"

"Or suppose they know nothing of us, and we, knowing something of them, have the better view," said Len. He shook his head and walked over to Cloran, laying his hands on the wheel.

"Go to sleep Cap'n. We have many weeks to ponder such things, and we have other business that is more important to consider." Cloran nodded, gave the wheel to Len, picked up his plate and walked towards the cabin. Richards, Jenkins and Mallory came topside and climbed the riggings to tend to the sails and assist Len for the first half of the night, to be replaced by Turner, Greaves and Darrell for the second half, Cloran snuffed out the lamps, walked inside and closed the door, taking the light with him.

Len stood there before the wind. The rain had finally come to a stop, and with the lamps out, he could see the waves and the textures of the clouded sky. He saw the gray rain clouds shrivel away and thin translucent clouds pass over the face of the moon; he saw the stars above, in all the shapes he knew so well, shining like undying sparks against the black, blue tapestry of the evening sky.

"Why," he said, "it's not very dark at all."

During the night, the rain had left and returned. The only dry places on the deck were under Len's boots as he stood at the wheel. Morning had just peered up over the edge of the world and with it came calm waves and dark clouds. The sky was gray and no birds rode the winds. Rain still drizzled, though not as heavily as during the night, and Len stood at the wheel as still as stone, moving little, only to tweak the course of the ship.

Cloran was first to wake. He went through the ship waking the first shift, and Greaves came inside to start on the morning meal. The men walked out onto the deck and clutched their coats tightly about them.

"Still raining?" muttered Richards bitterly.

"Aye, it's been doing this off and on all night," said Darrel, and he shivered, hugging his body. Len just inhaled and laughed.

"Ah, rain is a cleanser! It gives the air a nice bath, which it needs ever so often. I don't begrudge the rain."

"Well I do. You may not mind being wet, but I'm grumpy when I'm soggy."

"How was the night? Dull?" asked Cloran as he walked to the wheel. Len handed it to him and stretched.

"Uneventful, but not dull. I had quite a fine conversation with a rain cloud actually. Too bad his rain was all spent long before I was finished talking to him."

"Yes, well let's just hope a flock of seagulls doesn't swing by for some light conversation," said Turner. "I'd hate to see my nice deck get all messy."

"Nah," said Mallory climbing the riggings. "By now we're too far from land for there to be any seagulls. There's nothing for them to perch on."

"Yeah, except for the ship."

"I don't think they would perch—" started Mallory, but just then, he set foot on a particularly wet piece of rope and slipped. As luck would have it, his hand got tangled in the riggings and his body jerked to a halt. He wailed.

"Mallory! Cloran!" cried Turner and the crew ran to where Mallory twisted in the riggings. As the ship sped by, its lurching stretched his arm, almost out of socket. He cried out and clutched his arm but he could not free it.

"Hold him still!" called Cloran. Richards was already in the riggings and swung towards Mallory.

"Don't struggle," said Richards as he grasped Mallory's hand. It was blue and swollen, caught between two ropes that wrapped around it. "Hold still and I'll get you out." Darrell and Cloran had reached the gunwale and tried to catch Mallory's legs as he flailed in the wind, but he was not close enough. Len let go of the wheel to come help, but the wheel spun around and the ship jerked. Len snatched it again quickly.

"Drop anchor! Unfurl the sails!" called Cloran and the sailors complied, dropping the anchor into the sea and releasing the wind from the sails. Richards grasped Mallory's torso to steady him and tugged at the riggings, suddenly loosing his hand from the ropes. The ropes snapped together and caught onto Mallory's ring finger. As Mallory wrenched his hand free, his wedding band slipped off his finger and fell, bounced off the railing and plunged into the ocean.

"No!" cried Mallory and he struggled.

"You fool, it's just a ring!" said Richards angrily while attempting to drag Mallory to the deck, but Mallory pushed off Richards' chest, knocking him backwards, and leapt into the sea. He hit the water with a splash and the ship sailed past.

"Mallory!" cried Turner again and the entire crew ran to the side, looking to the spot where Mallory had plunged. He did not resurface.

"That reckless idiot," said Richards angrily. He unwound some belayed rope and tied one end around his waist.

"Hold this!" he said, and Darrell grasped the free end. Richards dove into the water after Mallory. The rain began to lessen and the ship grew still. Len came from the wheel to assist where he could as Jenkins climbed to the top of the mast in hopes of spotting Mallory. At length, Richards' head reappeared on the water.

"Do you see him?" called Cloran, but Richards just spat.

"That reckless idiot!" he cried again and then dove. The rope went under and Darrell gave him as much slack as he could. Richards began tugging on the rope.

"Don't let go," said Cloran and Darrell nodded. Richards surfaced again and spit out a mouthful of water.

"Let go of the rope!" he cried between gasps. "I need to find him." Darrell shook his head.

"Let go of it Darrell!" he called again, but Darrell stood firm with a grim face and downcast eyes.

"I'm going in too; hold this Len," said Turner, and grabbing a loose rope he tied one end around himself and joined Richards in the water. Jenkins, Cloran and Len scanned the waves for any sign of Mallory and yelled out his name, hoping he would find them. Richards and Turner used the full length of their ropes and swam to every spot where they thought they saw movement in hope that it was Mallory. It never was, and after a while, Cloran called to them.

"Richards, Turner, swim back." Turner swam back reluctantly and the sailors pulled him aboard, but Richards refused.

"Just give me more time Cloran, I can find the fool if you give me more time!" He dove again and was under for a long while but resurfaced near the ship, gasping for breath and clinging to the rope.

"Come aboard Richards," said Cloran with a low voice. "If he was close enough, we would have found him by now. I won't lose any more of my crew." Richards bobbed in the water, breathing heavily.

"I had him loose," he said at last. "I had him in my arms, and he pushed me away." In a burst of rage, he beat on the side of the ship until he bruised his hand. Darrell and Cloran pulled him up onto the ship and untied the rope from around his waist. Richards sat with his head between his knees, panting.

"How is it that a man who hates to fight or do anything dangerous can turn around and drown himself, over a piece of metal?"

The clouds had parted and the sea cackled mockingly. The sailors kneeled around Richards but were too stunned to say anything. Cloran slowly shook his head.

"The ring was more than just a piece of metal to Mallory. Sometimes men do things out of love without thinking." Richards covered his eyes. Len didn't speak, but slowly stood and entered the lower parts of the ship to tell Greaves.

"Go, everyone; follow Len below. We can do nothing more here. Mallory is at the mercy of the sea now, but don't trust her. She has been merciless as of late." And so the crew arose, hauled the anchor up and went below deck. Cloran approached the wheel and gripped it in his hands. Without a word, he stood unmoving, but then shook his fist at the Sea.

"Your hatred is with me!" he cried out angrily, and his voice was full of despair. "Don't take it out on my crew." The Sea responded with but a calm laugh that lapped at the hull of the ship. *Wavegrazer* drifted in the calming waves, with neither crewman nor captain willing to move on yet, and all aboard thought Mallory to be dead. They mourned his loss, and none dared hope that the Sea would spare him.

Indeed, the Sea would not have spared him if she had her way. Mallory plunged into the water after his ring. He could see the glint of gold spinning and diving far beneath him, and though he swam after it, with every moment the gold band sunk further and further away. The shadow of a ship passed above him and an anchor sailed past him, but the ship moved on, and as he swam deeper, the darkness engulfed him. He released a final cry of despair. The sea filled his lungs and he choked. His vision blurred, but with his last remnants of reason he thought he saw a crab, a giant crab, and it scuttled underneath him, sifting through the sands. But the sea then twisted his body and his eyes were born upward. As he faded away, he thought he saw a horse with flowing green mane, and his ears heard the sound of waterfalls and of wind and rain, and he was lifted, caught in a swift current, or born away to where he knew not, and if it was possible to cry at that moment he did. The glint of gold disappeared and the crab vanished as all went black. To the sea was added one more tear, and she murmured.

CHAPTER FIVE

Staghorn's Rock

When Mallory awoke, he felt wind on his face and his back hurt. He was acutely aware of how hard it was to breathe, and when he inhaled, a sharp pain hit him, causing him to cough terribly. He slowly opened his eyes and sat up. He was sitting on a rocky beach, but it really wasn't much of a beach. It ended where he sat. Before him stood sharp rocks and they were covered with plants that he could not name. He struggled to his feet and his head swam, but he was a man of the sea and was used to walking on wobbly decks, so he straightened his back (which ached just a bit), shook his head (which made him just a little dizzy) and focused his eyes.

He was on a small island. It consisted of large, bulky rocks strewn and piled about. Stiff leafy plants of all colors covered the place, but green and sea-blues were dominant among them. The most curious thing, however, was the peculiar man sitting atop the largest rock, snoring up a terrible racket.

Mallory was startled at first. He didn't know where he was or how he got there. He remembered being with his crew on the open sea, and the last thing he expected to see was this strange fellow. He was tall and bulky. He looked like a man, but his features were strange. His nose was short and broad. His eyes were large, but more wide than tall. He was clothed in blue plants and mosses, as though they were growing on top of him. He snored

71

loudly and scratched his belly in his sleep, which wasn't overly large, but a prominent feature nonetheless. Mallory was about to speak to him but the man suddenly yawned, stretched, and opened his eyes.

"Oh! You!" he said with a wide grin. "Ah, you're up at last! I must say, you swallowed a good bit of seawater, you did, and I'm surprised you are up at all." In that moment, Mallory was hit with a flood of memory. Everything that had just happened returned and he grew frantic. He clutched his hand but the ring was gone.

"Where's my ring?" he said eagerly and the man on the rock snorted.

"Well, and a good 'thanks for saving my life Mister Man!' to you too!" he said.

Mallory blinked.

"Oh, right, well sorry then, I'm not exactly sure how I got here or what has happened to my friends. But thanks for saving my life."

"Actually you'll have to thank Gerbald for that. He's the one that found you floating and bore you up. Gerbald!" he called, and Mallory heard a whinnying far off. From the water nearby came a bunch of bubbles, and then a horse's head emerged.

"A horse! I remember him," said Mallory.

"No, no, Gerbald isn't a horse, my good fellow. He's a Sea Horse! Aren't you Gerbald?" Gerbald whinnied in response. Mallory nodded his thanks to Gerbald. Gerbald snorted water into the air, and then dove into the sea again.

"So 'Mister Sailor Man', how do you like my kingdom?"
Mallory looked around at the few scattered rocks. The island was
hardly an island at all.

"Kingdom?" he asked, and the man on the rock lifted his
chin.

"That's right! This is my kingdom. It may not be much, but
I own it and it is mine! My name is Staghorn and this rock is my
throne. These plants are my garden, and Gerbald is my loyal
subject. Now what is your name, or shall I continue to call you
'Mister Sailor Man'?"

"My name is Mallory," he said, "and I fell from my ship. I
am a sailor on *Wavegrazer* and Cloran Hastings is my captain."

"Cloran Hastings, eh?" said Staghorn. "Yes, I think I have
heard of him. He has passed by my kingdom a few times before in
that big floating log of his. But I've always hid my island to make
sure he never found it. They say he knows everything about the
sea, but he doesn't know of me!" At this he laughed hard, quite
pleased with himself.

"Well Staghorn, do you know what happened to my ring?"
Staghorn finished laughing and stretched again atop his rocky
throne, and as he did, the blue plants and mosses on his body
wriggled.

"Oh yes, I know what happened to it. It's that fellow
Krackaman. He took it."

"Can you tell this Krackaman to give it back to me please?"
asked Mallory eagerly.

"Nope, sorry, I can't help you."

"Why not?"

"Because Krackaman and I aren't exactly the best of friends," said Staghorn. "You see, it all goes back to when he stole my little golden javelin. He has a craving for anything shiny you know, and has a big pile of odds and ends in his rock circle. I asked him to give it back, but he wouldn't have stolen it in the first place if he didn't want it now would he? Anyhow, I tried to get it from him but he's a fast one."

"Can you at least tell me where he lives?"

Staghorn looked at him strangely.

"Why do you want to go there? You won't convince him to give it back and Krackaman could snap you in half. Why waste your time over a little golden ring? I can give you a coral one if you want. I have a few that the mermaids like to throw at me. You see, they think I'm awfully handsome and burly." He stood up and flexed, but the blue moss on his arms really didn't show much muscle. Mallory sighed and sat down on a bare rock.

"It's my wedding band, the one my wife picked for me. I appreciate your offer but it just wouldn't be the same. I must get it back. It was pulled from my finger and fell into the waves, so I dove after it. She'll be devastated if I don't retrieve it."

"Hmmm, that doesn't make much sense," said Staghorn. "Wouldn't your wife be more devastated if she found out you were dead? You're lucky my Gerbald was grazing near where you fell."

"I know, I wasn't thinking. I just reacted. And now I've gone and lost my captain as well as my ring. But please, you must tell me where this Krackaman is."

Staghorn sat back in his throne and thought about it. He tapped his chin with his big bulky fingers and made a long dramatic deal about it.

"Well," he said at last, "I guess if you're going to go, you're going to go. Besides, while you're there you can find my golden javelin!"

"Of course I will, just tell me where to go."

Staghorn laughed happily and stood up. He rummaged around his throne for a bit.

"No, no, not this one, no that's no good either, ah! here," he said and he pulled a spear out from behind his throne. It was long, silver and bulky. "You will have to use this. It's a good spear and it should suit you fine." He tossed it to Mallory and Mallory reeled when he caught it.

"Why will I need this?" he said with a groan.

"Krackaman will not give up your ring easily I'm afraid. You may have to crack a crab to get it!" At this Staghorn burst into a bout of laughter again.

"This is too big for me. I'm only a man, not a…whatever it is you are."

"Mmm, quite right, let's see," said Staghorn and he rummaged through his spears again. "Ah, good, take this then." He threw Mallory a short javelin—short as far as he was concerned, but it was a full-length spear to Mallory. It was long and had a wooden shaft and its tip was oval with notches in it. "Much better. Now, Gerbald knows the way better than I, and unless you can sprout a set of fins real quick, I doubt you will do well getting there on your own. Gerbald!" he called, and there was a whinnying far off. Soon Gerbald's head popped up from the waves again.

"Hey Gerbald! This is Mallory and he wants to have a nice discussion with our good Krackaman." Gerbald whinnied, but seemed a little scared. "Bah, don't worry; I'm sure the lad is up for it. After all, he's one of Cloran's sailors."

"Let's hope this Krackaman is reasonable. I'm not much of a fighter," said Mallory, but nevertheless he gripped the javelin in his hands tightly. Staghorn peered at him with a strange look and smiled to himself.

"Right, of course not. Well then, be off with you now—go to your death! I'm sure our good crab is a bit hungry. Hop on Gerbald's back, and hang on tight! He has no saddle and his mane is slippery when wet." Mallory thanked Staghorn and walked over to Gerbald, who fully surfaced. He looked like a regular horse, only instead of hooves, he had large, stretchy, fleshy fins on the ends of his feet, and he crawled on his knees when on land. His hide was all blue and his mane was all green, and it trailed from his head down his back to his tail, which looked like a wide paddle. Mallory pulled himself onto the back of Gerbald and clung to his mane tightly.

"Oh, Gerbald," called Staghorn from his diminutive spec of an island, "Mallory can't breathe underwater, so be sure not to drown him!" Gerbald whinnied, crawled towards the water and then quickly dove in. Mallory clung to the Sea Horse's mane as tightly as he could, and Gerbald slowly paddled away from the island, gradually increasing speed. When Staghorn's Rock was well out of sight, Gerbald leapt into the air and dove into the sea. Mallory hardly had time to take a breath before he was fully submerged, but then he felt himself lifted upwards and they resurfaced, and he inhaled deeply before they plunged into the waves again. Gerbald continued to hop in and out like this for a long time, traveling incredibly fast, but poor Mallory was having a hard time of it.

"Please—*gasp!*—stop—*gasp!*—doing—*gasp!*—that!" he said, but Gerbald just whinnied (or laughed, as Mallory thought) and continued on his way with Mallory struggling to breathe whenever they surfaced.

It wasn't a very long swim, but to Mallory it was an endless age. With all the strength in his fingers, he clung to the slippery neck of Gerbald as the Sea Horse dove in and out of the waves, having a splendid time, and an even better time than had Mallory not been there to torment. Gerbald whinnied before plunging and spat water when he rose, but all poor Mallory could do was to time his breathing. At last, Gerbald's frolicking ceased and he began to swim slowly, skimming the surface of the water.

"I don't know what I ever did for you to try to drown me!" said Mallory between gasps and sputters, but Gerbald wasn't listening and in fact began to tremble. They swam into a mist, a very thick one that seemed to spring right out of the sea. As Gerbald slowly paddled, the *plop!* and *swish!* of his feet in the water were muted. His breathing was heavy and he snorted.

A short but wide mass of gray rock slowly grew out of the mist before them. As soon as Gerbald saw it, he stalled and refused to move any further.

"Run off then you trembling horse! I'll go alone," said Mallory alighting and plunging into the water. "But don't think that I won't tell Staghorn about this!" Gerbald just glared at him and then submerged. Mallory took the javelin in his right hand and began to swim towards the rocks. They grew larger as he swam near, but they were never anything but gray and shrouded. The mist filled Mallory's lungs and it was hard to breathe. He felt solid stone underneath him at last and he stood up in the shallows, wading towards the watery crag before him.

The gray outcropping formed an outer ring, but all he could see was the first half of the circle. There was a break in the rock ring and Mallory passed through. Inside were piled large stones, some sticking strait out of the sea and piercing the sky, and others sat strewn about in large clumps. There was no green life past the outer circle, not even barnacles, but there were bones, many bones—the bones of fish, whale, and others that were quite indiscernible—and there were shells everywhere, from the smallest of clam shells to the largest of snail shells, some even large enough for Mallory to fit inside comfortably.

The air was dank and heavy but Mallory continued to wade into the very center of the ring. At length, he thought he could hear a voice, or what sounded like a voice. It was low and quiet, and had other sounds intermingled with it—sounds like the cracking of shells on rocks and the snapping of twigs. Soon, he thought he could pick out words through the harsh and hardly intelligible sounds:

> *"Fish and whales and dolphins mine,*
> *Walking beasts and succulent swine,*
> *Crunchy bones and juicy meat,*
> *Tasty critters so divine!*
>
> *I snap and twist and mar and break,*
> *Sitting within my rocky lake.*
> *Oh such vittles are a treat,*
> *And their lives are mine to take!*
>
> *Shiny, pretty gold in hand,*
> *Strewn about my rock like sand.*
> *Ah, such treasures form my seat*
> *For I am the mighty Krackaman!"*

The voice went on singing its song and Mallory could see a large flat stone appear before him in the mist. He waded within reach of it and saw that it was heaped with shining things, some silver and some bronze but most gold, shimmering in the mist and reflecting off the sea in waves of dazzling color. On top of this pile sat a large and fat crab, and he walked all over the mound, picking up pieces that were slipping into the water and placing them on the top of the stack, or picking out pieces of bone and meat and throwing them into the sea. He would scuttle to the very edge of the water and strike it with his giant claws, making such a splash that the waves nearly covered Mallory's head, and every time he did this, he would make a crackling and snapping sound that terrified poor Mallory, but the crab was just laughing. It didn't take much to humor him.

The crab turned and scuttled over to the top of the pile. Mallory summoned all his courage and strode out of the water onto the crab's wide rock, covered in gold. The crab was dancing now atop his mound and singing a new poem he had just made and took no notice of Mallory. Mallory stood with the sternest face he could muster, and then smote the heap of gold with the butt of his javelin. All the gold that was so delicately stacked began to tumble into the water off the side of the rock, making a terrific noise. The crab lost his footing and began to slide down the pile towards Mallory, and when he saw Mallory, he shrieked a cracking, snapping shriek and opened his claws. But Mallory took the javelin in his hand and braced himself, pointing the tip of the spear towards the giant crab sliding his way. Seeing this, the crab scrambled to right himself and the sliding of gold stopped. There stood Mallory, face to face with the biggest crab he had ever seen, larger than a horse, and not just any crab, but a very, very angry crab.

"My gold! My perfectly stacked gold. You ruined my pile!" cried the crab, and he made swatting motions in the air. "Why did you ruin my perfect pile?"

Mallory stood strait up and lifted his spear.

"Are you Krackaman?" he asked. The crab snorted and tucked all his claws and legs in under his body, looking like a very distinguished crab.

"Why, yes I am! I am Krackaman, and this is my domain. This is my rock circle and my mound of gold and you're in my home, uninvited. Now tell me why I shouldn't snap you in half!"

"Because you took something of mine and I would like to have it back."

Krackaman roared a hideous laugh and Mallory could see the claws and cutters in his mouth swaying around.

"Took something of yours, did I? I probably did! I take many things that are not mine, but they become mine. What is it that you think I should give back to you?"

"I lost my ring in the water not long ago and I saw you take it. I would like it back." Krackaman stared at Mallory and then shook his whole body.

"Bah, lost it did you? Lost indeed! You lost it and that's that; now it's mine! It dropped into my sea and now I have it and shall keep it." He reached into his pile of gold and took out a small ring that he placed on the sharpest tip of one of his claws. It didn't fit very well but Krackaman held it right in front of Mallory's face and laughed. Mallory gripped his javelin tightly but didn't move.

"Not only will I take back my ring," said Mallory through his clenched teeth, "but I will retrieve a long lost spear of a friend of mine. I believe you know him? Staghorn is his name."

Krackaman yelped and smote his pile of gold with his claws, sending gold flying in all directions.

"Staghorn! Staghorn! Spear-hoarder, nuisance bringer! I am not surprised that he recruited a lackey like you—bah! And now he wants my golden spear that I stole very fairly from him. Well, he won't have it! And you won't have your ring! And now the mighty Krackaman will crack a man in two!"

Krackaman swiped at Mallory with one of his big claws, but Mallory ducked and dove underneath the brute. The crab spun around and stomped down with his many legs, trying to squish Mallory, but he ducked, crawled and evaded the floundering feet. He raced to the middle of the gold-covered rock and faced the crab with his pointed spear in hand. Krackaman grumbled and growled and sped after Mallory, leaping into the air and crashing down on top of him with his big, knobby belly. Mallory sank into the treasures and the crab leaned over him, snapping at his face, but Mallory fitted the tip of the spear against the crab's hard belly and pushed with all his might.

He did not pierce all the way through the shell because it was too thick, but he lifted the grumbling crab up and thrust him backwards so that he toppled over onto his back. As Krackaman lay there, flailing his limbs, Mallory dug himself out of the treasure and stood to his feet. Seeing the crab on his back, Mallory charged at him, swinging the spear, but just then, Krackaman righted himself and leaped forwards with a snapping claw. It missed Mallory but snagged his shirt, and Mallory spun around and stabbed into the crab's claw. When he pulled out his spear, with it came chunks of white, bloodless flesh. The crab roared and spun around in circles, but Mallory jumped onto the crab's back.

"My claw! You bit my claw!" cried the crab. Mallory climbed forward towards the crab's face and dangled the spear in front of his big, black eyes.

"See here! I have your eyes. I could easily pop them right now and take them home with me. I will have stolen them from you very fairly indeed! Shall I take your eyes?"

"No! Not my eyes! You can't take my eyes. Without them I won't be able to see my pretty gold and shiny things; please don't take my eyes!" Mallory pressed the spear tip against the crab's left eye and Krackaman shrieked and swatted the air with his claws, but he could not reach Mallory.

"You will give me my ring," said Mallory. Krackaman lowered the trembling claw that held his ring and Mallory snatched it quickly.

"Now, you will give me Staghorn's golden javelin."

"No! I won't give the spear. I've had it too long, it is mine!" Mallory pressed the spear tip into the eye harder and it swelled, about to burst.

"To your left! Left! There's the shaft sticking out of the pile, see? Take it, take it!" Mallory reached down from the crab's back and pulled out of the pile the golden javelin, which was quite large.

"Lastly, you will no longer steal from men."

"What! But they have such pretty—" said Krackaman but Mallory thumped his shell hard.

"You will eat fish and snails and other sea life, but you will neither attack men, nor capsize their boats, nor take their things. Promise me!"

"I promise; now leave my eye alone!" cried the crab, trembling. Mallory slid off his shell. Krackaman waddled over to the middle of his pile with his wounded claw and sore eye, feeling downright conquered and hurt, and wouldn't look at Mallory.

"Now that's a good crab. I will rename you! You are now called Munchafish, and if I ever hear of you harassing Staghorn or other men that ride the waves, I will come back and take your eyes with me!"

84

"Just go!" said Munchafish sniffling. "Now I have to organize my pile again because of you! My poor claw, my poor, poor claw…" Mallory didn't stick around long enough to listen to him sniffle and whine. He waded back into the sea with a spear in each hand and a ring on his finger and called for Gerbald. The Sea Horse surfaced with a startled whinny.

"There now, Munchafish wasn't that bad of a crab, he just needed a little smack. Our good crab knows now that he isn't lord of the sea and he won't act like it any more. Let's head back. I have a golden spear to give to your master, and swim on the surface this time! No more diving!" Gerbald obeyed and didn't dive anymore. He had never met anyone to live through a conversation with Krackaman (or Munchafish, as he was told to call him now), and found a new respect for the sailor that fell into the sea.

CHAPTER SIX

How to Get Rid of Nuisances

C loran was at the wheel and the crew was quiet. They had never lost a fellow shipmate before, and Mallory had been with the crew from the very beginning. The only thing they knew to do was keep their eyes forward and sail on, without looking back.

But there was one member of the crew whose job it was *to* look back, and not only back but ahead, and to each side. Jenkins the lookout was doing just that when he spotted a shape off in the distance.

"There's an island to our port Cap'n," he called down.

"Aye, there are many small islands that dot the waters in this area. None have any life on them."

"Maybe this island has at least one life on it," said Jenkins. The sailors thought of Mallory but knew it was unlikely to find him. Still, Cloran nodded and spun the wheel.

"If there is even a chance, we will take it," he said, and sailed towards the small island.

As they grew closer, the island became clearer and larger. It was not as small as it first had seemed, and even more surprising, it appeared to be inhabited. As Cloran had said, there was little natural life there, but he was surprised to see man-made gardens, and many huts made of thin branches, woven together with rope made from what appeared to be hair and cloth. The gardens grew

87

many different kinds of edible plants, a few which Cloran recognized, but some that seemed wholly alien. In the center of the island was a tall, flat hill. In the middle of the hill was a basin of clear water, and it overflowed onto the rest of the island, making small streams that ran through the huts to meet the ocean.

Cloran dropped anchor a ways offshore and ordered the men to lower the dinghy. Len stayed aboard the ship to watch her while the rest of the crew left with Cloran aboard the dinghy. Greaves took to the oars and rowed towards the strange island. As soon as they reached the shore, Darrell and Richards pulled the boat out of the water, and the sailors walked inland upon the black, rocky soil.

"Where are the people who built these huts?" wondered Turner aloud. Richards walked over to one of the clear streams that issued out of the basin of water. He placed his cupped hands into the stream and brought them to his mouth.

"Fresh water," he said.

"And gardens for growing food," noticed Jenkins.

The men walked into the midst of the rickety shacks, and suddenly one of the doors opened. A man stepped out and gazed at the sailors with unblinking eyes before fastening the door shut behind him. He came up to the men in a disinterested fashion, as if they were already annoying him.

"Newcomers, are you?" he said, eyeing them up and down. "Well, you can't have any of our shacks. Go over to the east side of the island, and there you will find bits of rope and wood and other things that the sea has washed ashore. You can make yourselves some huts out of that, or at least a lean-to. Shade is our most precious commodity here. Find a nice place that no one has claimed and you can plant a garden, but you only get a few seeds of each kind of plant we have! We don't grow enough to give whole plants away. My name is Wellard, and if you have any questions about the laws we have on this island, let me know. But not now. I'm heading back to bed."

"Whoa, hold a moment, you must have us confused with someone else," said Cloran. "We aren't coming to live here. We are just looking for a friend of ours. Mallory is his name. Have you seen him?"

Wellard laughed at him unkindly.

"Not here to live, are you? I am afraid you folks are in for a sad shock. You are here forever, as are we all."

The sailors glanced at each other.

"How did you come to be here?" asked Jenkins confused. Wellard shook his head.

"Hey Timson! Get out here!" One of the other shacks opened and a large, burly man stepped out. The shout took the attention of other men, and soon a good dozen had surrounded Cloran and crew, eyeing them up and down.

"Yeah? What is it?" asked Timson.

"Tell these newcomers how you got here."

"I got here the same way they got here. The marauders sacked our ship and dumped us here when we surrendered."

"That's right," Wellard said, facing the sailors again. "That's how I got here too; that's how we all got here and that's how *you* got here. Face it newcomers, you are here for good, just like us. You will never see your homes again, and if you want to live harmoniously with the rest of us, I suggest you don't cause any trouble."

The sailors were now standing in the middle of a circle of men who were admiring the sailors' fresh and crisp uniforms. The inhabitants gazed at the newcomers curiously, making the sailors just a tad uncomfortable.

"Are you saying that you are all victims of piracy?" asked Cloran in surprise.

"No different from you," said Wellard. "We are lucky to have our lives. To this day I don't understand why the marauders let us live."

"That surprises me as well. We just passed a burning ship at the Reef of Many Graves with dead men arrayed on the shore. We think the marauders are responsible."

The inhabitants of the small island looked surprised.

"Strange," said Wellard. "The marauders that attacked us made a point of keeping us alive. They said that they may be thieves but are not murderers, yet they would kill us if we gave them an excuse to. That's why I surrendered without a fight, as did most everyone here. It would amaze me to think that the marauders would go and kill some other sailors, after putting so much effort into providing us with seeds and finding us this island with fresh water."

"Maybe the dead we found were sailors who fought back," said Greaves. "Or perhaps there's more than one ship terrorizing these waters."

"Maybe, but I can't imagine anyone deciding to actually fight the ones that attacked us. Dressed in dark clothes with menacing eyes and a frightening captain..." The inhabitants all shuddered. "Terrifying."

"Aye, most of us have been here since before the Nurith Wars ended," said Timson. "That is when these marauders first found the courage to raid merchant ships. I don't know what they will do when this island gets full. They dump their new victims into the shallows here and sail off without ever looking at the state of things. I hope you fellows can find room to build a hut and make a garden."

"Do not worry about us," said Cloran again. "We won't be staying long. We were just looking for our friend Mallory, and should be on our way." The inhabitants all laughed.

"No, there is no Mallory here that I know of, and unless you have your own ship, there's no way you're getting off this island. And I tell you, I'd kill for a ship after being here so long." The inhabitants all nodded and sighed. The sailors looked at each other warily and began to back away.

"We do have our own ship, so—" started Richards, but Turner kicked him and he shut up.

"You do?" asked Wellard. Cloran cringed. The inhabitants all leaned to the side and look behind the sailors. Floating offshore sat *Wavegrazer*, clean and proud, with her sails gently churning in the breeze. The inhabitants stood with their mouths agape, hardly believing what they were seeing.

Cloran coughed, gave a short, nervous laugh, and then without another moment's hesitation, he and the crew turned and sped towards the dinghy.

The inhabitants cried out and chased after the fleeing sailors. The sailors leapt over the rocks that were in their way and reached the dinghy before the inhabitants. They jumped aboard and Greaves pushed the small boat into the water with all his strength before leaping aboard himself. But the inhabitants were at their heels, and as Greaves took both oars and was about to row away, other hands reached up at the dinghy from the sea and tried to pull the sailors overboard. Richards and Darrell kicked at them but the hands grabbed their legs.

"Don't make us fight you!" yelled Cloran from the bow of the boat. "We have no quarrel with you; just let us go and we will send help your way." But the men groaned and panted and strained to reach them, pulling the small boat back towards the shore.

The sailors drew their curved swords then and the ringing made the inhabitants fall back, afraid. Greaves quickly regained the oars and rowed away, but a few of the larger men leapt after the small boat and grabbed at the sailors' legs.

"Off!" called Darrell angrily, but the men did not get off, and so Darrell swung down his sword. The hands deftly avoided his quick strikes, but still clung firmly to the boat. The sailors kicked at the inhabitants, smashing their fingers, and the men recoiled with cries of pain, but Timson did not heed the pain of his wounded hands and would not let go of the ship, trying to pull them back towards the island. Greaves growled, picked up one of the oars, and swung it down and at an angle, smacking Timson in the head. He lurched and let go, freeing the small boat.

The sailors looked back at the island with pity as the captives moaned and cried out for help.

"We will send help as soon as we can!" promised Cloran, but the men just cursed him and shook their fists.

"What was that all about?" asked Len as the sailors climbed up the ropes and stood once again on the deck.

"It seems we've found more victims of those marauders," said Greaves crossly.

"More bodies?"

"No," said Cloran, "these were still alive, and set up with everything they needed to survive, for that matter." Len scratched his head as Cloran reclaimed the wheel. Cloran pointed the ship away from the island as the inhabitants tossed stones into the sea, never quite reaching *Wavegrazer*.

"It's a pity we can't send them any help," said Turner. "Being secluded on that island...it must be horrible."

"Bah," said Jenkins irritably, nursing his bruises. "I am loath to send those cretins help of any kind. They can build their own boat for all I care."

"We can't be too angry with them," said Cloran. "They were desperate, and desperate men only think of themselves. It would be like trying to rescue someone who was drowning. He'd cling to you like a child and you'd both end up dying."

"I think it's too early to use drowning men as analogies," said Turner quietly.

"Um, Cloran?" asked Jenkins from atop the mast. "Are you sure that the islanders didn't have their own ship?"

"Of course, that's why they wanted ours. Why?"

"Because a ship just appeared from the far side of the island and is heading our way."

"What?"

Cloran handed the wheel to Len and turned towards the stern of the ship. The island was fading into the distance, but just before it rested a ship with three masts, bearing no flag. It was in the process of turning and soon it was pointing right at them. While the island grew smaller, the ship grew larger and more distinct, and Cloran grunted.

"We may be able to settle our marauder problem sooner rather than later," he said.

"Is there any way we can outrun it?" asked Jenkins but Cloran shook his head.

"No, they've got three sails, but I wouldn't want to even if we could. I'd rather take care of this here and now." He turned to his crew. "Ok lads, get your weapons and bring them topside. Keep them hidden but handy for when we need them."

The men quickly went below and returned with a myriad of weapons. They hid the spears behind the masts and the swords behind the gunwale, then made themselves look busy, fiddling with the riggings.

Soon the approaching ship was nearly upon them. A tall man with a red beard stood at the prow of the ship and called to them:

"Drep yer enker!" called the man, but Cloran ignored him. The ship came closer, edging in on *Wavegrazer's* port side, and the man cupped his hands over his mouth.

"Drep yer enker!" he shouted again. Cloran faced the man and put his hand to his ear, shaking his head.

"Drep yer bleemin' enker!" shouted the man again. Cloran shrugged and turned back around.

The ship was soon side by side with *Wavegrazer*. It was longer than her but not much taller, just long enough to accommodate the third mast. It had a pitted and filthy hull, as if no one had ever cared for it, and carved into the prow and painted with faint white letters was the name *Rough Waters*. Men littered the deck, crowding against the starboard gunwale, and dangled from the riggings. They laughed and cajoled in words muddled and twisted, hardly recognizable.

There was a *snap!* and a *whirr!* and hooks came from the ship, over the side and onto *Wavegrazer's* deck. The surly looking men began to turn some cranks and the hooks pulled tight against the gunwale, drawing the ship closer to *Rough Waters*. Richards pulled out a knife to cut the ropes but Cloran motioned for him to stop. Instead, he had his men loosen the sails, and the wind escaped.

"Ey told yeh to drep yer enker!" said the man with the red beard. The hooks were pulled tight and *Wavegrazer* was now side by side with *Rough Waters*, which dropped its anchor. They both slowed to a stop.

"Oh! You wanted me to drop my anchor!" said Cloran, and he slapped his head. "Silly me, I thought you were telling me to drip my ankle."

"Den't be smert," said the man callously. "Meh nehm be Ceckeyed Ernst, and these be meh fehthfull mereuders." The surly men on board all laughed and cheered. "New ye knew why we're here, en' if'n ye knew what's best fer ye, ye'll givehs wet we went."

"Really?" said Cloran, and he scratched his head. "Well it was awfully rude of you to stop us while we were so busy, but no one can say that I'm discourteous host. I know, as all men do, that all filthy marauders like you really want is a nice cup of tea, and I am sure that we can accommodate. Greaves! Do we have any tea for these fine chaps?"

"Yes Cap'n, I have plenty," said Greaves with a grin.

"Good," said Cloran. "Would any of you like cream and sugar?"

"Shet yer filthy mewth!" shouted Cockeyed Ernst, and he spat. "Ey den't thenk ye enderstend yer predecement. I etteh cut yer smert teng et!"

"Ooo, that sounds like a threat, doesn't it Len?"

"Why yes Cap'n, it sure does."

"Do we take threats lightly Len?"

"No Cap'n, we don't."

"There, you see? Len says that we don't take threats likely, so I'm afraid I have to ask you and your dregs to bugger off."

"Thet's et!" cried Cockeyed Ernst, and he drew his sword. "Ehm e gut yez and yer hewl crew!"

Cloran reached for a sword and so did his men. They faced the marauders grimly and the sun flashed off their bright blades. The marauders glanced warily at their captain. They weren't accustomed to prey that actually fought back. But Cockeyed Ernst laughed.

"Ye den't scehre meh weth—"

"Listen up Ernst, I'm done playing," said Cloran angrily. "My name is Cloran Hastings and I have authority under King Bozin of Menigah to arrest you and your crew for piracy and murder. Put down your swords and we will spare your lives."

Cockeyed Ernst didn't move. He glared at Cloran with wide, bloodshot eyes, and his head twitched in rage.

"Kell em!" he ordered, and three wide planks shot from the ship and fell onto *Wavegrazer's* deck. The marauders started to walk across, but Cloran and his sailors lifted the boards and threw them down the small gap between the ships. Most of the marauders were knocked backwards and fell to the deck, but a few dropped between the ships. The ships bumped together in the rocking waves, silencing their screams.

"Aie!" cried Cockeyed Ernst and his marauders all screamed in anger. Some leapt over the sides and others swung from ropes into the riggings.

Greaves and Darrell reached for the weapons behind the mast. Darrell skewered a marauder who was climbing down the mast with his spear and Greaves hacked another down with a long-handled axe. The marauders in the riggings tried to fight back with their swords but couldn't compete with Greaves' and Darrell's reach. Three of them dropped to the deck at once and attacked Greaves, but Darrell came to his aid and pierced one all the way through. Greaves hefted up his mighty axe and swung sideways, felling the other two with one stroke.

Cloran and Len clashed with the leaping marauders at the gunwale and fought back to back. Cloran pierced his first assailant through the heart and then swung at another that appeared to his left. Len chopped off the arm of one that lunged at him and the marauder screamed and fell to the deck. The marauders ganged up on Cloran, each wanting to be the one to fell the captain, and Len turned around to assist him. They backed towards the middle of the ship and four marauders chased after them, then all at once Cloran and Len ducked and lunged forward, cutting two of their assailants out from under their feet. They turned, faced the other two and charged before the marauders knew what had happened, and these also fell.

Turner had a sword in each hand and defended himself against two marauders that had pinned him against the cabin door. Just then, Jenkins appeared with a pointed mace and smashed a marauder in the back of the head. Turner lunged at the other and cut him down, but then tripped and stumbled to the deck. He saw a sword flash above him and a shadow pass by and so he kicked upwards and sent something heavy flying. As he regained his footing, he saw Greaves and Darrell chasing down two that had gone after Richards, and he joined them.

The sight of their comrades dying enraged the screaming marauders. They fought ferociously and hissed and spat. Richards leapt into the riggings and turned to face the marauders that were chasing him. He parried two attacks simultaneously with his long stabbing sword until one was run through by Darrell who appeared behind him. Richards lunged at the second and pierced his throat before Greaves' axe cleaved him in two. The five sailors looked around panting but they had no more attackers. It was then that they noticed Cloran and Len with their backs to the main mast, surrounded by six marauders.

"Cap'n!" they all cried at once, and they raced to aid him. Cloran and Len had felled many of them but were now surrounded. Yet none of the marauders had the courage to make the first strike. Seeing this in their eyes, Cloran lunged at the nearest one. They stepped backwards quickly but then regained their courage and attacked. Cloran parried one, then two, then three swords at once, until a fourth appeared and knocked off his hat.

Jenkins arrived first and swung down with his mace unceremoniously. He flailed his arm wildly and the sight frightened the marauders who scattered. Jenkins bashed one in the head, then switched targets and caught another in the stomach. Richards thrust deftly with his sword and stuck one marauder, but another knocked his sword sideways and then lunged at him. Richards stepped back, dodged then thrust, but was blocked with a parry. The two exchanged blow after blow but could not get through each other's defenses, until at last Richards became enraged, roared and threw his body into the marauder, piercing him through.

The rest fled. Cloran and crew chased them to the gunwale and the marauders leapt back onto their own ship. The seven sailors stood facing *Rough Waters* with their weapons ready, but did not move.

Cockeyed Ernst hadn't budged. He watched the spree from the safety of his own ship and cursed his wretched marauders. Twenty or more bodies lay on *Wavegrazer's* deck, none of them moving. This had never happened before. Men usually surrendered upon seeing them, for fear was a marauder's greatest weapon, and the ones that did fight were either brash and unskilled or rebellious and alone. He didn't know what to do. He felt powerless, and he hated that feeling. He turned towards the three remaining marauders that had fled back to the ship.

"Kell em!" he screamed, but the men just backed away. "Kell em ye cewerds! Kell em!"

The marauders refused. In a fit of rage, he drew his sword and lunged at his men, but the men dodged and slashed at their captain. Cockeyed Ernst fell to the deck with a wail and his remaining men slashed him to bits.

When the marauders stood, they backed up, startled. Cloran and his sailors had boarded their ship, weapons drawn.

"You have a choice," said Cloran sternly.

The men instantly dropped their weapons and kneeled to the ground.

"Good choice," he said.

Jenkins found a holding cell on board *Rough Waters* and he, Greaves and Darrell threw the captives inside, then set to fixing the ship to sail. Cloran had the bodies stripped of weapons and valuables and then stacked them on the deck of *Rough Waters*. He, Len, Richards and Turner began to clean *Wavegrazer's* deck, and the men were quiet. All except Richards, who was feeling rather excited.

"Hah, they had no idea who they were messing with," he said as he kneeled, scrubbing the deck. "I mean, we fought harder battles than that during the Nurith Wars. These guys were pitiful, truly pitiful."

"Richards," said Len, "stop gloating."

"I'm just saying; if that's the way all marauders are, I say we hunt them down one by one. That fight was—"

"Was what?" said Cloran irritably. "Fun?"

"Well…not fun like…" started Richards, but he knew he had dug himself a hole.

"Look around," said Cloran. "We are washing away the blood of twenty or so men. Men who all had mothers, fathers, brothers and sisters. Some of them might have even had wives and children. No, that was not fun. It was horrible."

"I'm sorry," said Richards meekly. He stared at the deck. "I didn't mean it like that."

Cloran sighed and stopped scrubbing.

"I know Richards, and I'm sorry for snapping at you. It's a shame things had to end this way, but this is what happens when you stand up to those who live only for themselves, at the expense of the rest of the world."

"Yes Cap'n," said Richards.

The deck was now clean and the men washed the blood from their hands.

"We're all set over here," called Jenkins from the deck of *Rough Waters*. "I think we can man it with just three."

"Good, we've just finished cleaning up,"

"So what are we going to do with the extra ship?" asked Richards.

Cloran grinned.

"Oh, I'm sure we can think of something."

Back at the island, Willard excitedly boarded *Rough Waters*. He and the other inhabitants had nearly completed loading the ship with food from the island, had buried the twenty marauders near their old shacks and were gleefully exploring every inch of their new vessel. Timson wore a broad grin as he clambered through the riggings, learning every knot and rope, and he said over and over, "At last! At last!" Willard walked to the prow of the ship and faced *Wavegrazer*, which rested not far away.

"Thank you Captain Hastings!" he called, and he bowed low. "Please forgive our behavior earlier. After spending so many years on that wretched island, our self-control had waned. I do hope you will not hold it against us."

"Apology is accepted," called Cloran with a smile, standing with his crew against the starboard gunwale. "I'm just glad I was able to fulfill my promise. Now you have the very ship that took yours long ago!"

"Oh, no, this wasn't the ship that attacked us," said Willard. "That ship was larger."

Cloran frowned.

"Then it seems that there are more marauders out there," he said lowly.

"With you and your crew patrolling the sea, I have no fear of marauding vessels anymore," said Willard with a smile.

"Be sure to deliver the captives to King Bozin!" said Cloran. "I charge you with this *geasa*; sail strait for Stren, tell Bozin everything that has happened and deliver the captives into his hands."

"You have my word, Captain Hastings, and everyone on board is forever in your debt. Farewell and safe journeys!"

Rough Waters unfurled its sails and lifted its anchor. As the ship passed by, all the men on board cheered and waved at *Wavegrazer* and swore oaths of perpetual love and loyalty. Cloran and his men waved as the vessel sped past, and Cloran sighed.

"Well lads, the sun is setting and we've made little progress on our journey today. But at least we were able to help out these poor souls and make the sea a little safer."

"I hate the thought of there being more marauders out there," said Len. "I was really hoping we had taken care of it."

"Same here," said Cloran. "But for now, we have a long journey to finish, and if the sea throws another obstacle in our path, we will deal with it. Until then let's set sail and make up for lost time. To your posts! Raise the anchor! Make dinner! Let's see what's in store for us tomorrow."

CHAPTER SEVEN

A Day with the Archineans

I t was just another night at sea, and Len stood motionless at the wheel as the ship rocked beneath him. It was close to dawn. Greaves, Turner and Darrell hung in the riggings, tending to the ropes and minding the sails, but were quiet, sometimes closing their eyes and nodding off, or lost in deep thought, as men tend to do when on the silent sea at night. They couldn't see the moon. Dark, billowy clouds had appeared just before sunset and obscured both moon and stars. All Len could see were the dark lapping waves and the foam that accosted the ship's hull, but he didn't heed the darkness and sailed strait on through the night.

He closed his eyes and inhaled deeply, as was his wont before the sun rose, to smell the sea, the clouds and the air, and to glean all their secrets in one moment, but this was a different sea air he smelled, and he opened his eyes abruptly. He glanced around but didn't see anything. He looked out to sea, but nothing stirred save the churning waves.

The sea trembled and the ship jerked. Len let go of the wheel and ran to the gunwale to look over. He could see better now because the darkness was lessening with the onset of dawn, but still all he could see was ocean. The ship creaked and the wheel spun. The ship shuddered again and the sails moaned.

"Enough games!" called Len to the Sea, but there was no answer, unless the roaring of the wind was a laugh or taunt. The ship abruptly reeled, throwing Len to the deck and tossing the crew down from the riggings. *Wavegrazer* listed to the starboard side, and the whole ship trembled as the masts swayed. Cloran was first to burst out onto the deck.

"What's wrong?" he asked, but the ship shuddered and he too was thrown to the deck. Jenkins and Richards stumbled out of the door, awakened from their sleep too early.

"Len, what did you run into?" asked Richards and he clung to the railing.

The ship jerked again and threw the crew forward. There was a loud scraping underneath them. *Wavegrazer* rocked and it felt as if she was rising, and the sea disappeared beneath her. Out of the waves came a black rock, and it lifted *Wavegrazer* up, out of the water, and the ship flipped onto its side. All the men on deck tumbled onto the new ground below. The rock kept rising and it grew large and wide. It groaned beneath them and the sea receded swiftly in all directions. Cloran could see new land appear below them. *Wavegrazer* rested atop a large and tall hill of rock that dove steeply and smoothly onto a long, flat stretch.

At last, the rumbling stopped and water drained from all around them. The clouds above parted and the early morning sun peeked out of the sea. Cloran saw to his amazement that an island lay before and underneath them, long but not terribly wide. It was all of a single stone; there were no pebbles or earth but just solid, hard and black slippery rock. At the base of the hill were houses made of coral and other sea rocks, stacked upon one another or welded together. They were scattered in no particular order but all faced east, the direction the island pointed, and at the very end was a circular impression in the stone with a long shoot of coral sticking up from the center.

The sailors regained their footing and walked to the edge of the high rock hill, and stared out at the length of the island in awe.

"What just happened?" asked Jenkins. "Did we run into this?"

"I think it ran into us," said Cloran

"Look at the ship!" cried Turner in dismay. He ran to *Wavegrazer* and clutched his head in worry. "Look at her! She's toppled over and the masts are all broken!" The crew huddled around the ship and moaned.

"It will take a week to repair her, and a day just to right her," said Cloran and he sighed.

Just then, there was a blast—the sound of a horn blowing or something close to it—and the sailors faced the island to see what it was about. To their astonishment, the stone and coral houses began to open and out came some peculiar creatures. They were long and had the shape of men but the appearance of fish, and they had different colored scales all over their bodies. On their backs were fins and spines, and along their arms were the same, stretching from their shoulders down through their elbows to their wrists. Their bodies were blue, some darker blues some lighter blues, and their heads were round with narrow eyes, round chins and sharp snouts. They were bald and had no legs, and they flopped out onto the smooth, dark rock as the horn blew.

It was then that the sun fully rose, the whole of its disk burning brightly on the horizon, and it shone upon the island, heating it. The rocks steamed and the creatures began to wail. At once, they all underwent the same strange contortions. They screamed and cried and flopped onto their backs. Their tails stretched and then ripped in two, and the two halves grew knees and bent, and the fins turned into feet. They reeled to their knees and the crew saw from atop the hill the creature's fins and spines become soft, and they receded into their backs or shriveled into hair that streamed down from the creature's heads. They stood and all scales fell from them or turned into hair. Their eyes grew wide but their bodies remained in tints of blue and green. They stretched and flexed their new bodies and growled at the sun. They shook their fists and stomped on the ground, but soon their frenzy ceased and they examined their bodies, running and leaping about on the rock. They put kilts of kelp and other sea plants around their waists, drying in the morning sun, and they brought their hair back and tied it.

The sailors stared in astonishment from atop the stone hill. The creatures below walked about greeting each other and talking. But then one noticed Cloran and the ship. He cried out, and the whole community of creatures turned and saw them, and began to run toward them. Cloran and his men did not know whether in hostility or excitement they came, but their faces were fierce and wild as they ran violently up the hill.

Cloran quickly faced the ship.

"To the ship lads, get your swords! They don't look like they're trying to say 'hello'." The crew scrambled towards the ship to fetch their weapons from inside, but the creatures overtook them and laid hands upon them, dragging them back. They seized Cloran first but he planted his feet firmly on the rock and pushed upwards against it, throwing one of the creatures off the hill to the jagged rocks below. But three more appeared before him and restrained him, taking his arms and wrenching them down. The crew cried out and came after him, freeing him from the creatures, but for each sailor there were three assailants and soon they were all bound in ropes made of kelp—all except Darrell, who had hid himself in the ship. He found his curved blade and returned to see his comrades being dragged away. Fierceness took him then. He smote the rock beneath with his sword, showering sparks at the creatures, and he dashed his body into the crowd, killing three with one strike. He cut the bonds of Greaves who scrambled to his feet, and with his massive arms crushed one of the creatures, then picked up another and threw him. But for all their might and skill, they were overborne. The creatures struck Darrell's sword from his hand and it fell clattering to the ground. Four creatures, two on each arm, restrained Greaves, bound the men again, and led them off into the town of coral and rock houses.

"What a catch! What a catch!" the creatures called as they dragged the sailors towards the center of town. "We've cast our net into the sea of men, and pulled out quite a catch indeed!" They took the sailors to the steps of one of the larger houses. It had no doors and no windows, but had tall coral spiraling pillars and flattened rock walls. Gaps and slits were in the walls, large enough for one of the creatures to swim in and out of, but a large oval opening was in its very front, fit for someone to walk through. The roof was thatched with shells and the fins of fish, and dangling plants stuck to the walls, hanging over the oval opening. The creatures threw Cloran and his crew down before the opening, and their captors continued to chant, "What a catch! What a catch indeed!"

Out of the door came a frail creature, but he held himself nobly, obviously considering himself to be of great importance. He was clothed in a long robe, all red, sewn together with starfish skin.

"A catch already! A fine one eh?" said the creature. He came up, inspected the crew, and nodded to himself muttering. "Yes, they look strong and fierce. I hope they did not put up too much of a fight."

"They killed six of us! Six of us!" wailed the creatures, and the man at the steps seemed startled.

"And many more would we kill again, if you had caught us armed," said Darrell, with a growl. The frail creature smiled and came close to Darrell, then slapped him across the face.

"Such vigor! All the better. These are fitting sacrifices to Nodde, yes, fitting sacrifices they be."

"Sacrifices?" said Cloran and he snorted. "We won't be sacrifices to a silly sea folk or their silly gods. I am Cloran Hastings and this is my crew. Release us now! We are on an urgent journey and cannot afford delay." At this, the creatures laughed, a bubbling, gargling laugh, and the noble looking creature in the starfish robe grinned wide.

"Oh, we will not release you, not now or ever," he said, "and Cloran Hastings is your name? Splendid! Rumor of your deeds has reached even the bottom of the sea, and perhaps your sacrifice will be enough to last the whole year."

"I'm warning you," said Cloran. He stared directly into the eyes of the proud creature. "You will not succeed in this sacrifice. It would be better for you if we were released and leave on good terms, than for us to free ourselves and slaughter this entire encampment." Cloran stared at the man sternly and the man in the starfish robe looked sternly back, but when he spoke again, his voice quavered.

"We are the men of the sea! We are the coral-molders, the rock-hiders, the trap-layers! We are the shark-flayers, the whale-riders! We are the Archineans, and I am their chief; Archeen is my name. Every year on this day, we arise from the sea and catch what we may, to sacrifice to Nodde. Look!" he said, and he faced the sun, which had risen high by now and was no longer red but golden. "Behold Nodde, he who has power over us all!"

The Archineans fell to one quavering knee in reverence and fear, and some even in hatred.

"He resides within the burning sphere and watches over all our deeds. It is he that curses us with the man-shape, which only the sea can cure, and so we make sacrifices to ease his anger and return us to our natural form. No, we will not release such a prize as was given to us this day. Nodde would not allow it, and would doubly curse us all. You shall be our scape-men, our offering, and we shall live another year in peace under the waves, with prosperous raiding and pillaging." And with that, Archeen raised his hand and the Archineans took hold of the sailors, hitting them across the head with rods of coral until the men saw nothing but darkness.

Cloran awoke to the soft, pale gaze of moonlight upon his face. He heard the quiet lapping of water and felt a cool breeze, which chilled him. He sat up and his head swam. He reached up and felt a bump starting to grow on his forehead, and he winced. He was lying beside Jenkins, who was either asleep or unconscious. The Archineans were holding them in a cage of some sort made of fish bones and tendons. Looking around, Cloran saw that his cage was atop a pedestal and around him were three other cages with the remainder of his crew within. He nudged Jenkins and Jenkins groaned, holding his head.

"My eyes hurt," he said blinking. He sat up and looked around. "I can hardly focus; those creatures better not have messed up my eyesight." Cloran woke the rest of the crew by throwing bits of bone at them from his cage.

"How far are we off the ground?" he asked, for he could not see over the ledge of the pedestal he was on.

"Not far, just a short drop," said Len, peering over the side.

"A bit of a tumble, but we should be fine. Let's see if we can get these cages to fall and break open."

Cloran and Jenkins stood and leaned against the side of their cage that was closest to the edge of the pedestal, and the other crewmembers did likewise.

"Ram your shoulder against it, but don't let the weight of your feet hold the cage down," Cloran said, directing them. Cloran and Jenkins backed up then ran and jumped against the wall of their cage. It skidded closer to the ledge.

"Good! Just like that." The sailors did this over and over until their cages were teetering over the edge, ready to fall with one more nudge. But just then, the sailors heard the blowing of horns or shells. They saw the coral houses empty in the moonlight, and the creatures with their new legs came walking up towards the three sailor-filled cages. The Archineans were dressed in long robes with broad, flat collars. As they walked towards the sailors, Cloran could see many different designs in their robes made from shark and whale skin. They looked like worn tapestries of the sea, with drawn depictions of tales and histories of their people. When they reached the sailors, the crowd of Archineans encircled the three cages. One man walked to a small circular mark on the ground. He had a pouch of sewn skin and he poured a clear liquid from inside onto the circle. It filled the circle, letting out a cold chill, and a pale blue light issued forth, illuminating the whole of the area and casting long, flickering shadows. Then Archeen walked forward, casting a menacing glance at the sailors.

"Fellow Archineans!" he said, and the crowd of creatures cheered. "Today is the day we appease Nodde and ensure our prosperity for another year. Here are our sacrifices that were given to us by Nodde himself!" Archeen pointed at the sailors and the throng of seamen shouted and flailed their arms in the air. "Before we begin, we will now recite our clan chant, so that Nodde knows who it is that gives him this offering," and with that, he and the Archineans chanted the following:

> *"We are the strong Archineans,*
> *Who rule beneath the waves.*
> *We have striven with every clan,*
> *Since the ancient days.*
>
> *We wrest kingships from the weak,*
> *From those who are unwary.*
> *We torture those who inhabit the sea,*
> *And all the coasts we harry.*
>
> *Praised be the day Archeen,*

Took his seat of power!
We follow him in awe and fear,
And force our foes to cower.

Praised be our trial-law,
Given to every guest!
For due to it our king, Archeen,
Succeeded in passing his test.

And so forever we will fight,
To steal from those in need,
To dice all life to tiny bits,
And make the ocean bleed."

At the end, the crowd of Archineans made a gurgling sound and Archeen bowed his head. When they finished, Archeen raised his hand.

"It is time! The moon is full and we are ready. Now we summon Nodde, to see if this sacrifice pleases him!"

Two creatures in long, black robes adorned with white drawings walked forward with a censor each. Inside were smoldering pearls bubbling in the censors, and the two men kneeled before Cloran and Jenkins' cage. They emptied the censors with one motion and the pearls leapt out, bounced and hopped away, dancing around the pedestal. The three cages formed a circle and the pearls leaped and skidded across the rock making a horrible hissing and scratching sound, and everywhere they touched they stained the rock white, as if scorched by a searing heat. At last, the pearls collected into a little basin at the center of the three cages, and all went quiet.

The Archineans fell to their knees, and many bowed their heads. Only Archeen remained on his feet. A white glowing ring appeared around the basin where the pearls had collected. It shimmered in the moonlight and then a white cylinder of light shot up from the ring, encircling the pearls. The creatures began to gurgle again and some of them pounded on the rock with their hands and feet. None but Archeen and the sailors dared to look into the light.

The air groaned. The rock began to tremor and fear made the Archineans cower before the light. And then with a sudden hiss, the light vanished and steam rose from the circle where the light had been. Sitting on a stone in the middle of the circle and looking very uncomfortable sat an old man. He looked much like the Archineans, but he was older and his head was bowed. He sat in man-shape and wore a long yellow robe embroidered with red knots. Little red tassels hung from the hem of his robe and the end of his sleeves. His head was unadorned save for a full head of curly, rust colored hair—the only one of his nearby kindred to have such a hue—and he was snoring.

Archeen held his hands high and looked at the newcomer expectantly, but all he received was snoring.

"O Nodde," said Archeen finally, shaking his arms, "tell us, your followers, what we should do with this gift we have for you!" Nodde stirred and the creatures trembled and clenched their chattering teeth. He sluggishly opened his eyes and sat up in his knobby rock-seat.

"What is it? Och, my back, it's crooked. Is that the moon? Look there, it's night, so go away, I'm sleepy. What days are these when old men cannot get any rest..." With that, Nodde lowered his head to his chest and promptly continued his snoring. A blast of sound pealed across the night sky. The circle lit up and shot light skyward. As soon as it had started, it was finished, and as the light faded the sounds ceased; the man in the yellow robe was nowhere to be seen.

Archeen stood with his arms raised and trembling, staring dumbfounded at the spot where Nodde had sat. The Archineans around him slowly regained their courage and began to stand to their feet.

"What is it Archeen? What did our lord Nodde say?" they asked. Archeen regained himself and spun around.

"Ha!" he exclaimed franticly, and the light in his eyes was wild. "Nodde has spoken to us and we will obey!" He turned and faced the caged sailors and raised one clawed finger at them. "The sacrifices were accepted, and now they will be delivered." The Archineans cheered and ran forward with dried logs of sea plants and stacked them under the raised cages.

117

"That's not at all what he said you ridiculous urchin," shouted Darrell from within the cage.

"Your own revered leader cares little for what sacrifices you give him," said Cloran. "You would be wise to let us leave now, while we still have a chance to part peacefully."

"Oh, surely there are better ways than this to sue for your life!" cried Archeen, and he urged the creatures to build the fires faster. Cloran turned around and spoke to his crew.

"Well, we gave him a chance to let us go peacefully," he said. "It is best we break these cages and make for our weapons before they can catch us."

"Wait a moment," said Jenkins. "Let's see if we can do it another way, so that we don't have to destroy these creatures." Jenkins came to the edge of his cage and pounded against it.

"Archeen! Is this any way to treat guests?"

"Guests? You are no guests!" he said. "You are our sacrifices, and sacrifices should be silent."

"Ah, but still, we are in your company. We arrived here by misfortune and you have taken us in. As guests we demand a trial, the same as you were given when you came as a guest!" At hearing this, the Archineans stacking the logs ceased and murmured amongst themselves.

"He is right, as guests they have been mistreated," murmured the Archineans and, "Even Archeen was given his trial when he was our guest."

"But you are not our guests and we have no need to give you a trial," said Archeen, but the Archineans circled around him and called, "A trial, give them a trial, this is our way and we will honor it."

"That was a tricky bit of speech," whispered Cloran to Jenkins. "How did you know about this tradition of theirs?"

"Didn't you listen to their chant?"

"No, not really. It was hard to pay attention. They sound like pigs being stuck."

"Very well," Archeen said hotly. "You will receive a guest's trial. What boon will you claim of me if you should succeed?"

"That you release us," said Jenkins, "every man here, and that you will never again sacrifice men to Nodde."

"This I will grant you."

"And not just that," said Jenkins. "You will repair our ship and set us loose with good will."

"This I can manage."

"And something more," said Jenkins. "That you will never seek revenge." Archeen gritted his teeth.

"It was wise for you to ask me this, and if you pass the trial I give you, so shall these securities be assured. But now!" he cried, and he grinned widely and stood tall. "It is time for you to pass the trial I choose." Archeen put his arms behind his back and paced a bit in front of the cages. He stopped then, looked long at Cloran and then shot his gaze skyward.

119

"Men of Menigah," he said, "it is this which you must do. You will describe to me the face of the moon and what is upon it."

"Oh come on," said Richards angrily between his bars. "Give us something reasonable! No one can answer that."

"Yet it is the trial I lay before you, so answer it or die!" The Archineans murmured and the sailors groaned.

"The moon is it?" said Len facing his comrades. "How are we to know what is on the moon?"

"I suppose we can look," said Jenkins. He sighed, shrugged, and looked up at the moon. Cloran, Len and the rest of the crew looked up as well and held their gaze at the incandescent sphere.

"I see nothing," said Richards at last, and he lowered his eyes.

"Ha! Do you give up?" chided Archeen.

"You'd better wait until all of us have had a chance!" yelled Richards, so venomously that Archeen's smile faded quickly. But one by one, the crew averted their gaze from the moon.

"I just don't see anything," said Darrell at last. "It looks like a glowing white sphere to me." Cloran and Jenkins were left looking, Cloran with his hand over his brow and Jenkins on the tips of his toes. At last, Cloran turned away.

"Ugh, this is ridiculous," he said. "We'd better start working on getting these cages to fall."

"Wait," said Jenkins, and he pressed himself against the cage. "Cloran, lift me up higher. Let me stand on your shoulders."

The sailors looked at each other curiously, but Cloran came forward and knelt, and Jenkins climbed up onto his shoulders and stood. Cloran slowly pulled himself upright and they steadied themselves with the bars.

"What are you fools doing?" asked Archeen, but Richards eyed him darkly and the creature's voice quavered.

"Just getting a closer look," whispered Jenkins to himself. He and Cloran stood for a moment, with the entire crowd in a hush.

Len sat on the floor of his cage staring numbly at the crowd, when suddenly his eyes sparkled and he sat up.

"I can see…" whispered Jenkins to Cloran, "I can see water."

Len gazed at the two men with the black robes, the ones who had carried the censors containing the smoldering pearls. They were standing close together so that their robes almost touched, and faced Len so he could see them plainly.

"I see a long cavern of stone, with high cliffs, and a river," said Jenkins.

As Len looked upon the two men, he concentrated on their robes. Side by side as they were, the white drawings upon them came together and formed an image.

"I see holes and scattered stone. I see destruction."

Upon the meeting shoulders of the garments were, as now could be discerned, a white sphere, with rays pointing in all directions. Below them were three horizontal men, lying on their backs, their eyes closed and their bodies covered with a cloth.

"I see a mountain, an eminent peak, and upon it a gleaming tower."

In the center of each robe were lines in the form of waves, and under them a myriad of peoples with the tails of fishes, and spines on their backs and arms. They all faced towards the white sphere, and they pointed at the three lying men.

"I see five long silver strands coming from the tower, and they lead here, to earth, and they meet…"

At the bottom of each robe were three stones, and inscribed upon them were names in letters Len could not read. Below the stones was a long, bold white line, and below that it was black, and there were many eyes, eyes that stared back at the gazer.

"…the sea."

"I will tell you now," said Len standing to his feet and addressing Archeen. All eyes had been on the moon, but now the creatures turned to Len. "I know what is on the moon, and your followers will attest to this. On the moon are three graves, and in the three graves are three men. The men are from the sea, your forbears, and the patriarchs of your society. It would seem to me that they were ancient kings of your people, and were buried on the moon."

The creatures gasped and Archeen's mouth dropped. A cloud then passed over the moon and obscured Jenkins' vision. He reeled backwards, sending both he and Cloran tumbling to the floor.

"Attached to the sea? What do you mean?" asked Cloran but Jenkins rubbed his eyes.

"The ropes dove into the sea. The moon is connected to the sea by ropes, somehow." He covered his eyes with his hand. "I think I need to rest my eyes, I doubt they were meant for seeing that far." But when Cloran and Jenkins stood, they found Archeen standing aghast and the Archineans scrambling to the cages.

"They saw our forebears; they know what is on the moon. Let them free!" The cages were all unlocked and the sailors stepped out.

"Trickery!" cried Archeen. "No one knows what is on the moon but us. It is a secret that we alone guard."

"But not too well it seems," said Len, "and now that we have passed your trial, you owe us quite a debt indeed." Archeen was fuming and couldn't squeeze a word out of his clenched lips, but his subjects were praising the sailors for their knowledge. There was nothing he could do, if he wanted to remain in power. At last, he lowered his eyes and sighed.

"Free you are then, and tomorrow we shall repair your ship."

"Don't forget the rest of your promise," reminded Cloran. "You will take no vengeance, and never again will you wrongly take hold of men against their will."

"I will not forget."

The creatures went back to their homes and the sailors went towards the ship to stay the night. But Jenkins walked slowly, and every now and then he stopped and gazed up at the cloudy sky before continuing on his way.

CHAPTER EIGHT

Cache Cove

I t took many days before the sailors had refitted *Wavegrazer*. There was some deck and hull damage, though nothing drastic, and many food items were lost or spoiled when the ship tipped. It took a whole day for Cloran, his crew and the Archineans to right the ship and set it up on supports. The creatures worked hard during this time, but ever fearful of the strange sailors that had landed on their island, because Archeen spoke ill of them at the end of each day.

But at last, the ship was fully repaired and seaworthy again, and the crew boarded her. Their larder was refilled with the foods that the Archineans had on hand—dried plants, weeds and a small store of fish meat. The crew climbed the riggings and Cloran and Len stood at the gunwale overlooking the small stone island where Archeen and his people assembled to see them off.

"Thank you for helping to repair the ship," said Cloran to the Archineans, but the creatures trembled and Archeen shook his fist.

"Don't think too much of it," yelled Archeen wrathfully. "We only did it so as not to break our promise. Now get off our island, and I hope chance never has our paths cross again!"

"It's a pity you have to be so hostile. Are you sure you are able to keep the rest of your promise? Eat fish, kill sea-life, and stay underwater--that is your domain."

"Keep to your own business and ride the waves in your silly hollow log," growled Archeen. "We will live as we please, but never mind about our promise, we won't break it. And now I wish you rough seas, shallow waters and dead wind!"

With that, he and his Archineans retreated to their coral homes. Soon there was a shudder throughout the whole of the rocky island. Wooden braces propped the ship up on all sides, and kept her from tipping. The island then began to sink, as swiftly as it had risen underneath the sailors days before, and soon all the coral houses were submerged. Water veiled the length of the island, and the waves grew closer, climbing the rock whereon *Wavegrazer* rested until it lapped at the supports. Then they too were consumed, and as the sea engulfed the ship, she slid into it with a splash. The ship drifted free, and the tip of the rock disappeared beneath the waves. As the sea calmed, Cloran could hear the muffled wails of the Archineans underwater as they regained their former shape. Bubbles of air came bursting to the surface in a sudden rush until finally the sailors could see no trace of the island.

And so the ship's sails were unfurled and Cloran took the wheel in his hands once again, pointing *Wavegrazer* north.

Many nights floated by, and Cloran was making good time. He was upset, however, with the previous delays, and drove the ship as fast as she could go, straining the sails. The sailors worked quickly and efficiently. They did not complain but took to the task, for it was their job. They had been on longer journeys with Cloran before this one and trusted him completely. This was the last trip of the season, and when it was over, they would be home with their friends and relatives, the long hours of sea riding forgotten for a time.

On the fifth day out from their chance meeting with the Archineans, *Wavegrazer* sailed on calm seas. It was the middle of the day and Cloran was at the wheel. Len had just woken up and came topside.

"How far do you think we are from Miotes?" he asked.

"I would guess," said Cloran, "that if we maintained our course with little to no interruptions, we should hit the northern part of the Sea of Dirges in less than a week. From there it shouldn't be much longer at all--a day or so, perhaps."

"Great! At this rate we should get there before winter hits."

"It's not the getting there that bothers me, but the getting back."

The crew sailed on under the sun as it arced high above. At length, Jenkins caught sight of something.

"It's another small island Cap'n," he said, pointing east. "Smaller than the one that held those sailors."

"Any signs of life?"

"Aye, I think I see...a dock, with some ships tied to it. A great many ships."

"Way out here?" wondered Cloran aloud. He aimed *Wavegrazer* that way and sailed within a stone's cast of it. The crew furled the sails and took to the oars, and slowly sailed around the island.

They saw that it was indeed small--tiny enough to walk all the way around without ever seeing the sun move. What startled the sailors were the dozens of ships that were moored to the floating docks. A large wooden structure sprawled over the whole of the rocky island. It was dark and ratty, with no glass windows, but many gaping holes within its walls. A wooden stair led up from the docks to a door that was raised above the ground. Four long wooden docks extended from the island, and tied to each were ships floating listlessly in the morning sun.

"It's a fleet," said Jenkins in wonder.

"Why would sailors berth here?" asked Len. "There isn't any room to house them, unless they stay on their ships."

Suddenly Greaves yelped and pointed at one of the docks.

"Look, there!" he called. The sailors looked to where he was pointing and gasped. One of the ships was flat and long, just tall enough to match some scuff marks that had been recently made on the port side of *Wavegrazer*.

"Ah-hah!" exclaimed Len. "So *they* are the other marauders."

"Oh!" exclaimed Turner as a thought struck him. "Perhaps these other ships were seized by the marauders. There's twenty...twenty three...twenty seven ships here!"

"A perfect place to hide ships and loot, while avoiding the authorities," said Darrell.

"Should we do something Cap'n?" asked Richards, and Cloran nodded.

"It would be a great blow to piracy if we could catch these marauders unguarded. I would be irresponsible to ignore this," he said, and then he sighed, shaking his head. "Even though we don't have time to deal with it."

The men rowed *Wavegrazer* into a free spot at one of the docks and then tied up.

"Check these ships to see if you find anyone imprisoned or in danger," said Cloran. The sailors made sure that they had their swords, and some went to fetch spears. "If you find any trouble, don't fight alone. Call out, and get the rest of the crew with you."

"Yes Cap'n," the sailors said.

"Make your surveys brief, but search every chamber. When the ships are all checked, meet me inside that building," he said, pointing at the rickety shack. "I'm going to see if I can dig up any information on what kind of people we are dealing with."

The sailors lowered the gangway and the crew quickly scattered in all directions to search the moored ships. Cloran walked along the dock towards the door, looking for any sign of the marauders. The walkway around the building hugged its wooden walls. Cloran looked between the cracks in the dock and saw that the water was clean—no waste or rotting foods, no discolored spots or floating debris—and it was obvious to him that the marauders didn't spend much time here. He didn't hear any sounds of conversation, laughter, or other signs of human habitation coming from the building, and he realized that they might still be out at sea and could possibly arrive at any moment.

He looked at the ships nearest to him. All showed signs of a struggle—burned holes in the sails, broken rails and even a cracked mast here and there. He noticed that the one with the least damage was a large ship with three masts, and its most prominent sail was dyed all blue...

A sudden realization hit him. *"Blue Bane!"* he exclaimed, and a frightened horror as to what might have happened to Percy and his sailors made him halt where he stood. The last day he spent with them came to mind. The laughter his crew shared with Percy's men at the *Jade Unicorn* and their short reminiscing about old times filled his memory. The thought of these men wasting away on some remote island was unbearable. His face grew hot and he seethed in anger.

Cloran quickly strode across the dock and up the stairs towards the shack with one hand on his sword. He opened the door carefully and peered inside. Seeing no one, he threw it open and entered.

The room was dark, save the few gaps in the walls that let in sunlight. To the right, Cloran saw a stair descending sharply into the bowels of the wooden structure, and maybe into the very heart of the island itself. The small room he had entered was bare except for one wooden chair in a corner. He noticed a door in the center of the far wall, and out of it, Cloran heard a peculiar humming. The tune was soft and melodious, and Cloran recognized it somehow. The humming went on and every now and then he would hear a tinkling sound, like icicles falling off the rim of a ship.

Cloran warily stepped sideways until he could see into the room. The door was only partially opened, but he saw the form of a man sitting in a chair to his right. Cloran slowly drew his curved blade and stepped closer, ever so quietly. He squeezed through the doorway without making a sound and turned towards the sitting man. The man sat with his back to Cloran, but Cloran had walked right in front of a glassless window, casting a shadow upon the far wall. The man quickly stood, spun around and drew his sword.

The eyes of the tall man went wide, and his mouth fell agape. His wide, brown hat sat crooked on his head, and his left hand relaxed, releasing what it had held. Gold and silver coins dropped to the floor, tinkling as they fell. The two men were silent.

"Percy…" said Cloran confused, his sword raised. He looked at his old crewmate, but Percy didn't speak. Instead, his mouth quivered and his eyes remained wide as he searched for an explanation. Cloran's eyes then darted to the table, which was covered with coins, stacked high and against the wall. Other valuables lay strewn across the table—brooches, necklaces, rings and chains. A map adorned the furthest wall, and it was of the sea. It showed many small islands, the northernmost highlighted with a red arrow. It showed dotted lines that made up paths of common merchant travel—trade routes from Rogvelt to Stren, and even to Miotes. All of this Cloran absorbed in a brief, horrified moment, as

Percy stood before him wearing a guilt-stricken face and wielding no answers.

At that moment, Cloran felt a pain that he had never felt before. His heart turned cold and froze. His head throbbed and his eyes swelled. All trust he had in his friend vanished, dashed to bits. Any notions he had of friendship and kinship were stripped from him, extracted through a gaping wound in his heart. Fear and sorrow clenched his throat, and he breathed fire, taking many staggering breaths before he spoke.

"It was you...it was you all along?"

Percy dropped his sword and raced for the exit. Cloran threw his own sword and caught Percy's coat, sticking him to the door. Percy lurched, yanked backwards and fell to the ground. Cloran leapt over him and lifted up his old friend.

"Did you ever think of the lives you ruined!?" he cried, yielding to his anger.

"Cloran, you don't understand, I was having trouble, it was during the war and I had no means to live—"

Cloran lifted Percy and threw him against the wall, ripping his coat off. He realized then that his eyes were weeping, but it was anger that consumed his mind.

"Did you ever think of the children you left *fatherless?*"

"I never hurt anybody Cloran. I was always a considerate thief!"

Cloran threw Percy across the room and the man hit the far wall, falling to the floor.

"I saw the bodies at the Reef of Many Graves! I saw their broken swords and burning ship!"

"That wasn't me! All I do is give orders and count coins...it must have been another marauding vessel. You have to believe me!"

"And I'm supposed to believe this coming from a lying, thieving, backstabbing, treacherous—"

With renewed rage, Cloran picked up Percy and relentlessly beat him against the wall.

"Have you forgotten the old days? When we trusted our captain and thought ourselves invincible, when we did what we knew was right regardless of what harm might have befallen us, because it was what a noble and true sailor did? Do you not realize that you sacked ships identical the one we shared as shipmates? Have you forgotten Reuben?"

Cloran's eyes blurred and his body went numb as he beat Percy against the wall, his face contorted in anger and pain, for he was betrayed, and the memory of Reuben had been trampled. When he stopped to breathe, Percy's head trembled and his speech was halting, but his voice was clear.

"W-w-we never killed a soul. Even if all your trust is st-st-stripped from me, you must know that not a man d-d-died at our hands."

"Liar! After sacking and burning scores of ships, you managed to spare its defenders? Hah!"

The sound of many feet echoed up the stairs and suddenly a dozen men burst into the room. With one glance, they took in the situation and cried out, lunging at Cloran. They pulled Cloran away from Percy, who fell to the ground exhausted.

"Do not harm him!" cried Percy between gasps. "Bof, don't lay a hand on Cloran!" Bof, the first mate, let go of Cloran, and the other sailors did as well. But Cloran was unrelenting and attacked the whole lot of them feverishly. It took four of them to restrain the sailor. Percy stood with quivering legs.

"To the ship, quickly," he ordered, and his men let go of Cloran and helped Percy up. The sailors of *Blue Bane* ran outside towards their ship, and Cloran lunged after them shouting, "Traitor!" and, "Backstabber!"

The men boarded the large vessel and kicked away the gangway before Cloran could reach it. The rest of Cloran's crew came out of the nearby ships to see what the commotion was, and joined their captain on the dock. Cloran dropped to his knees, panting, as *Blue Bane* gained momentum and sailed away.

"You will pay!" shouted Cloran across the waves. He bowed his head and held his eyes. "I will make you pay."

Percy came to the side of his ship and leaned over. His face was wrenched in sorrow and guilt, but still he fled, avoiding the consequences of his deeds.

Blue Bane was soon out of sight, and the sailors stood on the dock, confused.

"What on earth happened?" asked Jenkins.

Cloran stood up slowly. His face was red but stern, and all anger had passed from him. He wore no expression, and didn't meet the eyes of his crew.

"There were no marauders in long, swift boats. It was Percy. It was Percy all along."

CHAPTER NINE

Finding the Captain

Mallory arrived back at Staghorn's Rock, heavily laden with two spears, but proudly wearing his recovered ring. Staghorn clapped and laughed when Mallory leapt off of Gerbald's back and presented him with his long-lost spear.

"You got it back! And it looks just as I remember it. I sure hope old Krackaman wasn't too much trouble."

"He was an ornery crab for certain, but after we got to know each other a little better, he became more reasonable. He is now called Munchafish, however, and has promised to be a good crab."

"Ah! That's good then. You must have been persuasive to get him to promise that. Did you get your ring back?" Mallory sat down on a nearby rock and fingered the ring on his finger.

"Yes, I got it back."

He sighed and stared out to sea.

"What's wrong? I thought you wanted it back?"

"Oh I did, but I'm just thinking about my wife. Here I sit on a rock in the middle of nowhere, without my captain and without my wife."

"Humph, middle of nowhere, well I tell you, this is the middle of somewhere, that's for sure," said Staghorn with a snort.

"But why worry about your crew? You will find them again someday."

"How do you know? They probably think that I'm dead. They will never find me here."

"Then we had best find them, eh? Gerbald!" Staghorn cried, and the Sea Horse stuck his nose out of the water. "Hey Gerbald! It's time to relocate. Mind taking us for a ride?" Gerbald whinnied and spat water at Staghorn and the man laughed and slapped his legs.

"Good! Come here then."

Gerbald swam forward and Staghorn rummaged around the rocks behind him. He then pulled out a long rope woven from sea leaves, and he tossed the end to Gerbald. The end had a loop tied in it, and Gerbald nuzzled it and slipped the loop into his mouth. With a loud whinny, Gerbald swam north until the rope snapped taut. The small rock island began to tremble, and then it moved, and Gerbald slowly pulled the island through the water. He picked up the pace and swam harder, and soon Mallory and Staghorn sat on the rock island gazing north, with the wind whipping their hair about. Staghorn stood up and the plants on his body flapped in the wind.

"There you go Gerbald! That's a good Sea Horse!" he called. Gerbald whinnied, and Staghorn sat back down.

"My, he sure has some strength in him," said Mallory in wonder.

"Yep, his whole race does. I found him one day while I was searching a deep cavern on the sea floor for old sunken warships, to see if I could find a new spear. He was a baby at the time and looked deserted, so I snagged him, brought him here and raised him on starfish, urchins and sea plants. We ran into a herd of Sea Horses like him one day, but he didn't want to leave with them and instead stayed here with me. Which made me happy. He is good company and doesn't argue, although he snorts water at me every now and again."

"Does he know where we are going?"

"Of course! I think. Hey Gerbald, do you know where we are going?" Gerbald spat water and snorted.

"Yeah, he knows. North to Miotes right? That's where we will find your beloved floating log. So in the meantime, sit back and enjoy yourself! I can guarantee that you won't be chauffeured around on a big floating rock ever again."

Mallory did sit down, but his thoughts were always towards his wife, and there was nothing he could do about that.

CHAPTER TEN

The Lady with the Red Hair

Pⁱercy's betrayal still deeply affected Cloran. He refused to give up the wheel to Len and sailed all through the night, every night, and all day every day. What thoughts went through his mind during those nights only the waves ever heard. The sailors were downhearted by the treachery of Percy and his crew, but even more so by the morose mood of their captain. Days spent on deck were, for the most part, quiet and uneventful, with no one wishing to speak and everyone keeping to his own thoughts.

Len didn't like this one bit. He hated seeing his captain so quiet and the crew so miserable. He tried to come up with a plan to lighten the mood a bit.

"Do you boys remember," said Len one day, "the tale of Old Roper?"

"I remember," said Greaves. "At least, I remember some of it."

"Sing it for me Greaves, because I have forgotten."

Greaves was hanging in the riggings, tying and untying ropes, but he stopped and tried to recollect the verse.

"It's been long since I tried to recite this one, but I think it went like this;

Old Roper was tall, as tall as a tree,
And no house or hall could hold him.

141

He lived his life mining and charging a fee
To the smiths who bought metal from him.

He laid his head on smooth round rocks;
The earth he had for a bed.
Birds made their nests in his curly locks,
And drank from the tears he shed.

'Oh lonesome wretch,' to himself he would say,
'Whose company is birds and beasts,
You won't last long, living this way,
Shunned from the little men's feasts.'

And thus Old Roper forsook the hills,
Seeking a comfortable hearth,
And looked for a place to offer his skills
In mining and digging up earth.

He looked for busy cities and towns,
So he wouldn't be lonely again.
And so he approached a place he found;
A busy town of men.

'Good morning townsfolk,' he said to the men,
With his deep voice outward booming.
'Is there anyone here who would be my friend?"

Asked he, with his tall form looming.

But the townsfolk shrieked and ran far away,
And many came back with nets,
Casting them at Old Roper that day,
Tugging him down with threats.

'A man-eating giant, as tall as a tree!'
They yelled while pointing at him.
And so they cast Roper deep into the sea,
Declaring that he must swim."

Greaves stopped then and scratched his head.

"I know there's more to it than that, but I think I have forgotten it."

"You spend too much time in the kitchen sniffing the steam from your pots!" said Darrell. He stuck his legs into the riggings and then dangled upside-down. "I'll finish it for you since you seem to have forgotten, and let's see how fast I can do it before I faint and fall!" Darrell inhaled deeply and then with one breath recited the rest quickly, as the crew clapped along.

"Swim he did for many days,
Until he could swim no more,
And then all things became a haze,
As he sank to the sea floor.

He lay there sleeping for the longest while,
When a lovely fish-lady came by.
She sat at his feet and gave him a smile,
Until he opened an eye.

'Oh lady,' said he, 'what is your name?
You're as pretty as can be.'
'I am,' said she, 'a woman of fame.
My name is Lanalee.'

'Oh Lanalee, I'm from the earth,
And no good can I sail.'
'Well then sir, come to my hearth,
And here now, have a tail.'

The lady gently touched his knees,
And from them sprouted a tail.
And so the two swam through the sea
To reach her seaweed vale.

One day Old Roper said to she,
'My dear, there are many others like me,
Who would like to travel the open sea,
And of the land to be quite free.'

'Of this there is nothing I can do,'
Said Lanalee to her lover true.
'The gifts I have to give are few,
And the gift of a tail I gave to you.'

So Old Roper came up with a scheme
To help mankind fulfill their dream;
To travel the seas and follow the stream,
Or wherever else the waves might gleam."

At this point Darrell exhaled loudly and his head grew red and he moaned, falling to the deck with a crash. The crew laughed as Darrell stood to his feet and stumbled about dizzily.

"Ah, I think I'm done for now," he said holding his head. "Remind me not to do that ever again."

"Then who's going to finish the song?" ask Len, and the crew thought, trying to remember the last verses. Cloran sighed and stretched his arms, coming out of his melancholy. He looked around at his sailors who were all thinking about the last verses to Old Roper and he raised an eyebrow.

"What is it you boys are doing?"

"We're trying to remember the last bit of Old Roper," said Turner. "Darrell would have finished it but he went and got himself dizzy." Darrell moaned, sitting on the deck and holding his head.

"Old Roper is it?" said Cloran. "I remember the end to that one." Cloran mumbled to himself as he went through the song from the beginning until he reached the end. "Ah here it is:

> *'Since I can't give men a tail,*
> *For them to use on the sea to sail,*
> *I think I'll give them something pale,*
> *And call this thing a sailing sail.*
>
> *A sailing sail for sailors to sail,*
> *Upon the sea like the mighty whale;*
> *To challenge storms and face the gale,*
> *Wherever the sailing sailors sail.'*
>
> *And thus ends Old Roper's tale."*

The crew laughed and clapped and Len smiled. His captain was out of his mood.

Cloran had finally gone inside to sleep. It was still daylight but Len took the wheel nevertheless. High-flying white clouds obscured the sky and the air was starting to get chill; not too cold, but the bite was noticeable. They neared Miotes with every wave that crested and the longer they sailed strait on through day and night, the sooner they would reach their destination.

The crew was singing bits of Old Roper and other songs when Jenkins gave a cry.

"It's Mallory!" he exclaimed and pointed out to sea. The crew scrambled down from the ropes and ran to the edge of the ship.

"I don't see him," said Turner.

"Neither do I," said Greaves. "Are you sure it's Mallory? We lost him quite a ways south of here."

"I'm sure of it," said Jenkins earnestly from the crow's nest. "I see a small island far away and...and it seems to be moving north, faster than we are. Mallory is on the island and so is another figure...no wait, maybe it's just a lump of sea plants. I can't tell. But that is Mallory, I am sure!"

"Len, head towards the island, let's get Mallory!" said the crew.

"The island has stopped moving. It is far away now. Len, turn the wheel a bit to port...that's it, he is directly in front of us now."

"How far Jenkins?" asked Len at the wheel. "If we maintain this direction we will reach the northern seas too far west of Miotes."

"It is far, but not unreachable. I'd say it should take the better part of the day to reach him, if the rock he is on stays put."

"This'll add a good bit to our trip for sure," mumbled Richards, "and none of us see him but Jenkins."

"Quiet you," growled Jenkins, "I know what I see and I see Mallory. If you don't trust me then maybe I shouldn't be the lookout."

"Aye, sorry, I never meant any harm. I'm just saying that we don't have time for this. But I wouldn't abandon Mallory to the sea, if we have even the slightest hope of saving him."

"I never said he was alive," said Jenkins from atop the mast. "All I said was that I saw him, but he isn't moving as far as I can tell."

"Maybe he is sleeping," said Greaves.

"Or maybe he is passed out," said Turner.

"Whatever he's doing, if he is there at all, we will get him," said Len, and the ship made for the point Jenkins had described. Thirty waves went under them, then fifty, and after what felt like forever Darrell yelled up to Jenkins.

"Is it getting closer?"

Jenkins strained his gaze.

"Really, I can't tell," he said. "The stone has stopped moving but it doesn't seem to be getting any closer. Maybe it's just far away. I still see Mallory on it."

A sudden rush of wind hit the ship from head on so that the sails puffed inward. Even the waves toppled over and rippled like still water, and the ship came to a sudden halt. Len clung to the wheel and Jenkins to the top of the mast but the rest of the crew fell over.

"What's that? A storm coming in?" said Richards, but the wind stopped. The waves were still and the sails drooped with nothing in them.

"I can't see Mallory anymore," said Jenkins in alarm. "Something has obscured his rock, but I can't tell what it is." From far off, a distortion on the water came at them. It wrinkled the water and warped the sky and suddenly it was upon them, right at the bow of the ship. There was a loud splash and a wave rippled outward towards them. *Wavegrazer* rose swiftly and climbed the looming hill, and then dove, and as it dove down the wave, an island was unveiled before them where there had not been one before. *Wavegrazer* rushed towards the shore of the island at a great speed.

"Hold the ropes!" called Len, and he twisted the wheel so that the stern of the ship came out and to the side. The ship lurched violently and *Wavegrazer* skidded across the wave horizontally, until its crest dove underneath the ship and crashed into the island. After the ripple there were no others, and the sea quietly gurgled much as it always had. The crew stood aghast, looking at the island.

"How could you see a rock a day's sail away Jenkins," said Richards, "but miss this?"

"It wasn't there Richards; you saw how it came up on us."

Cloran burst out onto the deck.

"What's all this ruckus?" he said. "Why did we—"

He leaned over the gunwale and looked at the island, blinking.

"There shouldn't be any islands in these parts," he said quietly, and he turned to Len. "Where did this come from?"

"We don't rightly know Cloran, it just sprung up out of nowhere."

"That's right Cap'n," said Jenkins. "First there was ocean as far as any of us could see, and then this thing appeared." Cloran closed his eyes and rubbed them.

"Giant rocks popping up underneath us, whole islands running into us from nowhere... I can't get any luck," he muttered to himself. He sighed and looked up at the island. "We had better sail around it then."

There was a small breeze, just enough to fill the sails. The sailors took to the oars and turned the ship west, and Cloran grasped the wheel.

"I sure hope we *can* sail around it," said Darrell, "but I don't see an end to it."

Beyond the beach was a low lawn that went deeper into the island, and there a few trees began to shoot up. Further inland the earth rose, and at the top was a small lake, but the crew couldn't see past it. *Wavegrazer* sailed along the shore and many waves passed beneath them, but the island remained where it was. Its scenery did not change. The sea parted on either side of the ship and they could feel the wind on their faces, but the sand stayed unmoving, the trees never changed and the lake was always in sight.

"Are we moving?" asked Greaves at the oars and Len nodded.

"It seems there's more to this than just a simple island."

"Aye, the circumstances of reaching it might have clued you in on that one," said Richards chuckling, but Len just glared at him.

"Drop anchor," Cloran finally said. "We aren't making any progress, so we had better see who or what is keeping us from our journey."

The sailors dropped anchor and put the dinghy into the water. The sailors climbed aboard and set off for the island. Greaves rowed towards the beach and upon reaching it, the men pulled the boat out onto the shore.

Out of the lake flowed a small silver stream that wound its way through the grass and emptied at the beach where *Wavegrazer* rested just offshore. The land was beautiful. There were no stumps or split trees, no broken or crumbling stones, no holes, pits or animal remains. There were no weeds strewn about the beach at all, just white sand as fine as salt. The sailors could see a ridge of mountains in the distance, blocking the sky.

"I don't see anyone," said Turner when the sailors reached the shore. Darrell stomped the sand.

"Seems real enough, but I've never seen sand this white before."

151

Cloran looked around with keen eyes and then pointed at the river.

"Come, let's follow it. If there are any people on this island, they will live close to water. Maybe we can find out why we can't move."

The crew marched towards the heart of the island, following the stream. It began to climb and the going became tougher. The lawn had disappeared and now the land became rocky. To their left was a dense forest of squat, leafy trees with smooth brown trunks, but none bore fruit. There were no trails, which made the going particularly slow. At length they reached level ground and looked behind them. The ship was smaller now as she rested in the water offshore.

The lake they had seen from the ship was now before them and it was large, much larger then it looked from afar. In the middle of the round lake was a stone statue of a woman holding a jar, and out of the jar poured water.

"At least we found signs of humanity," said Len.

"Look there!" said Jenkins and the crew stopped at the edge of the water. From the far end of the lake, they saw a woman walking towards them on top of the water. She had long, wavy red hair, deep and stunning, and it draped down her back. Her skin was as white as the crest of waves, and she wore a green robe with a red sash. Her cheeks and lips were pink and her eyes were fiercely green, and she walked slowly and carefully over the water with bare feet, carrying a stone jar in her hands. She walked to the fountain and began to fill her jar from it, glancing at the sailors periodically.

The crew stood motionless, stunned by her beauty, most of all Darrell, who couldn't contain himself.

"Cap'n, can we take her with us?" he asked, and a bit too loudly. The Lady with the Red Hair turned to them.

"Indeed!" she said, and she shuffled off across the water back in the direction she came.

"You scared her away!" said Jenkins, thumping Darrell on the head.

"Sorry, she was just so pretty."

"What kind of woman is she who can walk on water?" wondered Cloran aloud, but Len interrupted.

"Shhh! She's coming back."

The woman came again to the fountain and began to fill her jar, eyeing the strangers suspiciously. But poor Darrell couldn't help himself and he burst out again.

"Ah! Such a beauty. She would be a fitting wife for Cloran!"

"Oh, mighty are the powers of Cloran!" she said turning to them, and then she scurried off again.

"You twit!" said Jenkins. "Can't you keep your mouth shut?"

"What makes you think that I want her as a wife anyway?" said Cloran. "Have you forgotten about Adaire?"

"I know, I'm just saying that this woman would suit you well, that's all."

"Be quiet, here she comes again," said Len, and they all fell silent. This time she passed the fountain and walked straight to them. The men backed up a little, but the woman stopped in the shallows.

"Greetings Cloran Hastings," she said. "We have been looking forward to your arrival."

The crew glanced at each other.

"My arrival? But how did you know I was coming?"

"We knew of your coming some time ago, and would be honored if you would stay for the evening."

Amid his confusion and the many questions he had, Cloran kept the journey foremost on his mind.

"I am afraid that would be impossible, Lady," he said. "My crew and I are on a journey of great importance, and we cannot be delayed."

The Lady with the Red Hair looked surprised.

"But we were told you would help us," she said. "If you do not, then no one will."

"I truly am sorry Lady, but unless we can be of assistance at this moment and for no longer than an hour, we cannot stay. An evening is too long. Winter approaches whether we are sailing or not. Now tell me, why have you held our ship here?"

The Lady with the Red Hair averted her eyes and said, "It is not we who hold you here, but the island, which we do not control. If you wish to loose your ship, appeal to the island, but he won't let go until a certain task is met." She turned her gaze back upon Cloran and her eyes were piercing. "My girls are in danger, as am I, as is this island," she said sadly, "and I fear we will not last until morning. If you will not help us, then we must resign ourselves to destruction."

Cloran sighed and shook his head.

"Come with us now, men of the waves," she said, "and join us in the feast that is already set out for you."

"What's that? A feast!" said Richards eagerly. "I'm sure we can spare one more day to help this lady out, can't we Cloran?"

The Lady with the Red Hair smiled brightly.

"Thank you sailors; now follow me to the feast!"

"Wait, I didn't—" started Cloran, but the Lady with the Red Hair turned around and walked across the water towards the other side of the lake. The crew stood puzzled.

"Hmmm, well you heard what she said guys," said Len. "It should be easy enough to follow her." With one bold leap he stepped onto the water, which held his weight, and ran after the woman. The crew shrugged and ran after Len, sending out ripples wherever their feet touched. Cloran was now alone on the shore.

"Bah!" he shouted raising his fists into the air, and then he ran after his men. As fast as they chased her, she always seemed to be just out of reach. She led them past the flowing fountain and towards the center of the lake. She then turned and led them towards a small patch of lawn at the lake's furthest edge. The land sloped upward as soon as the water ended, and the hillside was heavily wooded with many twisted and gnarled trees that never lost leaves. They stepped onto land but the woman did not stop, and continued on into the forest. Following, the sailors found a stone stair that wound up what looked like the whole length of the hillside, but the end was much further than any of them but Jenkins could see.

"Don't tell me we have to climb that," said Turner, bent over and panting, but Cloran and Len began the climb and the crew followed, less eagerly than they had been at the other side of the water. The stair wound through the lowest parts of the hill, and at every turn, they caught a glimpse of the Lady with the Red Hair rounding the next before she would disappear.

At last and with the loss of much sweat, they reached the top of the hill. There the forest ended, save a few trees dotted here and there, and looking about the sailors could see far in every direction. But the object that took their attention at the moment was a grand structure in the center of the lawn.

It was built upon white stone and rose high into the air. The dimensions were baffling and the sailors could not tell how long or wide it was. Looking at it from the front, the sailors surmised that it was about as wide as four horses standing nose to tail. The length of the building appeared to go on forever, to an undefined end. But when the sailors moved to the side, they lost all sense of size and depth. Now the length looked to be about as long as seven horses standing nose to tail, but the width was baffling, and the sailors could not comprehend it.

It was a wooden building and looked strong. A stone step led up to a long wooden porch at the front of the building with a wooden door in the center of the wall. It was an oval door, taller than the tallest man and wider than the widest one. It was painted green, as were the oval window frames. A beam ran down the middle of the face of the structure and the walls met it at an angle, like the prow of a ship. It was paneled horizontally with wood of an unknown grain, and many beams were either carved with twisting shapes and knots, or adorned with painted decorations in shapes that were flowing and elegant, but symmetric. The roof rose high at a sharp angle and came down in a curved slope to end pointing horizontally, and it was thatched with the wings of swans.

The Lady with the Red Hair stood on the porch with her silken robe waving in the breeze.

"Come, sailors of the sea, and join us in this feast!"

With that, the oval door opened and six other ladies emerged wearing long green robes and white sashes, and each chose a sailor to escort into the building. The Lady with the Red Hair escorted Cloran.

When they entered, the warmth stunned them, as did the smells of foods long cooked. The Lady led them down a hall with many doors in it, but between each door was a tapestry and above each tapestry was a torch. Cloran studied the tapestries as he walked past, each one depicting a new part of a growing story.

Upon the first were ten women standing tall in a boat riding churning waves. Upon the second, the boat reached a land covered with trees. The third depicted the ten women carving a stair out of stone, the fourth of the construction of a hall, only it was built with the stems of flowers. The fifth depicted a multitude of women dancing on a beach at night. In the sixth tapestry, men from the sea interrupted the dance, and the dancing women were running towards the stair of stone. Upon the seventh, a red haired woman stood alone in the hall made of flower stems. The eighth tapestry showed the woman forming something on the beach using flower petals and thorns. On the ninth tapestry were many more women, dancing again on the beach. The tenth tapestry was not complete. On the bottom of the tapestry was a ship, and on the beach were some women and seven men, and there was also some commotion depicted, but Cloran could not make sense of it since it was not finished. The Lady with the Red Hair led them past the tapestries and the hallway ended.

At the end of the hall was a large room filled with many tables laden with meat and cheese and other foods the sailors could not recognize. Out of that room went three other hallways in addition to the one they had come in through, and each of the three were painted a different color—one dark red, another navy, and the third a forest green. Cloran glanced down each and could not see their end, then turned and looked down the one he had just come through. The tapestries went on forever, and only darkness met his gaze at the end.

The ladies seated them at the longest table in the middle of the room, and next to each sailor sat the lady that had escorted him. Three women played instruments at the head of the room, making music the sailors had never heard before but that comforted them. Servers came into the room and filled each sailor's goblet, and then everyone sat down.

"Welcome Cloran Hastings and his men," said the Lady with the Red Hair. "Thank you for staying with us this day, even though you are pressed for time. Consider us in your debt, and consider this feast part of the payment!"

The room filled with talking, laughter, merriment and music. The sailors were pleased to be able to talk with such ladies after so long on a stuffy ship with only each other for company, and made much of their time with them. Only Cloran seemed annoyed to be there and he mumbled to himself about time and winter, picking at his food. The Lady with the Red Hair turned to him, troubled.

"You've been quiet this whole time while your sailors have been enjoying themselves," she said. "Is the feast not pleasing to you?" Cloran sighed and shook his head.

"That's not it at all. The feast is wonderful, more than I could hope for. It's just that I am concerned about the coming of winter. I don't want to be at sea when it hits. Winter can surround a ship with no warning, and every delay brings me that much closer to it."

"Why don't you stay here with us then? There is no need to be sailing all winter long."

"That is a tempting offer," Cloran said respectfully, "but really, I can't. The king of my land has told me to fetch something of importance to him and bring it back before winter, so I have no choice but to continue my journey." The Lady looked at him surprised.

"Why is it that the great Cloran Hastings is doing something he doesn't want to," she asked, "based on the whims of another man?"

Cloran smirked.

"The 'great' Cloran Hastings is still subject to those with authority over him, Lady. I will not disobey my king and lose my honor in the process. King Bozin is a good man, but sometimes he allows his personal desires to override wisdom." Cloran stared off distantly. "We shouldn't even be here, really. We should be home for the season, resting, or retired in my case. But we have this last thing." Cloran nodded to himself, and mumbled quietly. "This one last thing."

The Lady with the Red Hair looked at his face and leaned towards him, touching his arm.

"I am glad you are here, even for a little while," she said quietly so only he could hear. "I heard rumor of you and your deeds long ago, and have loved you ever since."

Cloran turned to her shocked, but tried not to show it.

"Lady," he said, "I have love waiting for me back at home."

"Yes, but I am here *now*, Cloran, sitting beside you. And we are in a place far away from your home, where no one need ever hear of you again. Look at me," she said, and he did. He looked at her face, and it was as white as snow, beautiful in that beautiful place. Her red hair draped over her shoulders and made her stand out even more. "Am I not beautiful to you?"

"You are," he said.

"Does this place not please you?"

"It does."

"I have loved you long, Cloran, even from afar, for your reputation precedes you."

Cloran broke his gaze away from hers and stared at his lap.

"Lady," he said, "you love me for what others say of me, but you do not know me. Yet I have a love waiting for me, who loves me *and* knows me; who loves me knowing all my faults, all my fears, and who has been faithful to me even during my long months at sea." He looked at her now and held her gaze. "Would you have me give her up for a fleeting moment with you?"

His words pierced her and she recoiled, turning her head.

"I am sorry Cloran; I didn't know how much she meant to you." She took his hand and met his eyes earnestly. "Forgive my advance, I didn't know."

Cloran smiled.

"I will do that gladly Lady. And now, if you still welcome my company, let's continue with this meal that you have graciously set before us." With that, Cloran began to enjoy himself and the Lady with the Red hair proved to be good company.

The feast went on for the better part of the day, until the sun hid in the sea and twilight crept upon the sailors in that baffling hall. The feasters were finishing their meal, and the Lady with the Red Hair rose from her chair.

"Now that feasting is over, we shall continue the celebration on the beach. The time has come for dancing!" The women in the hall all clapped and stood from their chairs and ran in different directions down various halls, leaving the sailors at the tables, except Richards who ran off with his escort, of whom he had become quite fond.

"Lady, if you pardon my asking," said Cloran, standing from the table, "you mentioned when we arrived that you needed our help with something. What is it you need from us?"

"All in good time Cloran. You shall soon see," she said.

Len stood and looked down each hallway but could not see an end.

"Which way is out?" he asked. The Lady with the Red Hair pointed down one of the halls.

"That way," she said, and they looked where she had pointed. A door stood where there had not been one before. Cloran and his sailors walked towards it, and as he passed the tapestries, he noticed that the tenth one had been further completed during their meal. A fire was on the beach, and figures were running in all directions. Dark shapes with bright eyes were in the sea, but Cloran could not make out the rest.

The sailors left the strange hall and walked down the stairs lightly. They came across a dozen women carrying wood and the sailors took their burdens and followed them across the lake, past the fountain, along the river and down the hill to the shore where their ship still bobbed, anchored a little ways from the beach. There they piled the wood and struck a fire. More ladies came until all those that had been in the hall were there, along with Richards holding the hand of his escort, and they piled more wood onto the burning blaze. The musicians had come down too and set up by the water. They started to play a lively tune and the women all began to dance, but the sailors did not know the dance and could not join in.

"Hey now Esmer," said Richards to the lady who had been his escort, for that was her name, "show us the dance you are doing so we can join." Esmer came to the men and showed them step by step how to do the dance, and after a bit of awkward stumbling around, most of the sailors got the hang of it and joined with the ladies dancing around the fire.

"Come on Cloran!" called Len, but Cloran waved his hands and shook his head.

"No thanks, you all have fun and I'll sit here and watch." He sat down on a rock a little ways from the fire and the Lady with the Red Hair sat next to him. She wore a worried face and looked out to sea constantly.

"What's troubling you Lady?" Cloran asked, but her eyes flitted across the horizon.

"This is how it happened last time."

"How what happened? If something is going to happen, tell me so I can be ready."

The Lady just shook her head and said, "You are ready."

The sailors were having a good time dancing around the fire. They had taken to the dance easily, except Greaves who was having an awkward time of it. He stumbled around and bruised more than a few of the poor girl's toes, but seemed to be having a grand time nonetheless. All of a sudden, and partially due to the amount of ale he had consumed during the feast no doubt, he tripped and toppled over into the fire. The girls shrieked and the sailors scrambled to get Greaves out of the flames. They pulled him out quickly and kicked white sand over him, and the flames went out. Greaves stood up dazed, but none the worse for wear, with just a few burned holes in his clothes and very red skin.

"Look what you went and did you oaf!" said Darrell, laughing.

"Hopefully he can still cook with those hands," said Jenkins with a wink.

"No, hopefully we won't have to eat his cooking anymore," Richards said, half seriously. "Maybe this will give us an excuse to find a new cook!"

"No worries, I can manage; keep going!" Greaves said and the girls laughed, but Turner insisted that Greaves go jump in the water for a while in case his burns were worse than he thought. Turner looked at his blackened hands he got from pulling Greaves out of the flames.

"Ugh, now I'm filthy, and soot is so hard to get off," he mumbled, and went to wash his hands in the water.

They were at a part in the dance that required the dancers to leap about, and Richards and Esmer fell over onto the ground. They laughed and regained their balance, but Esmer tugged at Richard's shirt and took him away from the fire. They ran west along the beach until it turned around an outcropping of rock, and the fire went out of sight. There, Richards and Esmer lay on their backs against some rocks, regaining their breath and looking at the stars.

"That one is called Goldenhæm and looks like a tree," he said, pointing out the stars and constellations to her, "and that one is called Oggrank the sea giant. There is Goondagk the miner, and there is Justarn the forester. See, that one is Jarnok, and it points north. We often use that one when sailing, to make sure we are headed in the right direction."

"I never knew the names of those," said Esmer. "I often sit out at night and look at these stars, but I didn't know what they were called."

"As sailors, the stars are important to us. We have to know all about them so that we can make it to where we need to go."

"Where are you going?"

"Before we stopped here, we were headed north to the island of Miotes," Richards said. "The king has us on a big mission, and Cloran personally asked me to accompany him on this trip."

"Oh, so you're important on the ship?"

Richard's chest puffed out.

"Yep, one of the most important ones."

Esmer rolled over onto her side and looked at him.

"I'm glad you spent the day with us," she said. "We often get lonely out here."

Richards faced her.

"I'm glad we stayed too."

He looked at her for a while and realized that he never wanted to look away. He had never seen anyone like her before. He could best compare her to pale moonlight—soft and cool, but radiant and beautiful. She laid her hand on his. The sensation of her touch poured over him like a wave, only it was a warm, gentle wave. Richards was overwhelmed with a sense unlike any he had experienced before, and for the first time in his life, was at a loss for words.

"I've never been in love before," said Esmer quietly.

"Neither have I. Is this it?"

"I think so. What else could it be?"

The wind picked up and chilled them as they lay there, but they did not shiver.

"I wonder if you could come with us," said Richards abruptly.

"On your ship?"

"That's what I was thinking. I mean, wouldn't it be better than sitting on this island all day? Why, we would get into so many adventures, and you could see how we work, and you would be with me every moment of the day!"

Esmer sighed, smiled and grasped his hand.

"I think I would like that," she said.

From the blackness of the sea, Richards heard a *snap!* and a whirring sound, and then all at once a net flew through the air and entangled Esmer. She tried to stand with a cry but the net tightened and she was jerked to the ground and dragged towards the waves. Richards leapt up and drew his sword, cutting the ropes, but a second net flew through the air and ensnared Richards, pulling him to the ground.

"Richards!" cried Esmer franticly. Laughing and singing came from the waves and Richards saw dark shapes arise from the water, twisting into hideous forms as the sun crept over the horizon before assuming the guise of men.

"Cast your nets onto the land boys, cast your nets! Today is a fine day for a catch!" In the moonlight Richards saw them, with their dark blue skin, hooked snouts, tangled hair and shaky sea legs.

"Treacherous fiends!" he cried, but they just laughed.

At the fire, the dance continued until, in a sudden flurry of activity, dozens of nets came from the sea, entrapping the women and sailors alike. The Archineans came to shore and adopted their land legs, and at their head was Archeen.

"Faster sea scourges, let loose your nets! The bounty of land is ours for the taking!" The creatures stood in the waves and pulled in their catches. The women of the island shrieked and kicked, crying for help.

"Not again! Do not take them again," mumbled the Lady with the Red Hair to herself, and she tried to free one of the ensnared girls. The sailors did not take long to fathom what was happening and they drew their swords. They cut the ropes attached to the nets, freed the ladies, and then faced the sea.

"What devilry is this?" growled Archeen angrily, his starfish-skin robe fluttering in the early morning breeze. The sailors faced the Archineans with drawn swords.

"Archeen!" cried Cloran in anger, and he pointed the creature out with his sword. "It is you who gave me a promise not long ago, and are you now breaking it?"

Archeen looked confused and bewildered, but his eyes lit up when he recognized Cloran.

"Confounded sailor, pain in our plans! You know nothing of our troubles under the waves. We need these vermin to continue our lines, and we shall take them as we did before!"

"Then you shall pay for it dearly," growled Cloran, "and your leadership will be the cause of many deaths tonight."

Without another word, he raised his sword and the sailors leapt into the shallow waters.

Richards hewed at the net that ensnared him with what little reach he could manage as the Archineans came and groped for him. Esmer was hefted over one of their shoulders and carried out to sea as she flailed and kicked. She grasped the side of her kidnapper's head and wrenched at it and he screamed, dropping her to the sand.

"If you don't play nice, you won't play at all!" the Archinean yelled, and he kicked her in the side. Richards freed himself and roared to his feet with his glinting blade swinging, killing a creature that reached for him. The others flinched and stepped back, not expecting to find anyone armed. Richards did not pause for speech, but lunged at the creature nearest to him, cutting him through. Three others were left having watched two of their friends fall at Richards' hand, and they squealed in anger and reached for the frantic sailor. In that first moment, he cut off two hands that grasped him, but others grabbed his legs and tripped him. Richards fell face first to the sand, but rolled over quickly as a heavy body fell on top of him. He hefted his sword and stuck his assailant in the heart, and with a screech, the Archinean slid down the length of the blade to the hilt. Richards rolled the body over, but his feet were ensnared and the Archineans were dragging him away. He kicked franticly and managed to pop one in the snout, who spouted dark blue blood out of his nose and let go. Richards wrenched his body and twisted around, loosening the rope, and as he stood to his feet, he swung sideways, slicing through his nearest attacker from collarbone to shoulder. The remaining Archinean watched his last comrade fall to the sand in two pieces, then turned and fled towards the sea.

Richards spun around looking for Esmer. He saw two dark shapes kicking something on the ground, and with a cry he rushed at them. When they saw him, one ran to the water and escaped, but the other pulled a long point of bone from his belt. The sailor and the Archinean clashed and Richards was stuck through the shoulder with the point so that it came out his back, but Richards stabbed his assailant up through the jaw and out his head. The creature fell lifeless besides Esmer, who was not moving.

*   *   *

Mallory sat on Staghorn's rock, bored and sad. He had retrieved his ring and restored the golden javelin to Staghorn, but now he had lost his captain and his only means back to Jessie. It had been days since Gerbald began to pull the rock northwards, but they did not seem any nearer to Miotes and had seen no sign of *Wavegrazer*. Mallory munched on dried sea plants and did not relish the taste, but it was all Staghorn had to offer.

"My, you sailors sure do eat a lot," Staghorn said from atop his rocky seat. "I can go for days without eating more than one leaf of seaweed, but you have eaten up almost my whole store! No matter, I can get more easily enough."

Mallory sighed and stood up. He looked out to sea but didn't hope to see anything.

"Why have we stopped?"

"I felt a cold wind from the North, and I don't like the cold so I had Gerbald stop here."

"But don't you understand? I need to go north; that is where I will meet my captain."

"Oh, I have a feeling you will meet him much sooner than that."

"What makes you so certain?"

Staghorn looked eastward. The moon had finally vanished and the sun was just edging into view.

"Look there," Staghorn said, pointing towards the sun. Mallory looked but didn't see much, although the rising did hurt his eyes. The light got more brilliant, far brighter than it by rights should have been, and Mallory squinted. But then in a flash, the light was obscured and a rough wind hit his face. Before him rested an island that had not been there a moment before. He was so close to it that he could see every detail. He saw a stream trickling down from a gentle slope and it wound its way through a lightly forested area to end at the whitest sands he had ever seen.

"My, that sure came upon us fast," said Staghorn, and he laughed.

"There, what's that?" said Mallory, pointing to the northern side of the shore. "It...it looks like *Wavegrazer*!"

"No, really? Here? Amazing," said Staghorn with a chuckle, and with the piercing look Mallory gave him, he burst into laughter again.

"You really need to stop keeping so many secrets you weed-covered rock-dressing."

"Do I? Oh dear, I'm no longer allowed secrets, how terribly boring that will be. Well then, look there by the ship—there's a secret you should deal with yourself."

Mallory looked, and at that moment he noticed a fight on the beach. Cloran and his crew were fighting blue-skinned creatures and were far outnumbered.

"Ah! They're in a scrape and I'm not there!"

"Gerbald!" called Staghorn and he gave a mighty whistle. In less than a moment, the Sea Horse arrived spouting water with a whinny, and snorted at Mallory.

"Hey there good horse-fellow! Mallory is in need of a steed again and you might actually have some fun. Are you willing to bear him once more?" Gerbald sneezed water at him in response.

"Good! You two have fun; I'll watch from here and root for you. Oh Mallory, here, take this." He reached behind his rocky seat, but stopped and looked Mallory dead in the eye. "Now, this is my absolute favorite, so you be careful, and I want it back when you're done!" He pulled out a long lance. It was blue, made of coral, and looked quite ancient. He hesitated for a moment but then handed it to the sailor and waved at him. "Go now, help your friends, but bring back my lance! It is my favorite. I really like that lance."

Mallory didn't pause to thank him but took the lance and leapt onto the slick back of Gerbald. He left Staghorn on the rock mumbling about his favorite lance, and with Gerbald skimming through the water faster than even *Wavegrazer* could go, he raced to help his friends.

*   *   *

The sailors and the Archineans clashed on the shore, but the creatures were unarmed and fell fast to the flashing edges that gleamed before them. By sheer numbers alone, the sea-men pressed onward and put the sailors to a hard fight, but the Archineans' mounting casualties were incredibly demoralizing.

Archeen stood upon the water nervously, and while his Archineans fought the sailors, he eyed his escape. At last, his spine failed him and he turned and ran. Seeing this, the Archineans howled in despair and chased after their leader. The sailors sped after them as far as they could go but they could not match the speed of the fleeing creatures as they ran across the top of the waves.

The Lady with the Red Hair appeared at the shore, and suddenly her eyes flared green. Before the sailors knew what was going on, she stood atop the waves, and she chased after Archeen with a rod of coral in her hands. She moved with an incredible speed, but the sailors could not see what motions her feet made on the water's surface.

They glanced at each other in frustration, cut off from their attackers and not knowing what to do. But Cloran didn't hesitate, and he brought a leg up out of the water and lifted himself onto the surface. The sailors did likewise, and then with a roar they chased after the fleeing Archineans. They did not have to go far, however, for the Archineans had turned from their flight and, as it appeared to the sailors, were fleeing back towards the island.

"Looks like they are coming back for more!" said Darrell eagerly, and Greaves laughed beside him. The sun heated the sailors' backs as the Archineans came rushing at them, but behind the fleeing creatures, a shape appeared over the water. The sailors heard a loud whinny, and they saw a man riding what looked to be a blue horse with green mane. The horse reared up, gave a snort, and spouted water high into the air. The man on its back hefted a long blue coral lance and roared with a loud voice.

"Mallory!" the sailors cried and their hearts were lifted. Redoubling their efforts, they charged the Archineans, who halted in their tracks. Surrounded on both sides—on one by six men with curved blades and fell voices and on the other by a terrible man on a horrifying steed with a cruel looking weapon—the Archineans braced themselves and, cornered as they were, let out such terrible growls that the waves beneath them sundered. There, on the top of the waves, the sailors reunited and fought bravely against the Archineans, who were ferocious and unrelenting.

But Archeen was not in that fight. He dove beneath the turmoil and assumed his natural form. With a mighty swish of his tail, he shot away like a bolt from a bowstring, diving deeper into the bottomless depths. His robe of starfish skin fluttered away. The sun above him faded and all was blue and clouded except for a few beams of light that penetrated into the depths of the ocean. But he was not alone in his flight.

The Lady with the Red Hair dove into the sea after Archeen, and without even the tiniest movement she sped after him, overtaking him at every swish of his tail, until at last she came upon him. She outstretched her hand and smote him on the tail with her rod of coral. His tail shriveled and turned into coral, and he screamed in agony as he sank with the dead weight. As he sank, the Lady sank with him.

"This is retribution for your evil deed many years ago," she said, and she held aloft her rod. "You took what family I had to places where they could not survive. Neither you nor your brood will do this again to my girls."

"Mercy!" he cried, but his bubbling gurgle was in vain. She smote him on the head and in an instant, his being turned into coral. He sank to the very bottom of the sea where over time he crumbled into sand.

On the waves, the sailors cheered. Many of the Archineans had been slain and their bodies melted into the ocean, but many also had surrendered and accompanied the sailors back to shore. Since their leader was gone and they were disarmed and weakened, Cloran warned them sternly never to take up arms or use force against mankind ever again, and let them go back to the sea where they shrieked, screamed, assumed their natural shapes and swam to the very depths of the ocean.

But the crew didn't give the Archineans a second thought and instead surrounded and embraced Mallory, having thought him dead.

"You ridiculous lover, your heart almost dragged you to your death!" said Jenkins. He slapped Mallory on the back and embraced him. "We thought you were long gone."

"I would have been if not for this fellow," said Mallory, and he walked over to Gerbald, who sat on his knees in the shallows, and scratched his snout. "Thanks again for the rides. Oh, and here," he said, placing the blue coral lance in Gerbald's mouth. "Make sure Staghorn gets that back." Gerbald gave a final snort of water and then dove into the sea, swimming back to his master. Mallory saw Staghorn's rock in the distance and the large man sitting on his stone chair. He heard him laughing away, and Mallory smiled and waved his thanks before the rock island vanished from mortal sight.

"Richards was so angry at you when you fell," said Darrell. "He swam around looking for you for hours."

"Really?" asked Mallory with a raised eyebrow. "That surprises me."

"Where is Richards anyway?" wondered Cloran. They looked around and saw no sign of the ladies either, only the smoking remains of the beachside fire.

"There," said Jenkins pointing to a multitude of tracks on the beach. The sailors followed them along the shore and around an outcropping of rock. There they saw the women of the island crowded together, looking at something on the ground.

When the sailors reached the place, they found Richards lying on his knees with a bleeding shoulder and Esmer outstretched in his lap. Esmer was battered and bruised. Her joints were swollen and her face was streaked with blood. Richards sat sobbing. The Lady with the Red Hair came up from the sea and the morning sun glinted across her shining skin. She walked over to where Esmer lay, knelt down and touched her forehead. Esmer's eyes opened. She blinked and looked around before catching Richards' gaze. Without saying a word, she smiled and reached up to touch his face, but her strength failed her. Closing her eyes, her spirit departed.

Cloran took off his hat and the sailors bowed their heads. The women stood around their sister crying, but Richards most of all. A gentle breeze licked at their feet, and in that moment, Esmer's body dwindled into a bundle of flower petals and thorns. Caught up by the wind, they scattered over the beach, filling the air with the loveliest of scents.

CHAPTER ELEVEN
Pale-Faced Hospitality

C loran and crew stood aboard the dinghy in the shallows of the island. Arrayed on the island was the host of women, downcast and sorrowful due to their loss, but striking in the morning sunlight. The Lady with the Red Hair came forward to bid the sailors farewell.

"I wish our parting could be a more joyous one. Perhaps you could stay longer?"

"If only the sea could give us the time," said Cloran, standing tall at the front of the dinghy. "But there is an important matter that we must attend to and time is not on our side. I fear we have delayed too long already."

The Lady nodded.

"I understand. Go then, and fulfill you duties. Thank you for your help with the creatures from the sea. This is not the first time they have raided this island, and had you not been here, today would have turned out just as bad as before."

Abruptly, the Lady drew close to Cloran and spoke softly, so only he could hear.

"As special as your relationship is with the Sea, I know her much more intimately," she said, looking Cloran in the eyes. Cloran frowned and raised an eyebrow, but the Lady kept on talking, quickly but quietly. "She chooses her objects of hatred on a whim, and once she has chosen, she never relents. She has chosen you, Cloran, and so be on your guard at all times. You never know what menace lies crouched and waiting behind each wave. For my part, I will watch and wait. You will not come to harm, as long as I am able to intervene."

Cloran nodded and smiled. Certainly she did not intend to ride with them. There was no room on the ship for her, especially if they would be bringing a princess back. Perhaps the best thing to do would be to thank her, and then set sail as swiftly as possible.

"Thank you Lady, your help is always appreciated. And now I must leave and sail north to Miotes. Farewell!" With that, the crew rowed towards the ship. They boarded her and raised the anchor. Cloran took the wheel and with the sailors at the oars, eased away from the island. The island got smaller and smaller until it disappeared completely. A large wave appeared behind them and soon overtook them. It lifted *Wavegrazer* and then lowered her, and the wave continued to go out before them until it collapsed back into the sea. They lifted the oars, pulled tight the halyards, and Cloran spun the wheel north. *Wavegrazer*, catching a strong wind, cut through every wave before her like a knife.

But when the ship had long gone and the sea showed no ripple, a head peeked out from the waters. The face was adorned with long, braided red hair, and the owner fully emerged and stood atop the waves. She closed her eyes, inhaled, and then faced north with her green, piercing gaze.

All that afternoon the crew discussed their adventures with Mallory and exchanged tales of what had happened to them while he was gone. The only sailors who were quiet were Cloran, who was concerned with the weather and focused on his sailing, and Richards, who kept to himself, high in the riggings near the top of the rear mast, nursing his shoulder. At last, the sun extinguished itself in the sea and the moon came out, along with the stars, which were not veiled by clouds that night. Cloran gave the call to turn in for dinner and the crew went below. But Richards caught Mallory by the shirt before climbing below and took him aside.

"Mallory, I want to apologize," he said softly.

"Apologize? For what?"

"For calling you a coward before. You see, I didn't understand why you were careful before jumping into danger." He looked at his feet and spoke with a strained voice. "But now I know, if only slightly, what it is you are protecting your wife from ever having to live through. The love I knew was formed and taken from me the very same day, and if it stings this badly I cannot imagine the sting of broken love formed over a lifetime. I apologize, Mallory."

Mallory couldn't meet Richards' eyes and was choked with emotion, but he smiled and embraced him.

"All is forgotten my friend. Waves far behind us."

Cloran didn't speak much in the days that followed. He stood all day every day at the wheel, gazing northward at the horizon, sailing strait without break. He would sail all night without rest, much to Len's displeasure. The trip itself went smoothly. There were no rough waves and the sky had not been clouded for days, and so the sailors found themselves hanging leisurely in the riggings and discussing idly what they would do when they got home.

"When I get home," said Mallory, smiling with his eyes closed, "I'll buy a new house for Jessie, right on the outskirts of Stren. It will be on acres of land, all level with no hills and no rocks. We will have animals there, with sheep and horses, and we will have lots of children and each one will have a pony."

"I suppose that works well for you," said Turner, "but animals stink, and I certainly wouldn't want to live amongst stinky animals. I'll tell you what I would do. I would buy a tall building right in the heart of Stren, and turn it into a museum. Why, we have lots of Menigan history in Stren but no proper place to keep it. I would build large tables and lay on them artifacts from the Nurith Wars, arranged nice and orderly. I would keep the place spotless at all times, and hire a full-time staff to clean the dust and grime from the city. I'll stay at the top of the building and write stories of everything that I have seen, and take old texts from years ago and assemble them, order them and, if need be, translate them. Yes, that's how I would spend my time."

"How boring!" said Richards, dangling in the riggings. "What a dull way to spend your days; reading and writing, ordering and cleaning—bah! You need some excitement. I would become a diver and collect things from the ocean floor. I'd buy a place right on the water by the docks, and every day I'd dive to the bottom and search for colorful rocks and oddly shaped coral. Maybe I'd even find some riches that have dropped there, or old treasures that people have long forgotten."

"And you can put them on display in my museum!"

"Sure, if you like, but I'll also go down there and find rare fish that none have ever seen, and put them on display in big tanks. And maybe I'll find some new fishes that are good for eating, and come up with a recipe that no one has ever heard of before."

"You can leave that to me," said Greaves, leaning against the railing. "I'll open up a restaurant, right on the water, and I'll be the lead cook. I'll serve the best foods in all of Stren. Richards can give me whatever rare fish he finds and I can turn them into splendid dishes! I'll become renowned through all of Menigah as the finest cook around, and tourism will boom in Stren just from all the people coming to eat at my place."

"All those ideas are fine and good," said Darrell, "but they lack manly vigor! I would become a fighter in the ring, and I would fight the mightiest warriors in the land. They would all gather at the arena in Stren and people would come to watch me fight them one by one and send them back home to their families in shame. No one would be able to beat me. I would be known as the definition of strength, endurance and valor."

"That's silly," said Jenkins from the top of the main mast. "Such a life lacks intellectual challenge. I think the greatest life

183

would be that of an explorer, which is why I have enjoyed my time here on *Wavegrazer*. But when we return, I'd like to spend my money on a tall building, miles away from Stren. It would have a flat roof where I could sit and study the moon and the stars. I would write down everything I saw and name everything that was unnamed. Maybe I would find new constellations, or perhaps, if I gazed long enough, I would discover things that no man has ever seen. And then I would draw great maps of the sky, and sailors could use my detailed maps for perfect and precise navigation. People would know me as the greatest watcher of the stars that ever existed and my findings would go down in history. What about you Len?" he asked, turning to the first mate. "What will you do?"

"Me? Well," he said thinking, "I can't imagine myself doing anything other than what I am doing now. I love sailing. I love battling the ocean, and I love adventuring to faraway lands. I love the freedom that the sea gives me, the ability to move wherever I wish and to be subject to nothing but the fancies of the sea." Len sat down on the deck and leaned against the cabin door. "When I get home, I will just count the days until I can go back out to sea. Don't you all like being sailors?"

"I don't mind it," said Darrell. "It keeps me busy, is exciting and I never go hungry."

"I think most of us are glad we are sailors," said Jenkins, "but I don't think any of us want to be doing this for the rest of our lives. It is a good job and a satisfying way to live, but there are many other things I would like to accomplish before my short years are through."

Jenkins frowned and stood erect at the top of the main mast. He put his hand over his eyes and gazed northward.

"I see something."

"What is it?" asked Cloran, "and don't tell me it's a ship or island or rock with ridiculous half-man, half-fish creatures."

"Oh, it's none of those Cap'n," said Jenkins, "but it...well, it looks like a castle."

"A castle? On the water?"

"Yep, it looks like a castle, or some sort of tall stone structure...I can't rightly make it out."

"You can't make out something on the water before us, but you can see what's on the moon?" chided Richards, and the sailors laughed.

"There wasn't a mist between me and the moon that night. But there's a mist here. Look, it's coming at us." As soon as he spoke, a mist developed before them and engulfed the whole ship. The sails drooped and *Wavegrazer* cut slowly through the dead waves. The air was stifling. Every footstep the sailors made was magnified, but the sound of the sea was soft.

"I can't see anything beyond the nose of the ship," said Jenkins.

The sailors came down to the deck and walked to the bow. All they could see was gray, and all they could hear was the gloomy lapping of the water against the hull.

"This isn't a natural mist," said Greaves lowly. "Not natural at all."

"Can we turn back?" asked Turner.

"I don't know where back is," said Cloran. "But don't worry, all mists dissipate. I am more concerned with where we will drift to in this mist. I have no sun or stars to guide me."

Just then, the sailors felt a strong wind on their faces, coming from in front of them. The sails puffed inward then drooped down, and the ship bobbed dead in the water. Suddenly a dark, wide opening appeared before their bow, and it came right at them.

"Look out!" called Jenkins, and Cloran twisted his wheel to the side, but with no momentum the ship did nothing. The dark space opened before them and grew large. The crew could now see clearly a stone wall, built of many large, rectangular blocks, erected on a small bit of earth. In the side of the wall was carved a giant opening, large enough to swallow many ships. Before the sailors could do anything, they were enveloped. The light behind them quickly vanished and all went dark.

The sailors scrambled about on the deck, bumping into each other, but then a light was lit. Len held up a lantern and lit two others that hung from the cabin wall. Cloran took off his hat and threw it on the deck.

"Things just can't go smoothly, can they? Why can't a journey ever be easy?"

"Because that would take all the adventure out of it," said Richards with a snicker, but Cloran glared at him.

"I'm not in the mood, Richards. We don't have time for another delay." He rubbed his eyes and then looked around. "All right, so what have we stumbled upon this time?"

On either side they saw the gray, brick walls of the structure, but above them there was no roof—just darkness. When they spoke, their voices echoed deep into the depths of the castle. Everywhere around them, they could hear drips and splashes. The air was cold and dank, and the moisture in it choked their lungs. There was no room in the channel for the ship to turn around, but even if they could, the entrance behind them was out of sight.

"Take up the oars lads, let's paddle our way through. Push against the walls if we drift too close; I'll do my best to keep us centered. Let's see if we can find an exit."

"Let's hope this labyrinth *has* an exit," said Mallory, and his voice returned to him three times in that hard, hollow channel. But other voices echoed through the labyrinth, and they weren't of the sailors' making. At first they sounded low and far away, like a humming under one's breath, but as they rounded a turn in the channel the voices became louder. The sailors realized that they were hearing many voices—low growls and yelps, and now and again a bellow would peal through the air. Cloran stiffened and listened in the dark, dank air.

"Get your spears boys," he said, "and quickly."

187

"What are they?" asked Turner, and the crew set down their oars, scrambling below to get their weapons. They came back with a spear each and their curved swords strapped to their belts.

"If I am correct, those are the calls of—" Cloran started, but as they passed by a dark ledge on either side of the ship the sounds intensified, and there were more growls than yelps, and bellow after bellow pealed through the air.

"Sea Lions," he said.

The crew looked at him confused.

"Sea lions?" asked Darrell. "Those don't sound like sea lions."

Cloran moved towards the railing of the ship and Len tossed him a spear.

"Not *that* kind of sea lion," he said. In the torchlight, the sailors could see pale eyes looking at them from the dark crevasses surrounding them. One pair grew larger, and with a growl its owner came into view. A Sea Lion leaped over the side and onto the deck. It had a shimmering, silvery coat, and clawed flippers. It had the head of a lion with a pointed snout and long teeth. Flowing blue mane graced its head and stretched down its back to its pointed tail. It roared and two more Lions leapt onto the ship."

"Oh," said Darrell.

The Sea Lions lumbered towards the sailors and attacked with guttural growls. The men faced them with their spears, and forced them back. Darrell gutted one and cast it over the side with the point of his spear, and when he did, the howling and baying from the stone shelf grew louder and angrier. A dozen more came into sight. Turner and Mallory ran to the side and fended them off, but as the ship drifted through that narrow channel, more eyes appeared in the darkness to either side. Before the sailors knew it, angry roaring Sea Lions had overrun the deck. Len and Cloran stood back to back and gutted any Lion that came near them, but soon they were up to their elbows in Lions and had no room to use their spears.

The sailors drew their swords with a sharp ringing, and the curved blades chopped through the hides of the Lions as if they were melons. Greaves and Darrell laughed, and together they made piles of the corpses around them. But in doing so, they trapped themselves. As more animals came onto the deck, the two men had to climb into the riggings just to have swinging room. Silver blood flooded the deck and made fighting slippery work. Jenkins tied a rope to his left arm and flung the other end around a mast so he could keep his footing. Slipping about, he used his momentum to his advantage and thrust deep within the flesh of his assailants, sending Sea Lions flying overboard. Richards was the only sailor who still used his spear. He hung in the riggings and skewered any creature that came near.

The sailors made piles of the attacking creatures and sustained their fair share of scratches and bites, but no matter how hard they fought, the Lions kept coming.

"Sail us out of here!" called Jenkins. The current in the channel pushed the ship closer to the stone walls until it scraped against them, coming to a halt. "I doubt they will stop coming. We need to move from this place!"

Greaves pushed the carcasses aside and made a path to the wheel. Cloran and Len worked their way towards it, through tough opposition, kicking overboard bodies and live Lions alike. Cloran finally reached the wheel and gripped it in his hands. Greaves picked up an oar and pushed away from the wall, using all of his might. The ship shuddered, scraped, and finally lurched away from the wall, and Cloran drove the ship back into the center of the channel. The sailors took up the oars and some used them to keep the ship away from the walls while others paddled hard in the narrow channel. Greaves swung his oar around his head, smacking Sea Lions and flinging them overboard.

Before them, the channel split into four paths. The water began to move faster, forcing *Wavegrazer* along. Cloran quickly looked down each path before him and chose the furthest to the right. Twisting the wheel sharply, he nosed *Wavegrazer* into the dark, new path.

The sailors killed the remaining Sea Lions on deck and the bellowing, growling, snorting and baying soon faded behind them. The deck was slippery with the silver blood of the creatures and the sailors found it hard to keep their footing.

"How did you know which one to take?" asked Jenkins, kicking corpses overboard. Cloran shrugged.

"This was the only one without a dark shelf on either side. I figured we would be rid of the Sea Lions this way. But I don't know where it leads and have no idea if this is the right path."

"Oh, look at my poor deck," said Turner moaning. "And after all the work I've spent keeping it spotless."

"Killing Sea Lions is messy business!" said Darrell, wiping his sword on one of the corpses nearby and sheathing it.

"Let's get rid of these bodies," said Turner and he kicked a few overboard.

"No, don't get rid of them all, I want to try something," said Greaves. "I want to see if their flesh is worth eating."

"We can bother with cleaning and eating later," said Jenkins who had climbed up the main mast again. "Look!"

At the end of the channel there was a dim light—daylight. Drawing near, they saw that the channel opened up into a large, square chamber. As they entered the chamber, they saw that the daylight came from an opening to the left that led outside, but before them was a wooden dock attached to a stone stair. It wound upwards to a stone shelf, and on the shelf was a stone door. On either side of the door was a torch, and the door had a silver knocker in the shape of a man's head. The sailors rowed the ship alongside the dock until she came to rest.

"Looks like you chose the right channel," said Jenkins.

"The exit is over there boys," said Cloran. "I don't want to further explore this castle. Help me push away from this dock, for we're heading out!"

The sailors lifted their oars and used them to push away from the wooden dock. But just as they did so, the stone door opened and a frantic man came out and ran down the stairs. He was the palest man the sailors had ever seen. His skin was white, devoid of any pigment, and his hair was even whiter. He wore a high-collared, dark blue coat with silver buttons, and it flapped as he ran down the stairs.

"Whoa, whoa, whoa!" he said frantically, reaching the dock. "What are you? How did you come? Why are you here? What is this?!"

Cloran sighed.

"My name is Cloran Hastings," he said, turning towards the excited little man, "and this is my crew. We came through that opening there behind us, and found it...well-guarded."

The pale little man's eyes went wide and he covered his mouth.

"No, not *the* Cloran Hastings! Flayer of the Giddendrach and slayer of the Horned Whale!"

Cloran cringed.

"That's what people say."

The pale man paced along the deck quickly and then raised his eyes.

"Amazing! What good fortune! You must come with me; I must show you to the king."

"Oh no, we haven't the time," said Cloran quickly. "Send him my greetings but we really must—"

"Do not deny me!" said the man loudly, tensing his body. "You came through our back door uninvited and killed our pretty pets. The least you can do is meet the king."

Cloran groaned and glanced at Len.

"I suppose we owe them at least a greeting," said Len. "Let's just be quick about it."

"All right," said Cloran turning to the pale man. "We will meet your king, but we haven't got much time and need to make this brief."

"That's just fine!" exclaimed the man. "That's all I require! Come now, follow Philip; yes that's me, I am Philip the doorkeeper, but you can call me Phil. Follow Phil!"

Greaves leapt onto the dock and tied up *Wavegrazer*. The gangway was lowered and the sailors disembarked.

"Stay close boys, let's not wander and get lost. I don't want this to take more than a moment." The sailors made silver footprints as they followed Phil up the short stone steps. When he reached the door, Phil gave the silver man-head-knocker two quick knocks and three long ones. The sailors heard shuffling on the other side, and then it opened. The man that greeted them was also pale, with hair just as white as Phil's. The two men whispered together and then the porter smiled and greeted the sailors.

"Greetings sailors! I am Marvin the porter, but you can call me Marv. Come, follow me; I will show you to the king!"

Marv led them down a gray stone hallway. It was lined with torches that had blackened the walls. The walls were tall and the ceiling was far above them. Silver doors appeared in the walls as they walked, some being tarnished, but others were polished, and below these were scrape marks in the floor from their constant use. There were no decorations or furnishings anywhere to be seen, but it didn't feel like the sort of place that wanted furnishings.

"Cloran!" whispered Richards. Cloran slowed his pace to walk alongside Richards.

"What?"

"They referred to the ruler of this castle as a king."

"Aye, they did."

"But, isn't Bozin the only king? We are still in Menigan waters, right?"

"Yes we are."

"So should we do something about it?"

"No, I don't think so. I mean, it's not as though this fellow were claiming the throne of Menigah. At least, not to my knowledge. Perhaps he is just the king of this castle, and I suppose there's no harm in that. Besides, I don't think Bozin would mind some unknown floating castle inhabited by pale men floating around, ruling their own affairs."

"If I were king, I wouldn't want someone else calling himself king too."

"When you're already the ruler over much, there's no need to bother yourself with ruling over just a bit more."

"It's just the principle of the thing. It bothers me."

"Well don't pick any fights about it, Richards. I don't need you making a scene and delaying us further!"

Richards nodded sheepishly. As the men walked, Darrell kept staring at Marv, and finally couldn't contain his wonder.

"What type of creatures are you?" he asked his guide as Marv led them through the castle towards the throne room. Marv stopped and faced Darrell. After a moment, he smiled.

"We are men just like you. Isn't it obvious?"

He continued leading the sailors.

"But if you are men, why are you so pale?"

Marv laughed.

"We live inside of a floating castle and we never come out. This is what happens when the sun doesn't reach your skin for many years. But don't you mind that, we are just as human as you."

A narrow hall appeared in the wall to the right, but Marv led them past it. At length they entered a square stone room, with a well-polished door in each wall. Couches also lined the room between the doors and they looked soft, made of cream, brown, white and even light blue leather. In front of them was an ornate door made of wood and beaten gold, worked into twisting shapes.

"Here we are, this leads to the throne room," said Marv. "King Mundin only allows one supplicant in his presence at a time. Cloran will follow me and the rest of you, please take a seat. Servers will be in shortly to offer refreshments."

"Don't bother sitting boys, I won't be gone long."

195

"Won't be gone long, ha! Not gone long, *he-he-he!*" said Marv with a chuckle, but he avoided Cloran's sharp glance and opened the door for him.

Cloran walked into the throne room and the double door shut behind him. A long, silver and blue carpet led to the throne. Tall, slender pillars of white stone lined the long carpet, and as Cloran walked past he could see silver workings within them glint in the daylight. The light came from four long and thin slits in the top of the arched ceiling, which led outside where he could hear the sea slosh. Cloran could see that the sun was just on its way down, but he gritted his teeth and hurried along to get it over with as soon as possible.

The hall was not very long. At the end was a white throne, and hanging on the wall above it was a flag. It had an azure field and was trimmed with silver. Three silver chevrons pointed down in the middle of the field, and affixed in the center was a rather queer rendition of a pale head. Cloran frowned and looked away. It wasn't a particularly attractive flag. On either side of the throne stood a bored-looking guard, wielding a silver halberd and wearing a long, high-collard blue coat with silver buttons. On the throne crouched a thin, wiry looking fellow with frumpy clothing—regal enough compared to the guards but unkempt and faded. He was asleep and slouched to the right, and on his head was a white, spiny crown made of, apparently, bone.

As Cloran approached, the two guards looked up from their thoughts and immediately stood at attention. Cloran stopped at the foot of the throne and nodded at the guards.

"Should I wake him?" he asked, but the guards glanced at each other awkwardly.

"Yes. Er, no," said the guard on the left. "That is, he should be woken, but you are not the one that should do it."

"No, he should," said the guard on the right, turning to the guard on the left. "We don't normally wake him when he sleeps, so he may be mad at us when he wakes. Let this newcomer wake the king."

"You're not thinking," replied the guard on the left. "If the newcomer wakes him, Mundin could very well get angry at us for not properly introducing him before being addressed. You know how he doesn't like to be spoken to by people he doesn't know."

"What do you know!" replied the guard on the right. "Nothing, that's what you know, and I know you know nothing for I've known you not know it. You are the guard on the left, after all, and why are you the guard on the left? Because you are never right. I, however, am always right, which is why I am the guard on the right; so, being right, I know what is right to do, and I say he should wake him."

"Is that really why you are the guard on the right?"

"Yes it is. Mundin told me when he hired me."

"Now I feel awful. I thought he liked me best."

"Why would you think that?"

197

"I don't know. I suppose I always just assumed. And now I'm just a worthless guard, being on the left!" The guard on the left started to cry and the guard on the right walked over to comfort him.

"There-there, I'm sorry you weren't picked to be the guard on the right. You are a fine and proper guard as far as I am concerned. You stand more erect than any guard I have ever known!" The guard on the left stopped his sniveling and looked up.

"Is that true?"

"Yes it is! And to prove it, I will let you stand on the right today, because you are my friend, and the most erect standing guard I have ever known."

"I think that is the kindest thing I have ever heard!" said the guard on the left, and with that, they switched places.

"But only for today," said the guard on the right, who was now on the left.

"Right."

Cloran stood and waited, but the guards looked straight ahead and didn't seem to know that he was even there.

"So, shall I wake him?" he finally asked again.

"Yes," said the guard on the left, who was now on the right, but "No" said his counterpart, and at the same time. They glanced at each other.

"No."

"Yes."

They glanced at each other again.

"Yes."

"Yes."

Cloran hesitated for a moment, and then addressed the king.

"Sir," said Cloran loudly, but the king did not wake. He did, however, begin to snore.

"King Mundin," said Cloran louder.

"I don't think he can hear you," said the guard on the left.

"Yes, I am aware of that," Cloran said annoyed, "so maybe you two can help me." The three of them shouted, yelled and called for Mundin over and over, but the small king did not stir. Finally, the two guards gave their halberds to Cloran and shook the king so vigorously that King Mundin finally yawned and opened his eyes. He sat up in his chair, stretched, and looked around with a frown.

"Were you two shaking me?"

"No sir," the guards replied.

"Oh. Well then, that was either a really bad dream or a really good one. Where are your weapons?" Cloran outstretched his arms and the guards quickly retrieved their halberds. King Mundin sighed and slouched in his throne.

"My, I feel so safe. So why are you here? Are you going to give me tribute?"

"Um, no," said Cloran slowly.

"Are you going to sing for me?"

"Not at all, I'm here because—"

"Well then you are no good! Go away."

"Very well," said Cloran through his gritted teeth. "I am here because Phil sent me to greet you, but I shall return to my ship and leave then, if that is your wish." Cloran turned to leave but Mundin stood up from his throne quickly.

"Wait, wait!" he said earnestly. "I didn't know Phil sent you to me. You came through the back entrance then?" Cloran turned back around.

"I am not sure. We happened upon your castle by accident, and came through a channel swarming with Sea Lions. I apologize for killing your, erm, pets, as it were."

Mundin laughed and jumped back into his throne.

"Not at all! They breed fast so it is no worry. They are just here to guard our doors and to eat when we get hungry. And we are often hungry. But come! Tell me your name and of your travels."

"My name is Cloran Hastings, and I have come from Menigah. I am heading north to Miotes, and actually am in a bit of a hurry. If you don't mind, I really must be getting back to my crew now so that we can continue with our journey."

"Cloran Hastings!" exclaimed Mundin. "Here I have Cloran Hastings! You must stay and eat with us tonight. I have much to...discuss with you!"

"Oh no, I really can't do that. I must be going now."

"Oh, no? Going eh? Humor me and answer a few of my questions. It's the least you can do after killing my…pets, as it were." Cloran couldn't say no to that, so he resigned himself to answer the questions Mundin gave him.

As soon as Cloran had entered the throne room, Marv turned and left the entry room, saying he needed to maintain his position as the porter. The sailors stood around for a while, waiting for Cloran to return, but as he took so long, they sat in the soft leather couches.

"I wonder what kind of leather this is," said Greaves sitting down in one of the blue couches. "I don't think I've ever seen anything with blue skin before."

"They probably dyed it," said Jenkins.

"It doesn't look dyed."

"We should get some of these for inside the ship," said Richards, sinking into his couch with a smile.

"Who cares about couches, I just want to get to Miotes and back," said Mallory. "We've had far too many stops along the way."

"Ah, now you're starting to sound like Cloran," said Richards with a chuckle. "Always talking about time and weather."

"Poor Cloran, he just wants to get this trip over with," said Len. "I don't think we've ever sailed this late in the year before."

"Aye, usually we're unloading and cleaning the ship about this time, getting her ready for spring."

"Maybe you are," said Darrell, "but I'm usually at the Unicorn this time of year!"

"Bah, I'm going to get *Wavegrazer* ready for when Cloran gets out," said Len. He stood and went out the door that they had come through. As soon as Len had gone, the doors to the left and right of the throne room opened and out came two other pale men.

"Phil has asked me to serve you this wine," said one of the men, and they went around the room, handing each sailor a silver goblet filled with a clear liquid.

"Hey now, this isn't a bad deal!" said Richards. "Free wine and soft seats!"

"Enjoy," said the servers with a smile, and they left the room.

Len walked back down the hall to the very end, and opened the door to the small harbor where *Wavegrazer* was moored. Phil was there, and he stopped Len.

"I'd like to go back to the ship and get her ready to go," said Len, but Phil laughed.

"Your ship isn't going anywhere yet," he said with a grin. Len frowned.

"Why not?"

Phil's smile faded and he cleared his throat.

"Oh, well, only because it is a custom we have that our guests remain inside the castle until they are all ready to leave. And since your captain is still conversing with the king, it would be great if you could all just wait in that room until he is done. Besides, I sent some wine down for you all. Try some, it's really good, the best we have in this castle."

Len nodded.

"All right, if it is your custom, I won't complain."

Len went back inside and Phil closed the door. He shrugged and walked towards the entry room, but on his right he passed the narrow hallway that they had walked by earlier, and curiosity got the better of him. He looked around, saw no one, and went down the small hallway. It was dark and torches did not line it, as they did the main hallway. It went a short ways before turning a sharp corner. Upon turning the corner, he stopped abruptly. Marv stood there, blocking the way.

"You cannot come this way," said Marv sternly. "This is not open to guests."

"I'm sorry, I didn't know," said Len, but he paused. "Might I ask what is down here?"

Marv was quiet for a moment.

"Gold," he burst out. "Yes, we have gold back here. It is our castle treasury, and so we don't like strangers coming this way. I'm sure you understand."

"Sure, no worries. I'll go back with the others."

Len retraced his steps back to the main hallway and walked towards the chamber where the sailors sat. Suddenly the harbor door creaked behind him and he spun around. Phil had entered from the small harbor, and his face was excited. Without looking around, he darted down the narrow hallway where Marv was, and Len could hear them talking. Len silently walked towards them, hugging the wall, and when he got close enough to hear them, he hid behind a torch, lying flush against the wall.

"...and I was sitting there and saw it swim by, big and silver, as big as a man!"

"Wow, that big eh? I wonder if it tastes as good as one. How did you catch it?"

"I threw a brick at its head and stunned it, then dove in and grabbed it. He sure was a slippery fellow. I don't think I have ever caught a fish that struggled so much. But I smashed it against a wall until it stopped moving. Quick, come see! You won't believe me otherwise."

Marv and Phil flitted by and cast shadows down the hallway, past where Len stood flush against the wall. They opened the harbor door and went outside, leaving Len alone and confused. *A fish that tastes as good as what?*

He grabbed a torch from off the wall and quickly turned down the narrow hallway. The hall twisted, left, then right, then left again, until at length he came to a narrow wooden door set in the stone wall a few inches off the ground. He opened it and climbed inside, but as he shut the door he dropped his torch, and it went out.

"Blast," he said, and he bent down to pick it up. Feeling the ground for it, he came across many strange things. Some were round and some were long and flat. They all were hard and course.

"Gah, what an awful smell," he said, wrinkling his nose, "and these don't feel like gold bars. Where is it…"

He finally found his torch. He pulled out of his pocket a piece of flint and took his small knife. He struck the flint with the knife and sparks flew. At last, a spark caught hold of the torch and began to burn. Len blew on it until flame burst from the torch. Satisfied, Len stood to his feet and looked around.

What he saw in that room horrified him. Bones littered the floor, some still red with blood. They were scattered all over the place, some stacked in piles, others just strewn about. The bones had teeth marks in them, and it was clear that they had been chewed upon. Len gasped.

"Th-these are human bones! They have been eaten!"

The gravity of the situation dawned on him and his mind went towards the crew. He threw open the door, casting his torch aside. He ran down the narrow hallway, turned one corner and then another, but as he turned the last corner he stopped dead in his tracks. Marv stood in his way, but this time with his sword drawn.

"Despite my best efforts, it appears you have discovered our little secret, and sooner than we would have wished."

"Cannibals!" Len cried in anger, but Marv laughed.

"No, we are not cannibals. You must eat some of your own kind to fit into that category, but we are not human, not by any means. We are Man-wraiths, my friend, Man-wraiths! We may wear the visage of men, but we are creatures of another era, forced off the land by you wretched people. And now that your captain is dead and your crew is drugged by our 'special wine', we will be able to feast on their fat flesh without care!"

Marv giggled, thinking himself terribly witty, but a sharp hiss sliced through the air and silenced him. Len stood with his curved blade drawn.

"I have been to the edge of the world and the bottom of the sea. I have hitched a ride on the four winds, seen more than most could ever dream, and I will be damned if I let some measly pale-faced Man-wraiths make an end to my captain and crew!"

Marv was not used to his prey fighting back. After all, he usually fed on those that had drunken his 'special wine'. He no longer smiled, and with his sword pointing towards the floor, he stepped back.

"Phil!" he called over his shoulder, but the door to the harbor was shut, and Phil was not within earshot. Len lunged at Marv and the Man-wraith turned and fled down the hallway, crying for Phil. Len chased after him, but the Man-wraith was quicker and Len soon lost sight of him. Blood, however, was not foremost on his mind, and he turned and ran as fast as he could towards the entry room, shouting, "Don't drink the wine!"

"I think we should have a toast, before we drink," said Darrell. He raised his silver goblet. "To what should we toast?"

"How about to victory in battle, since we did just kill all those Sea Lions," said Greaves.

"No, too conventional," said Mallory. "How about we toast to a successful journey."

"Way too boring," said Richards. "We need an exciting toast, something unique. Let's toast to…fantastic adventures, above and below the sea, to fine foods, lovely ladies, mighty battles and strange sights."

"I, for one, hope we don't come across anymore adventures," said Jenkins, "and I bet Cloran would feel the same. Let's toast to no more adventures."

"Aye, and to no more messes," said Turner. "We have quite a bit to clean up when we get back to the ship. I hope that silver blood doesn't stain."

"Bah, forget the toast, now my arm is tired from holding this goblet," said Darrell. He put the goblet to his lips and drank the whole thing in one gulp.

"So then a few years later, we stumbled upon a hole in the water—not a place filled with land, mind you, but an actual hole that went through the ocean and came out the bottom."

Cloran sighed.

"That's enough for now, I really must be going."

Mundin glanced at the guard on the right, who was really the guard on the left, and nodded at him. The guard looked at him quizzically but then nodded in remembrance, and walked towards the throne room door.

"Wonderful story!" said King Mundin clapping. "I say, your adventures are so exciting. Perhaps you could tell me one more story?"

"I am afraid I must decline," said Cloran irritably. "I don't have the time."

Mundin's eyes were not on Cloran, however, but on his guard. The guard reached the throne room door, opened it, and peered through. He saw Darrell quickly chug the contents of his goblet. Closing the door, the guard turned to his king and nodded. Mundin grinned and leaned back in his seat.

"You have led an amazing life Cloran, and I thank you for answering my questions. But alas! I am afraid your run ends here, and I do hope you will hold nothing against me."

Cloran frowned.

"My run is not ending anywhere," he said, "and what is it I would hold against you?"

Mundin leaned forward wearing a broad grin.

"We are a simple people, leading simple lives. Our only joy in this wave-riding existence is when we can feast upon the most succulent delicacy of all."

Mundin's grin faded and his eyes were unblinking. His jaw was agape and the smallest trail of drool escaped the corner of his mouth. Cloran still wore his confused frown, but then the thought dawned on him and his eyes went wide.

"Oh, we are a responsible race, and we use every bit of our prey. Of them we make weapons, buttons, toys, dice and...couches." Mundin stood from his throne and slowly walked towards Cloran. "We eat only the finest and the fittest, of course. Phil makes sure to choose prey with the most meat on their bones."

Cloran drew his sword.

"If your intentions are what I think they are," he said angrily, "my crew will burst through those doors and cut you down."

"They are no threat to me!" said Mundin with a cracked voice, and he broke out in a string of jittery laughter. "By now the wine they drank has turned them into senseless sacks of meat, ah! and soon the feast will begin!"

Cloran sliced through Mundin's string of laughter with his sword. He stabbed Mundin in the chest and thrust him back onto his throne, sticking him to it.

"Guards!" the Man-wraith King screamed, grabbing at the hilt sticking out of his chest, but the guards on either side of him shrieked and ran around aimlessly. White, sticky blood oozed out of Mundin's chest, and he spit and swore.

"Help, I'm losing sap!" he cried, but Cloran did not stop to hear anymore. He turned and ran towards the door shouting, "Don't drink the wine!"

"You dolt, you're not supposed to drink until everyone has toasted!" said Greaves but Darrell just shrugged.

"You were taking too long." He frowned. "Bleh! That stuff didn't taste very good anyway."

Just then, Len burst through the rear door.

"Did any of you drink the wine?" he asked anxiously. The sailors stood quickly, confused.

"I did," said Darrell, "but the others hadn't toasted yet."

Cloran burst through the throne room door, much to Len's relief.

"Draw your swords boys!" he called. "We've got to cut our way out of here!"

"What happened?" the crew said, but they heard echoes throughout the castle of loud, hurried footsteps and the clanging of weapons. The doors on either side of them suddenly opened and out poured dozens of chisel-wielding Man-wraiths. Without another word the sailors dropped their goblets, drew their swords and, leaping atop the leather couches, fought off the Man-wraiths.

They came at the sailors boldly at first, but within seconds, the first few assailants had been stricken down. Their white, sappy blood oozed out of their bodies, and a fragrance of newly hacked wood filled the room. In dismay at the loss of their comrades, the Man-wraiths backed up to the end of the room, but larger Man-wraiths with clubs and maces entered and were not as timid. One lunged at Jenkins who deftly evaded the blow and struck back, slicing the Man-wraith along the neck, but the blade offered the big Man-wraith but a scratch, and with a laugh the Man-wraith swung low at Jenkins's feet, tripping him to the floor. The Man-wraith, however, did not get to finish him off. The rest of the sailors lunged upon him lustily and hacked at him so fiercely that bits of his fibrous body flew in all directions. The enraged Man-wraiths lurched towards the sailors, and Len opened the rear door as the fighting became more pressed.

"Out!" he called, and the sailors backed out between swings. With all the men out the door, they ran down the hallway towards the harbor, with the Man-wraiths in hot pursuit. But Darrell could not keep up with the sailors, and at last his strength failed him and he fell. He cried out, and Greaves skidded to a halt, turned around and ran to get his friend.

By now the largest of the Man-wraiths was upon Darrell as he lay there and hefted up a giant chisel, but Greaves threw his weight into the Man-wraith and they tumbled to the floor. They wrestled there until Greaves overturned him and then, taking the Man-wraith's own chisel in hand, hacked at the Man-wraith's trunk giving him large, gaping wounds that oozed sap.

With the Man-wraith lying there moaning, Greaves hefted Darrell over one shoulder, and with the chisel in his free hand, fended off the other Man-wraiths as they reached him. The smaller ones fell quickly and soon Greaves had carved up a pile of moaning bodies. With no room to go around him in that narrow hall, the remaining Man-wraiths backed off warily, cursing and hacking at the air. Greaves turned and fled after his shipmates.

Turner opened the door to the harbor and lunged at Phil, who was sitting there carving up the fish he had caught. With a cry, Phil dove into the water, and the sailors poured out of the castle and ran the length of the dock towards the ship. All climbed aboard and Cloran raced to the wheel. The sailors used their oars to push away from the dock, and Richards fumbled with the rope that held them.

"Where are Greaves and Darrell?" called Jenkins from atop the main mast, and in horror they realized that the two were not with them. But just then, Greaves leapt out of the doorway with Darrell over his shoulder and ran down the length of the dock towards the ship. The Man-wraiths came after them enraged, and some stopped to throw small darts made of bone at Greaves and the ship. Most missed or stuck to the ship's hull, but one caught Greaves in the thigh, and he cried out. Turner and Mallory grabbed the rope that was still attached to the dock and pulled the ship close again, but the gangway had fallen and dropped into the water. Greaves looked back and saw the Man-wraiths approach, and with the last bit of his strength he leapt towards the ship, casting Darrell over the side in the process. As Greaves came down, he caught the rope and dangled there.

"Go, go!" called Len, and he and Richards pushed away with their oars. Greaves hacked at the rope below him with his chisel until it snapped, and *Wavegrazer* was free. Cloran used the momentum from Richards and Len's push to ease the ship towards the exit. As the sailors plunged their oars into the water and rowed fiercely, he nosed the ship away from the dock.

The Man-wraiths had reached the end of the dock, just in time for *Wavegrazer* to drift out of reach. Turner and Mallory hauled Greaves aboard as the Man-wraiths hurled bone darts and spears at the ship, only to have them stick in the hull or sail harmlessly overhead. As the sailors emerged from the darkness of the castle, they heard the wails and groans of the angry, hungry Man-wraiths, and then a call went out; "King Mundin has died, King Mundin has been drained of sap!" But the ship sailed on, the castle grew smaller, and the calls of the Man-wraiths faded.

CHAPTER TWELVE

The Narcotic Effects of Silver Blood

Sea Lion corpses littered the deck. It was still slippery with the silver blood, so the sailors were sure to be careful.

"Is he all right?" asked Cloran. Turner went to Darrell, who lay on the deck in a pile, and stretched him out on his back.

"Hey buddy, are you alive?"

Darrell opened his eyes, but could not move his limbs or his mouth.

"Look at me, if you can."

Darrell blinked and looked at Turner. His eyes were clear and he was conscious, but other than that, he was motionless.

"What's wrong with him?" asked Richards. He leaned over Darrell and frowned.

"Blink once if you can understand me," said Turner. Darrell blinked once.

"At least he has his wits," said Richards. "Actually, I'm not sure about that. He *was* the only one to drink the wine."

"Blink twice if you think Richards deserves to be thrown overboard," said Turner, and Darrell eagerly blinked twice. The crew laughed and Richards stood up.

"Hah! He can throw me overboard when he can support his own weight."

"How long will he be like this?" asked Len.

"I am no physician," said Turner. "But maybe if we get some food in him the poison will more easily run its course."

"Don't feed him anything until he is strong enough to swallow," said Cloran at the wheel. "I don't want him choking to death."

"I suppose I should go fix something for the rest of us," said Greaves. He sat with his back against the door and pulled the bone dart out of his thigh with a grunt.

"No, you sit still," said Turner. "You managed to save Darrell, kill a few Man-wraiths and leap aboard with a dart in your leg, so I'll cook up something." Turner walked to the door and then turned around. "But you all had better help me clean this deck after we finish eating!"

Turner closed the door, and Mallory propped up Darrell against it so he could see everything. The sailors then piled the Sea Lion carcasses, but the sun disappeared and the moon started to fade into view. Cloran sighed heavily.

"Get Darrell into some clean clothes and put him to bed. The rest of you eat and start the night shift. There's no sense having us all out here when the sun isn't out." The crew obliged and went below deck except Len, who reached for the wheel.

"Not tonight Len," said Cloran, holding the wheel firmly.

"But you have been sailing without rest for days now. Get some sleep."

"I'll sleep easy when we're on our way back from Miotes. Right now, I just want to get there."

Len sighed, nodded, and went below, leaving Cloran at the wheel as night encompassed the bobbing ship.

Morning brought still winds and clear skies. The sails drooped and *Wavegrazer* moved but little while the sailors cleaned the deck. Greaves took a dozen or so Sea Lion carcasses below to see what he could strip from their bones to eat. Darrell leaned against the cabin door and rested while the crew worked tirelessly to get the silver blood off the deck. Richards tossed the remaining carcasses overboard one by one.

"Looks like the fishes will be getting a good meal today!" he said, hurling a Lion as far as he could.

"Oh, my poor deck," said Turner sadly, scrubbing off the blood.

"I'm not sure if fish eat this kind of meat," said Darrell. He had regained his ability to speak and eat, but he could not yet move his limbs.

"Some fish do. Like sharks."

"Is a shark a fish? I thought it was more of a...well I don't know what it is, but it seems to be too big to be a fish."

"My poor clean deck is clean no more," said Turner with a sigh.

"I'm pretty sure they are fishes," said Mallory, scrubbing hard. He and Turner had buckets of seawater and rough sponges and were scrubbing the silver blood off, washing it into the sea.

"The creatures of the sea can be divided into three groups—fish, squid and monster. I think fish fits better than squid or monster."

"They seem like monstrous fish to me," said Jenkins from atop the main mast.

"I'll never be able to see wood again, this accursed blood has stained my deck silver," moaned Turner.

Cloran stood quietly at the wheel, fuming at the lack of wind but thankful at least for a slow moving current. Once the deck was clean the sailors could man the oars, which would help a little, but it was wind he needed more than anything.

Just then, something in the water caught his eye. He looked to the right and raised an eyebrow.

"There are your sharks Richards," he said.

"Where? I don't see—" said Richards, but then he did. Mallory, Len and Richards walked to the gunwale to have a look. The sailors could see the long, white shapes of big fish just below the surface, slowly swimming alongside the ship. Some would stop and watch the sailors intently with black, unblinking eyes until the ship passed them, then quickly swim to the bow of the ship, stop, and again follow the sailors with their eyes. Richards laughed.

"I was right! These fellows look awfully hungry."

He picked up another Lion carcass and tossed it overboard. Three sharks swarmed it when it hit the water, and devoured it before their eyes.

"I've never seen sharks so...eager," said Len.

With a bit of effort, Darrell managed to turn his head towards the sailors, but he could not see the water from where he sat.

"Hey, I want to see. Someone bring me to the side." Len and Mallory lifted Darrell up and threw his arms over each of their shoulders. They brought the limp sailor to the edge of the ship so he could see.

"My, they are begging, just like dogs!" he said with a laugh, and Richards threw in the last of the Lions.

"That's it sharkies, no more food for you, so go away!" he said, but the sharks did not go away. Instead, they swam close alongside the ship, and every now and then faced the sailors, staring them down with their large, black eyes.

"Stupid sharks," said Turner, still scrubbing. He pushed bloody water off the deck to the sharks that had gathered on his side too. "They're here because of the blood."

"Stop cleaning the deck so that they go away," said Darrell.

"No way! I don't want this blood drying on the deck in the sun. Then I'll never get it off." The slow current that was carrying the ship suddenly dissipated. The sea grew calm and in a few moments, *Wavegrazer* lost all momentum. She slowly rocked in the churning waves and the sharks circled the ship.

"Perfect timing," said Cloran in frustration. He left the wheel and walked to the gunwale where his men stood. "Let's hope the wind picks up soon, or I'll have to stick you boys with the oars. We don't have another day to spare."

"I don't think I like these sharks staring at me," said Richards at last. "Turner, stop cleaning that deck."

"It's as clean as I can get it for now," Turner said, standing up and wiping his brow. "I am afraid we have a silver deck forever. This stuff acts just like dye."

He rinsed the deck with a bucket of clean water and then joined his friends at the ship's edge.

"They sure are acting odd," he said, peering over the side.

"Maybe it's something in the blood," wondered Mallory, but just then the ship trembled and a low groan came up at them from the waves beneath. In a flash, the sharks scrambled away and disappeared.

"Whoa, I didn't think sharks could make such a noise," said Len.

"They can't," said Cloran.

A second low-pitched groan sent the waves around them shimmering and the ship itself trembled.

"I think we need to go now," said Richards, stepping away from the edge.

"What do you want him to do Richards, summon the wind?" said Mallory, and a third bellow shook the ship so that the masts swayed.

"Jenkins, get down from there!" ordered Cloran.

Suddenly the ship lurched and an ivory spike pierced through the hull, coming out the other side. The ship tipped and the sailors slid along the deck. Len and Mallory lost hold of Darrell and he tumbled across the deck, caught by the gunwale on the port side. *Wavegrazer* would have capsized, but the spike held her in place, and when it pulled out of the ship, she rocked back upright. The main mast swayed and threw Jenkins as he was trying to climb down. With a cry, Jenkins sailed through the air and hit the water hard with a *splat!*

"Jenkins!" cried the sailors and they ran to the edge. Jenkins resurfaced and coughed. He held his chest and wheezed hard.

"Someone get him," ordered Cloran, "and get some weapons up here!" Greaves opened the cabin door and came onto the deck to see what was afoot, but the sailors ran past him and below to fetch their spears and harpoons. Before he could ask what had happened, the waters reverberated with that same, low groan. The sailors emerged with their weapons and Len prepared to jump in after Jenkins.

The waves grew angrier as a bulge appeared in the water beneath Jenkins. A white, gleaming ivory horn slowly emerged from underneath the wheezing sailor and lifted him into the air. Jenkins cried out hoarsely and clung to the horn as its owner surfaced. From the depths of the sea emerged a beast only known in tales—a giant, black, hard-nosed Horned Whale. Its face was rough and knobby, and barnacles grew all over it. Its body was black and it gleamed in the sun. Its horn was white and spiraled from the tip down to a thicker base that grew in the shape of an upside-down triangle. The crew stood aghast, but Cloran shook his head.

"Figures."

The Horned Whale bellowed and lunged at *Wavegrazer*, piercing her hull, although this time it didn't go all the way through. The impact flung Jenkins off the horn and into the largest sail, where he tumbled back onto the deck, landing near Darrell.

"You all right?" asked Darrell in his crumpled position, unable to move.

"I'll live," said Jenkins with a wheeze, holding his chest. "On any other day, something like that would be fun."

The ship lurched again and again as the whale tried to free its horn, but it was stuck and the whale groaned angrily. The sailors began throwing harpoons and spears at the great beast, but they stuck in its hide and did no more damage than a splinter would a man. It did, however, annoy the whale, and his bellows became louder and shorter.

"Spears won't work here," said Greaves, and he took up his great Man-wraith chisel. With a running leap, he cast himself overboard and onto the giant horn. He crawled along it and then climbed up onto the whale's nose. Hefting the weapon upwards, he came down with tremendous force, and blow after blow, chipped away at the hard nose of the moaning whale. The whale twisted and lurched, and the ship rocked back and forth, but it could not free its horn and Greaves' work finally drew blood.

The hard shell protecting its nose cracked, and red blood drained from the whale like a river. Jenkins tossed Greaves a long harpoon and, stretching his arms up, he came down with the pointed spear into the wound he had created, driving the weapon deep into the beast's face until the shaft disappeared. The whale squealed and shot out high-pitched peals through the waves, and the sailors covered their ears in agony, but Greaves managed to crawl along the horn, back to the ship. The sailors clung to masts and railings to keep from being tossed overboard.

"This will drive us mad long before he dies!" called Len over the din, but then the whale made a new noise. If the sailors thought its squeals were already frantic, they became even more so, and wave after wave of water lashed across the deck as the whale kicked its tale. The sailors peered over the edge to see what was happening.

"Look there!" said Turner pointing, and the sailors could see white gleaming bodies under the waves beside the massive whale. The sharks had returned and brought friends with them. Lured by the blood, they attacked the whale timidly at first, but then more fiercely until every shark tore off bits of the whale and devoured them. At last, the whale stopped squealing and with a final flip of its tail, became still.

"Can you believe it," whispered Richards under his breath. "My little sharkies have come to rescue us."

"Don't believe that for a moment," said Mallory. "They would devour you in a second if they could. But this whale is a much bigger target."

The wind finally picked up and Cloran helped Darrell up off the deck, propping him up against the door.

"Lower the sails quickly," he said to the crew. "The last thing we want to do is drag this whale around." The men lowered the sails and saw then that the corpse was gone. Only a bloody skeleton remained. The sharks had picked the bones clean and disappeared.

"It seems that they finally got their fill," said Richards with a laugh, but he didn't laugh long. The ship creaked, and then suddenly it tipped to the side. The bones began to sink and the ship was sinking with it.

"Get that horn out of the ship!" called Cloran, and the crew took out their weapons. Len, Greaves and Mallory climbed onto the horn and hacked at it, but they couldn't make even the smallest mark. The ship rose steadily out of the water and the men on deck began to slide towards the skeleton. At last the weight became too much, and with a sudden jerk the horn snapped at the base. *Wavegrazer* fell back into the sea with a splash, sending water out in a wide ring and up onto the deck. The bones vanished into the depths of the sea, but the ship tilted to one side and slowly began to sink.

"We're taking on water!" called Len. The sailors went below and found water up to their ankles. It was coming out of the crew's bunkroom, and Mallory waded in.

"Get me some boards and nails," he said. A giant hole went through the very hull of the ship, where the Horned Whale had skewered it through with its first attack. The sailors fetched some boards and tried frantically to cover up the hole, but the water rose steadily higher and the ship tilted sharply.

From outside the hole a shadow passed, and then the ship lurched. Something scraped alongside *Wavegrazer*, making a deafening noise, and it lifted the ship up until *Wavegrazer* leaned slightly the other way. The water stopped pouring in from the hole beneath the water line, and Mallory quickly and sloppily boarded it up.

"What's that? Another whale?" wondered Jenkins aloud, but Cloran, angry at the whale, angry at the sharks, and angry at the whole situation, stormed away and climbed on deck.

"Cloran," said Darrell who was lying on his side near the door, but Cloran could see what had happened. He stood in amazement as his crew joined him from below deck. There, side by side with *Wavegrazer*, sat a large ship with a blue sail. It held *Wavegrazer* up by supporting its side, and ropes had been cast onto her deck and pulled tight. Men arrayed in black uniforms lined the side of the blue-sailed ship. They wore somber but proud faces, and their dark eyes were both sad and sharp. Their leader, a man with keen eyes, a long brown coat and a wide-brimmed brown hat, took off his hat and saluted Cloran.

"Percy!" exclaimed the crew quietly, but Cloran stood motionless.

"Captain Cloran Hastings!" cried Percy from the deck of his ship, *Blue Bane*. "When we last parted ways, you swore to inflict justice upon me if we ever met again. We are here to offer our help, and receive whatever justice you deem fitting."

*   *   *

"Can you hear what they are saying?" asked Mallory to Turner. The two men stood in the dinghy that was resting by the side of *Wavegrazer*, working to patch one of the holes in the hull. Cloran and Percy sat on the deck of *Blue Bane*, talking lowly together, and the sailors strained to hear the conversation. Turner shook his head and turned back to his work.

"No, they are talking too discretely."

Mallory lifted a plank in place and Turner used long nails to set it. A head appeared in the hole they were covering from inside *Wavegrazer*—one of Percy's men.

"Here, use this," the man said. He lowered down smaller boards, a hand drill and some wooden dowels. "You can get a nice flush seam with these. Nails will rust out."

"Thanks," said Turner slowly, and the sailor left.

On deck, men from both ships were sawing, trimming and shaving wood, and a train of men with buckets bailed water overboard as they scooped it from below deck. Sailors dangled from ropes over the side of *Wavegrazer* and trimmed cracks and breaks, sanded seams and made broken edges strait as the men on deck got wood ready to repair the holes.

The majority of Percy's sailors, however, took to removing the horn from *Wavegrazer*. With ropes tied to the base of the horn and wrapped around back on deck with pulleys, they slowly extracted the massive horn from the hull of the ship. Three small dinghies were in the water below it, and when the tip finally emerged the sailors let go of the ropes. The horn crashed onto the boats, cracking in the center, and *Wavegrazer* lurched upward after shedding the weight. The sailors clapped and cheered.

"A Horned Whale!" exclaimed Bof, the first mate of *Blue Bane*, as he and many of Cloran's men sawed and prepared wood for patching the holes. "I always thought they were creatures of myth. I would love to have seen it."

"It was pretty intimidating," said Richards with a saw in hand. "I never imagined them being so big."

"What did you boys do to make it grumpy?"

"I think it was the Sea Lion blood we were washing overboard," said Len, who was also cutting wood. "It lured the sharks, and I bet it lured the whale too."

"Aye, that's probably what it was," said Bof. "That's how we found you. We followed a trail of silver film on the water. We didn't know it was blood at the time, and thought perhaps it was some menacing creature wreaking destruction on the seas."

Jenkins stood cutting wood, but did not say a word.

"So is that what you have been doing since we last saw you? Patrolling the seas to make them safe?" asked Len and Bof nodded.

"We figured it was the least we could do. Over the years, we've heard rumors of all sorts of dangers that we mainly avoided. We were just now hunting for a rumored floating castle when we stumbled upon you."

"Ha!" exclaimed Richards. "We just came from there, and I'll tell you, it was filled with some of the strangest creatures I have ever seen."

Jenkins threw down his saw and it clattered across the deck. He angrily walked towards the main mast, climbed the riggings to the very top of it and remained there, motionless.

Bof glanced at Len worriedly.

"Did I say something to anger him?" he asked, but Len shook his head.

"I'll go talk with him. Don't worry about it." Len set his saw down and walked to the base of the mast.

"Jenkins, are you all right?" he called up, but Jenkins turned away and did not respond. Len frowned and climbed up after him. A cold wind picked up and blew through Len's clothing, chilling him. At the top he found Jenkins sitting with his legs in the riggings, staring silently out over the water.

Len glanced around. He saw *Blue Bane* to the side of *Wavegrazer*, where Cloran and Percy were talking on the deck. *Wavegrazer* was now resting evenly in the water, and Percy's crew was hard at work repairing her. The small boats were hauling the two halves of the massive horn, taking one piece towards each ship. Far off, Len could see a silver trail leading away from *Wavegrazer*, and the filmy substance formed a path that went farther than he could see.

"Hey Jenkins, is anything the matter?" he asked. Jenkins remained motionless and stared out to sea, but eventually nodded his head.

"Yes, something is the matter," he said softly. "We sit here on our ship, having lived our lives as true and honest sailors. But Richards is down there sharing stories and jokes with a thief, one of the worst kinds of villain." He shook his head. "I would have rather seen *Wavegrazer* sink than to be saved by these vermin."

"Ah," said Len nodding his head. "I see."

"There were over twenty ships at that little cove of theirs. Each ship could easily hold a dozen sailors. Do you realize how many men that makes, trapped on island-prisons, scattered across the sea? Yet on the sea, they do not get justice. Marauders are rarely caught and punished. They can go on sailing as if they did nothing wrong, profiting from their evil while we work hard for years to earn an honest day's pay. I can't work side by side with these crooks and laugh and joke. I simply can't."

Len looked out to sea and nodded. Light clouds obscured the sunny sky, and the wind became chill.

"They've resigned themselves to Cloran's judgment," said Len. "King Bozin gave Cloran command of these waves and the ships upon them, until this journey ends, and I believe he will judge them wisely."

"He should have punished them when we first found out what they were."

"Cloran was taken by surprise just like we all were. I can tell you that he was more upset about all this than any of us. He and Percy go way back, and it was as if a brother betrayed him."

A lone bird descended out of the sky and, circling over the two ships for a while, finally perched in the riggings next to Jenkins.

"A bird!" called Mallory pointing upwards, and the sailors from both ships cheered; "Land, we are near land!" The bird sidestepped along the ropes, then leapt up and flew away. Len and Jenkins followed it with their eyes, while the sailors below cheered and hollered.

"It looks like we may make it to Miotes in time after all," said Len with a nod, but Jenkins still wore a stone face. Concerned for his friend, Len put his arm around Jenkins' shoulders.

"You are right," he said softly. "Justice needs to be brought upon Percy and his crew for what they did. But from what I can see, the sailors of *Blue Bane* honestly regret the deeds they have done, and are even taking steps to amend them."

"Their deeds can never be amended," said Jenkins.

"It does no harm for them to attempt to reform themselves," said Len softly. "Should we really hold this against them forever?" Jenkins said nothing. "Are even thieves beyond forgiveness?"

Jenkins looked down.

"I believe they are beyond redemption."

"It is not for us to decide who can or can't be redeemed. We can merely judge by what we know is right. These sailors have acted kindly and have been respectful ever since they got here, and I believe are truly sorry for what they have done. It is now up to us to forgive them, and go on with our lives. We may not, and probably shouldn't, ever forget what they have done. But we can't hate them forever."

Jenkins sighed and smiled at Len.

"I appreciate you coming up to talk. I'd just like to think about it alone for a bit." Len nodded and climbed down to finish helping with the repairs. When Jenkins eventually came back down he was still quiet, but his face was calm and he worked alongside Percy's men without complaint.

The men had patched all of the external holes and were now sanding them smooth. The inside of the ship was damp and messy, but the structural damages were repaired. The sailors in the dinghies below had taken the two halves of the massive horn and brought them on board the two ships. The men tightly tied the top half of the horn to the prow of *Wavegrazer* to be used as a figurehead, so that it stuck out like a gleaming pike, and the bottom half was affixed to the prow of *Blue Bane*. Cloran and Percy watched the working sailors from the deck of *Blue Bane*.

"They seem to be getting along fine, despite it all," said Percy. Cloran nodded but remained silent. He sat down with his back against the rail, and Percy sat beside him. At length, Cloran looked over at his friend.

"I want to know why, Percy, you resorted to piracy." Percy pursed his lips in thought, searching for words.

"That isn't an easy question to answer. Ten years ago, if you had told me that someday I would be the captain of a band of marauders, I wouldn't have believed you. I didn't intend for this to happen, but men do such things when need persuades them."

"Perhaps I can better empathize if you start from the beginning."

"All right. It was during the war and times were hard, as you know fully well. My crew stuck with me, but we had no consignments and nothing to eat. In desperation we sailed to Rogvelt in hopes that someone there had work for us, but there was none. We didn't have the supplies to sail back and were stuck there. So one night, Bof and I snuck aboard a merchant vessel that was moored at Ketubim and we stole some spices to sell in the market, just to get enough money for supplies to sail home. They caught us, however, and we fled Rogvelt before the authorities could catch us.

"Afterwards I was upset with myself for resorting to thievery, and so I tried to make amends by searching the nearby waters for marauding vessels. We came across other merchants who told us of a large vessel with a blue sail that was harrying the coast, and so we sought the ship. At last we found it, and we took it by surprise during the night."

"So you killed the marauders on board, took their vessel and became marauders yourselves?"

"Not quite. We had them at sword point and ordered them to surrender, which they did. But the captain of the ship requested to talk with me in private."

Percy sighed and bowed his head.

"Oh, how I wish I had never listened to the man. But at the time, the only thought on my mind was the aching within my belly, and so I met with him. He bartered with me, and suggested that I let him and his crew go. In exchange, he would pay me a tribute from every merchant vessel he sacked on the waters. He told me tales of riches and of enough food so that my boys would never be hungry again, and I was swayed, Cloran, by his slick words. We made a pact, and he swore tribute and allegiance to me under the most revered of their piratical oaths. He took my ship and I took his, for I had fallen in love with her." Percy fingered the deck and smiled, caressing the smooth wood. "She is the finest ship I have ever seen, and has served me well ever since."

"Didn't you think of the people that would suffer and die because of what you did?"

Percy's smile faded and he nodded.

"Part of the pact was that the marauders would spare the lives of the sailors they captured, and if it came down to it, to flee rather than take human life."

"Did you really expect a marauder to keep his word?" asked Cloran earnestly, and he was quickly growing angry.

"Well…yes. I know that it is foolish to put faith in the faithless, Cloran, and I make no excuses. I trusted in the oath they took with me, and hoped for the best. I do admit, reluctantly, that if I had heard of any deaths at the hands of my retainers, I would have probably turned a blind eye. As it was, I sailed the seas looking for other marauding vessels to capture and force to become my retainers. I have eight vessels under my authority now, and they report to me every month."

"Is a ship called *Rough Waters* under your employ?" asked Cloran slowly, looking him dead in the eyes. Percy cocked his head sideways.

"*Rough Waters?* No, I've never heard of it before."

"Mmm," said Cloran rather dully, but he was secretly relieved.

"Anyhow, I took my crew to the island where you found me, and I set up a storehouse there to keep our stolen goods. I sail between Rogvelt and Menigah to sell them. The marauders arrive at the island to drop off my share, and report to me how many ships they have taken. In the state I was in, I tried to convince myself that I was doing good, saving lives that the marauders would have otherwise destroyed, and taking wealth from the hands of the evil, even though by doing so, I became evil.

"But I never fully convinced myself. I always knew what I was doing, and I grew to hate it. I began to look for a way out, but if I showed any sign of weakness, my retainers would turn against me and destroy my men and me. I felt stuck in a world that I did not want to be a part of. In a way I was glad, Cloran, that day you caught me, for at least I wouldn't be living a lie anymore. I didn't have the strength to stand against these villains. I am glad you do."

Cloran stood and walked away from Percy. He stopped, gazed out towards the sea, and then turned around.

"We found an island," he said, "with many sailors on it. They told us that they had been captured by marauders and then set loose on the island rather than being killed."

"Good!" said Percy happily, getting up. "That means that the marauders have kept their word."

"But we also found wreckage by the Reef of Many Graves. The crew of the ship had been killed and their bodies arrayed on the shore."

Percy's face grew dark and he held is chin.

"It is possible," he said at length, "that there are other marauders patrolling the sea besides the ones under my leadership."

"Commanding a ship named *Rough Waters*, perhaps," said Cloran. "But I suppose we will never know for sure."

Percy stood next to Cloran and sighed, staring at the deck.

"I never thought beyond myself and my men," he said. "The day you stumbled upon my storehouse awakened me. Not only was I relieved to be freed from my secrecy, but the moment I saw your eyes, my heart sank to the bottom of my soul. I knew then how horrible it felt to betray a friend. I realized that I had betrayed my king and my crew, and as I sailed away from the cove to avoid responsibility for my deeds, horror struck me as I realized that I had betrayed the memory of Reuben."

Percy turned away from Cloran and talked softly.

"That is why I was hoping our paths would cross again. I could have sailed off in my fast ship and never returned. But the memory of Old Captain Reuben stung me in the heart, and I knew that I couldn't live with myself if I had betrayed him. It was he that taught me the sea and the stars."

Cloran sighed and rubbed his eyes, but at last, he lifted his gaze and grasped the shoulder of his old shipmate.

"I will believe you. I know I have every right to doubt you, yet I can't help but want to trust you. However, I can't let you leave without suffering the consequences for your deeds. Do you understand?"

Percy lowered his gaze and nodded. Both captains looked at their sailors, working side by side to repair *Wavegrazer*.

"I wish I could do it all over again," said Percy. "I am a horrible captain. I led my boys into wrongdoing. They'll never be able to forgive me."

"They are responsible for their own actions, just like you are responsible for yours. But perhaps you can find a way to redeem yourselves."

The two captains climbed aboard *Wavegrazer*, and Len and Bof assembled their sailors on deck. Percy examined the repairs done to *Wavegrazer* and nodded his approval, and Cloran stood before Percy's men.

"I want to thank you for saving us, and helping us with the repairs," he said first, and his own crew clapped in appreciation. Cloran held his hands behind his back, lowered his face, and began to pace along the deck.

"It seems that I am faced with the unpleasant task of righting the wrongs that are committed at sea. You, as sailors, followed your captain towards the end he chose for you. And that end was piracy."

The sailors of *Blue Bane* stood erect and silent.

"We have all been faced with hard times. Luck on the sea changes with the winds, and she can bring us prosperity one day or poverty the next. But it is what a man does when faced with such hardships that shows his character. Evil times are no excuse for evil deeds."

Cloran gazed at the men that stood before him, and was moved to pity. Some of them had families waiting for them, and Cloran was not eager to do what he was about to. And yet these very men, though now in repentance, had been instrumental in ruining the lives of other sailors. Justice must be wrought, even on the sea.

"You banished other sailors when you took their ships, to live their lives on cramped islands, and so now I banish you. From this day onward, you are forbidden to land on Menigan soil or sail through Menigan waters, upon penalty of death."

The sailors gasped and some wept, for Stren was their home. But they also saw the mercy in Cloran's decision, and though visibly upset, not one protested. Percy walked forward then with downcast eyes and a somber expression and spoke with a quiet voice.

"Lads, I am sorry that my leadership has brought this upon you. I'll never forgive myself for leading you astray, but if you will still follow me, I will lead you to greatness. It is my plan to flee to Rogvelt, where, with their government's permission, we will atone for our crimes by fighting piracy on the open sea. We have fought marauders before and defeated them. Let us right our wrongs and keep the seas safe. I remind you that we have an advantage. We know the habits of these villains and can recognize their ships. Together, we can make a new name for ourselves. No longer will people know us for theft and destruction, but instead when they speak of *Blue Bane*, they will think of justice and honesty. Our name will become a blessing to whichever land accepts us."

Though upset at being banished, Percy's men found his words encouraging and full of hope. At Bof's lead, they saluted Percy.

The sailors of *Blue Bane* boarded their vessel and got to work preparing to sail west towards Rogvelt. Cloran caught Percy before he boarded his ship, and slipped him a note.

"Give this to the elders when you arrive at Rogvelt. It is my personal guarantee that you mean no mischief, and it is a plea for them to work with you to rid the waves of the menace you know so well. Perhaps my endorsement will help in some way."

"Thank you, Cloran," said Percy with a smile.

The two men hugged and then Percy boarded his vessel. The sailors cast aside the ropes between the ships, and *Blue Bane* eased away from *Wavegrazer*, sailing west towards Rogvelt. Cloran, Len and the rest of the crew stood by and waved at the sailors as the ship sailed away.

"Was I right?" asked Len to Jenkins. The lookout nodded.

"You were. It was a fair punishment, and even I almost feel sorry for them. Almost."

As the ship grew smaller on the evening horizon, the men of *Wavegrazer* could hear them sing, and they sang the funeral song of the sea:

> *"We send you forth with fond farewell,*
> *atop the sea and amongst the waves.*
> *Through the storm and raging swell,*
> *we wish you love and brighter days.*
>
> *Atop the sea and amongst the waves,*

you go to rest in deep darkness.
We wish you love and brighter days,
as you sail through the abyss.

You go to rest in deep darkness,
though in our thoughts you'll always be.
As you sail through the abyss,
our prayers will be concerning thee.

Though in our thoughts you'll always be,
your spirit will forever sleep.
Our prayers will be concerning thee,
as you travel through the deep.

Your spirit will forever sleep,
through the storm and raging swell.
As you travel through the deep,
we send you forth with fond farewell."

CHAPTER THIRTEEN

The Ring of Ice

For the first time in many days, Cloran gave the wheel to Len when night fell. Len was overjoyed to see his captain finally ready to sleep, and when Cloran reached his bunk, he cast himself into a dead sleep so sound that no rising wave or trembling ship could wake him.

Night and morning passed, and Len did not wake his captain. Finally, when the sun was at its highest, Cloran awoke and climbed topside. The chill air stung him upon opening the cabin door, and he clutched himself tightly.

"Here Cap'n," said Greaves handing Cloran a bundle. Cloran unraveled it and saw that it was a coat made of dark blue fur with ivory buttons and green trim.

"Mallory and I made them out of the Sea Lions," Greaves said. "Now that the air is colder, these are much more fitting than the flimsy things we were wearing."

"You got the special cloak with the green trim," said Richards with a wink. "Ours are just plain old blue."

"It's a mighty fine coat boys! I'll be hard pressed to take it off even in warmer weather."

Cloran wrapped it around his body and then gazed out to sea. What he saw startled him, and he walked to the bow of the ship to peer over the side. During his sleep, they had sailed far enough north to hit ice. An icy film covered the water, but

Wavegrazer skimmed through it easily with a hiss. The sailors' breath froze in the overcast sky. The ship moved swiftly through the thin ice, and a thick layer of the frozen waves already coated her hull.

"It seems you made quite a bit of progress last night," said Cloran, and Len nodded.

"This ice sure came up on us fast, though. We were sailing on clear waters until we hit a line, then ice suddenly appeared."

"Let's hope we don't run into anything thicker until we reach Miotes," said Cloran. He walked back to the wheel and Len gladly handed it over.

"I think you let me sleep too late," said Cloran with a smirk. "I might just have to yell at you a bit."

The day wore on and Len went below deck to get a few hours of rest. The ice got just a bit thicker and larger bits of it bobbed here and there, but *Wavegrazer* deftly avoided them. Sea life began to appear on the ice. Both flying and swimming birds perched on the larger pieces, and dove or flew out of the way as *Wavegrazer* sailed past. They made an awful squawking and Turner was in constant dread of them messing up his silver deck, but the ship passed through without incident and Turner sighed in relief.

Other sea beasts climbed out of the water to rest. Large tusked walruses charged and batted each other with their fins, long-legged birds waded through them squawking, and even giant ice-turtles with fuzzy shells and beards climbed out of the water to look around with their long necks.

At last, the bobbing ice became too large and too frequent to sail at their present speed, and so Cloran lowered one of the sails and crept through the waters warily.

"We should be close to Miotes now," said Cloran. "If we do everything right, we should reach land before nightfall."

"Isn't this ice dangerous to sail through?" wondered Mallory aloud, and Cloran nodded.

"Yes it is, although not as dangerous as it could be. These chunks of ice are not tall, have narrow bottoms and sit high in the water. As long as we keep from touching them, we will be fine. There are other, more dangerous bergs in the area that we should avoid completely, if we can."

"Are they close?"

"Yes, just up ahead. They are part of the island's defenses, but the men of Miotes have made a way to navigate through them."

Only Cloran and Len had ever been this far north, but then it was under Old Captain Reuben. The rest of the crew had no idea what Cloran was referring to, but they soon found out.

At each passing hour, the air grew colder and the ice grew larger. The sky darkened, even though it was only in the mid-afternoon, and soon it sank completely out of sight. *Wavegrazer* dodged between the massive floating bergs, but Cloran's expert maneuvers kept the ship far away from any danger. At length, Len emerged from his short nap. He walked to the edge of the ship, stretched, and then shuddered.

"I see we've neared the Ring of Ice."

"Yep," said Cloran with a smile. "It will be the first time the boys have seen it."

"Is it normal for it to get dark this early?" asked Turner. It was now dark enough to see the moon and stars, and the pale moon-glow glinted through the nearby ice, illuminating them and casting a blue, soothing brilliance over the sea.

"Yes, the sun rises late and sets early in the far northern reaches of the world."

"Why is that?"

"I am not sure."

"I heard," said Jenkins, "that the sea gets stronger as you travel north, and it is harder for the sun to escape it and rise. It rises later and with more effort, and it is so exhausted afterwards that it sets much sooner than normal."

"Where on earth did you hear that?" asked Richards, cocking an eyebrow.

Jenkins shrugged.

"I think I read it somewhere."

Len cupped his hands around his mouth.

"Ho, ice!" he called to the north-west, but his voice was stifled. He walked to the starboard side of the ship.

"Ho, ice!" he called to the north-east, but his voice died in the waves. He walked to the very bow of the ship.

"Ho, ice!" he called due north, and in a moment, his voice came back to him. *"Ho, ice!"*

He called again and the rest of the crew joined him, and a moment later a chorus of *"Ho, ice!"* came back to the ship. As *Wavegrazer* moved forward, a jagged mountain came into view. It grew taller and wider as the ship grew near, and it filled the sailors with awe.

"That," said Cloran, "is the Ring of Ice, and we must now be careful. Man the oars lads. We have some tricky maneuvering ahead of us."

The ring stretched east and west as far as they could see. It was brilliant white on the rough surfaces but deep blue wherever the ice was smooth, and the ice did not bob or move in the water. It didn't seem to float, but looked as sturdy as solid rock, although water paths and narrow channels could be seen twisting through the ring.

"This is Miotes' main safeguard against unwanted visitors, but there is a man-made channel nearby that leads right to the peninsula. Let's see if we find it."

Cloran turned the ship and brought her alongside the ring, sailing around it with the crew searching hard for the man-made channel.

"What an obscure place to live in," said Darrell, leaning against the cabin door. He could now move his torso and his arms, but could not yet stand or walk and was too weak to assist with the rowing. He could, however, see over the gunwale, and he stared at the massive wall of ice. "Why would anyone want to live here?"

"The island was first inhabited many years ago, before the onset of the Nurith Wars," said Len. "It was during the time when the barons of Menigah scrambled for the throne after King Linus died. Bozin won, of course, but he gained his power with the help of the Noths, and Bozin's brother Sakal fled in fear for his life."

"Bozin had dealings with the Noths?" asked Jenkins in surprise, and the crew was stunned.

"Yes, long ago," said Cloran, "and that's how they eventually took control of Menigah. You all lived through the Nurith Wars, and you didn't know that?"

"I've heard many different accounts of the wars," said Greaves, "but this is the first time I've heard anything like that about Bozin."

"Aye, I wouldn't be surprised if Bozin didn't want it being known. But that's what happened. One of the Noths possessed him—Sheth was his name—which is what first started the third Nurith War. But Sakal fled here to Miotes with his followers until the war was over, and after Bozin was freed, they resumed contact and are close again."

Cloran looked at them, hoping a spark of remembrance would light their faces, but they stood there confused, hearing this version of the story for the first time.

"Bah, no one pays attention to history anymore..." he mumbled under his breath, turning back to his wheel.

There were no birds or visible sea life near the ring, and the wind had slowed to a gentle breeze. The nearby bergs bumped into each other, and the only noise that could be heard other than the sailors' conversation was the occasional *crack!* of colliding blocks of ice.

All at once, there was a low moaning sound over the waters, and the crew looked west towards it.

"Did you hear that?" asked Darrell from the deck. "What was it? I can't see that way."

The crew stopped rowing and gazed westward. There it was again! It was faint and far away, but it reverberated through the water and bounced off of the towering blocks of ice. At first it sounded like a moan, but then like a creaking noise, and then it sounded like neither and rather like a splash, or a rumble, and finally the crew couldn't tell what it was.

"Is it another Horned Whale?" wondered Greaves.

"Eh, I don't think so," said Len. "The whale had a distinct call, but this...this sounds like a whole mess of noises."

"Maybe it's the creatures we passed on the ice a while back," suggested Turner, but then he realized that the sound was coming from the west, not south, where they had come from.

"It's probably just the creaking ice," said Cloran at last. "Yes, that's what it must be. There is a lot of weight towering above us. I wouldn't be surprised if some of the bergs snapped or crumbled."

"Maybe it's..." started Len lowly, but then his voice trailed off. Cloran's explanation was suitable enough, but the sound didn't remind him of falling ice. There was something guttural, tonal and vocal about the noise. "Can't place my finger on it," said Len at last, shaking his head.

"Forget about the sounds—look there!" called Jenkins. As the ship passed by another outcropping of ice, they could all plainly see a wide channel that cut straight through the ice wall. The water was blue and unclouded by icy film, and the walls on either side were sheer.

"Ah! nice work Jenkins," said Cloran happily. "That's what we've been looking for."

Cloran spun the wheel, the sailors tugged at the oars, and the horn at the prow of the ship nosed into the channel. The sailors couldn't help being a little nervous as the ship passed between the two massive walls of ice. They were sheer and very smooth. The gaps between the giant bergs were small and the pieces fit snugly together to form the walls on either side of the channel. As they passed through, the men began to get an idea of how thick and otherwise impassible the Ring of Ice was and were grateful for the man-made channel.

At last, the nose of the ship emerged from the channel and *Wavegrazer* appeared on the other side of the ring. The sailors looked back as the ship left the harrowing hall of ice, but Cloran looked forward with a wide grin. He stood at the very doorstep to Miotes.

Land lay before them, not far away. A vast city stretched along the shore as far as he could see, and Cloran thought that it could almost rival Stren. The moonlight highlighted the snow-covered buildings, and to Cloran's eyes, it looked like a painting. Smoke poured out of the city's tall towers and sloped houses, making Cloran feel warm in spite of the ice all around him. The harbor was small with only a few wooden docks, and even fewer ships moored there. At the eastern point of the city stood the capital building of Miotes, tall and shining in the distance. It was made of stone and stretched out along the shore, then pierced inwards towards the heart of the city. The stone structure ended abruptly at the water's edge where it opened up into a wide passage, which was reminiscent of the opening of the Man-wraith castle, and Cloran assumed that it was a private, guarded harbor. Above the opening was a tall tower, and out of it gleamed a brilliant light.

The beauty of the city had so overcome Cloran that he hardly noticed a small ship approaching on his port side until it was upon them. The ship had the name *Ale Trodder* painted on its side, sat low on the water and had but one sail. It was fast and maneuverable, with eight oars poking out of its sides, and it circled all around *Wavegrazer*. A man in a bright uniform and a tall, awkward hat stood at the prow of the small ship and addressed the sailors.

"Identify yourselves!" he called with a booming voice. Cloran handed the wheel to Len and walked to the side of the ship to talk with the herald.

"I am Cloran Hastings and this is my ship, *Wavegrazer*."

The herald seemed taken aback at the name presented, but only for a moment. He still knew his job well.

"State your business here in the realm of King Sakal!" he cried.

"We are here by order of King Bozin of Menigah, and must urgently talk with your king."

The little man in the bright uniform muttered something to the other men in his boat.

"I assume you have the appropriate papers?" he called again, less earnestly this time.

"We do, and we have been sailing for weeks and would love to finish our journey as soon as possible."

"Of course you would!" said the herald, "but we have processes and procedures here in Miotes and they will not be forgotten. But you're in luck; I have no more questions for you now, yet I will need to see your papers when you arrive in port. Follow me Captain Cloran Hastings; you have reached your destination safely!"

"Did you hear that boys? We're here!" Cloran shouted, and the sailors cheered. "We're halfway done, and it's always faster sailing south. Today is a day of rest!"

Ale Trodder led them towards the covered harbor of the stone capital. The sailors looked up in awe as they passed under the high tower with the piercing light until it disappeared as they entered. It was darker in the covered harbor, but not much so, for torches lined the walls. There was only one dock inside and it wasn't very long. Past the dock rested a long, black metal gate and two guards stood beside it. The small ship moored to the left of the dock and *Wavegrazer* to the right.

The crew tied up the ship, pulled up the oars and stowed away everything on the deck while Cloran climbed ashore to talk with the captain of *Ale Trodder*. The man wore a uniform that none of his crew shared. He had on a yellow coat that was trimmed with red. His pants were red and trimmed with yellow, and bronze buttons adorned his outfit. He also wore a tall, black hat with a ridge that went from the front of his face to the back, and yellow feathers adorned the ridge. Three other men in uniforms came through the gate wearing gray pants, dark blue shirts and long gray coats with white fur trimming the collar and trailing down the edges. They met with Cloran and the brightly dressed captain and the five men talked for a while. At length, one of the men wearing a gray coat—the one with the highest collar—stepped back and saluted Cloran.

"Welcome to Miotes, sailors from Menigah!" he exclaimed. "Forgive us for the formality, but there has been word of marauders in these waters, as of late. We had to be sure you were legitimate. I am sure you sailors are quite weary. Follow me to be duly entertained!"

Greaves and Jenkins helped Darrell to his feet, and the sailors climbed down from the ship to follow the porter through the black metal gate. They stood inside a lobby of sorts within the capital building. People were running this way and that, looking very busy, but many stopped to stare at the newcomers wearing the strange Sea Lion coats. At the west end of the lobby was a white stone arch that led outside to the city, and through it the sailors could see buildings with tall smoke stacks and people talking, walking, running and riding, despite the darkness.

"This way," said the porter, and he led the sailors to a wide stone stairway with a blue carpet running down the center. At the top was a long, well-lit hall with doors and arches on either side and a grand arched door at the end. It was open and guarded, but the sailors could not make out what was through it. The porter led them through the nearest arch on the right side, which led to another long hall lined with eight doors and a window in the wall at the end.

"These are your rooms for as long as you choose to stay," said the porter.

"Where should we go when we want to eat?" asked Richards, holding his belly.

"There are many fine restaurants and pubs, as well as a market nearby where you can get some food. As guests, you will each receive thirty tokens that you can use as currency anywhere in Miotes. Just stop by the exchange office when you are ready."

"When will I be able to speak with King Sakal?" asked Cloran. "I'd really like to tell him why I am here and see how fast we can set sail for home."

"Oh, I do not think you want to sail home at this time of the year. It is too dangerous, especially this far north."

"Yes, I realize that. And really, it would have been wiser not to sail here at all, this close to winter. But I am bound by orders from King Bozin and I must return to Menigah before winter hits."

The porter gave him a funny look, but nodded.

"I understand. King Sakal is in a conference with an ambassador from Rogvelt at the moment, but I believe I can get you in to talk with him today, if you wish."

"That would be perfect."

"All right then, follow me. We will wait for the king to finish his conference."

"Do we have to come too?" asked Darrell, still propped up by Greaves and Jenkins. Cloran laughed.

"No, you boys go explore the city and enjoy yourselves. We will not leave until tomorrow, at the soonest, so get some food and relax!" The porter led Cloran and Len away, leaving the sailors by their rooms.

"I claim this room!" said Richards, and he took the one at the end of the hall on the left by the window. The sailors each chose a room, but didn't stay long and soon convened in the hallway before the window.

"Look, you can see the whole city from here," said Mallory.

Outside they saw it stretch out before them—a sprawling snow-covered city. Tall lamps with large, white glowing bulbs illuminated the roads with bright, flickering yellow lights. Men walked up and down the street with torches on the ends of long poles, relighting lamps that the wind or snow had extinguished. People scurried here and there, attending to their own respective business. A long and wide road lead from the capital in which they stood, and it wound throughout the city.

"Anyone see a good place to eat?" asked Richards, and Greaves pointed out the window.

"There is the market the porter was telling us about."

"Then let's go!" said Richards.

"Hold a minute," said Darrell. "Set me down." Greaves and Jenkins let go of Darrell and he leaned against the wall. "You guys go ahead, I'll stay here. I don't want to be a burden."

"Nonsense, you won't be a burden," said Mallory. "We can't leave you here all alone."

"Let's find you a physician, I am sure there is one in town," said Turner.

"No, I insist," Darrell said crossing his arms. "I don't want to be dragged around town all day. The poison is running its course and I will be fine in a day or two. Just place me in one of those rooms and I'll have a nap."

"Bah, stop it," said Greaves. "What are you thinking? Don't be ridiculous. Here…" Greaves stooped and faced his back against Darrell. "Put your arms around my neck…there you go, like that, now pull yourself up onto my back." Darrell pulled himself forward and as he stood, Greaves wrapped his arms around Darrell's legs.

"See? No burden at all."

"Oh fine, have it your way, but when I can walk again I'll get you back!"

"Sure you will, gimpy," said Greaves.

"Does anyone know where the exchange office is?" asked Jenkins, and the sailors shrugged. "Well let's find it. I may not be as hungry as Richards, but I could use a bite."

The men walked down the hallway and asked a random person where to find the exchange office. They were pointed towards an arch near the stairs, and there they found a long table with many men counting money and tokens. Jenkins told the men who they were, and they were each given thirty tokens to use in town.

The sailors went down the stairs and out into the town. It was cold and the men hugged their coats tightly. All around them, people flew by attending to their busy lives, and the street didn't look anything like what they saw from the window in the capital.

"It will be easy to get lost here," said Turner. "I bet this is how strangers at Stren feel when they see it for the first time. But this place looks a lot tidier than Stren."

"Let's follow this road and see where it takes us," said Jenkins, and they did. They passed many homes, which was peculiar to them, because the housing in Stren was set aside from the main city, but here residents were thrown in alongside the businesses. The sailors passed a carpenter's store, where two men stood cutting and smoothing a long beam of wood. They passed a stable where travelers could rent horses and mules for the day to travel from one end of town to the other. They passed a cart set up with many brightly colored cloths, some rugs, tapestries and clothing, but still saw no sign of the market. People stared at them as they walked by. It must have been a peculiar sight to see six dirty sailors in strange looking coats walking down the street together with Greaves carrying Darrell on his back, but Jenkins took advantage of their popularity.

"Can any of you direct us towards the market?" he asked aloud, and a few people quickly rushed off to continue with their business, but others pointed them north down a side road. Jenkins thanked them and the sailors walked on. The side road must have been a short cut because it was more of an alley than a road, but they emerged to find themselves in the heart of the market.

The scent of the different foods was overwhelming, and Richards ran off without a word to find something to eat.

"He had better not go and lose himself," muttered Turner, and the sailors all went their separate ways to find some food. Darrell and Greaves found a cart selling scallops-on-a-stick, and after buying an impressive number of sticks, they sat down at a nearby round table.

"I feel the strength coming back to my legs," said Darrell. He slid three scallops into his mouth. "Feels all tingly, like when your legs wake up after being sat on for a long time."

"Do you think you will be able to walk soon?" asked Greaves, eating his scallops one by one.

"Maybe. When we're done, let me walk on my own. I may be able to handle it." He had already finished off one stick and was working on a second. "That drug was pretty nasty. I'm glad we all stopped to toast when we did." Greaves raised an eyebrow.

"Enjoying those?" he asked as he watched his friend inhale the scallops. Darrell just grinned with a full mouth and nodded. Turner and Mallory found them and sat down. Mallory had a large egg and Turner had a neat, organized display of perfectly aligned fish.

"What is that?" asked Greaves, pointing at the egg.

"A heated octopus egg with parsley," said Mallory precisely.

"Octopuses lay eggs?"

"Evidentially some do," said Mallory. He pulled a sharpened bone spike out of his pocket. "They gave us these to crack the shell with. They say it's pretty hard." Mallory whacked and chiseled away at the egg before finally making a hole. Satisfied at his victory, he took out a deep spoon and ate the steaming contents like a bowl of soup. Turner wrinkled his nose.

"I've always hated eggs. That's revolting."

Despite Turner's disgust at the egg, he ate the blue and red fish on his plate eagerly. They were all hungry and happy to eat something besides Greaves' cooking.

"How long do we get to stay here?" asked Darrell between bites.

"Probably not long," said Mallory. "Knowing Cloran, he will try to take us out tonight, if he can."

"No, he already said we could rest tonight," said Greaves.

"Oh yeah. Tomorrow then, I'd imagine."

Jenkins and Richards arrived. Jenkins had a large bird on his plate. It looked like a sort of penguin, only it was fat, had a blue beak and blue webbed feet. It looked frightening, but it smelled great. Richards had a plate piled with steaming fried tentacles, and he sat down next to Darrell.

"Jenkins, did Cloran say when we are leaving?" asked Greaves. Jenkins was chewing the meat off of one of the bird's legs, and enjoying it, from all appearances.

"No," he said with a full mouth, "but I assume we will leave early in the morning, if he has his way. I suppose it depends on what King Sakal says."

Darrell had finished his scallops-on-a-stick and was eyeing Richard's tentacles greedily.

"We really should stay here the rest of the winter," said Mallory. "Especially this far north. We have no idea when the sea will just freeze over, trapping us, or whether some storm will come by and swallow us."

"Oh, don't think of such things," said Greaves. "Cloran has been doing this all his life. He knows when it is safe to sail."

Darrell quickly snatched a tentacle off of Richard's plate, and Richards glared at him.

"True, but he may forsake his better instincts and sail anyway in order to fulfill his duty."

"Even so, he has Len with him," Jenkins said, "and Len will talk him out of anything that is too dangerous. I'm not terribly concerned with the winter. No rational sailors would have sailed as late as we have already, and we made it here just fine."

"Well, 'just fine' if you discount all the marauders, Archineans, Man-wraiths, and islands of isolated women that are floating about," said Turner. The men laughed and Greaves got up to get them some drinks.

"We did run into an unusual amount of obstacles this time," said Mallory.

"Yeah," said Jenkins. "It's normally not as eventful as all that on the sea."

Darrell snatched another tentacle from Richards' plate, and Richards slapped his hand.

"Len told me that the Sea was angry at Cloran," said Richards, and he moved his plate away from Darrell. The men sat quietly, eating and thinking.

"If the Sea is angry at Cloran, she won't show us any mercy either," Mallory said, and the men grunted. Greaves came back with the drinks, and the sailors spent the remainder of their meal enjoying the new, yet familiar sounds of the busy little market in Miotes.

Cloran stood outside on a stone balcony, high above the covered harbor overlooking the Ring of Ice, where they had seen the bright light upon arriving. The sky was now as black as coal, and the stars stood out brilliantly. It was cold, but Cloran did not button his coat. He stood silent and unmoving, gazing southward towards home. The porter came up behind him.

"King Sakal is nearly ready to receive you, if you want to wait inside," he said. Cloran nodded and followed the porter, who led him through an arch, down a hallway and towards the throne room. But the porter passed the throne room and Cloran hesitated a moment in front of it.

"Isn't the king in here?" he asked, pointing into the room. The throne room doors were open and looked like they had been for a while. No candles or torches were lit inside the room, and the only light that could be seen was the moonlight that seeped in through vertical slits in the walls. The room itself was dusty and cobwebs adorned the hard throne of white stone. Cloran could see little beyond the throne. All was dark and it looked completely forsaken.

"No, King Sakal doesn't like the throne room very much. He says it's too big and regal, and prefers to conduct business in this conference room. I think it's the actual throne that he dislikes, being made of hard stone and all. He likes the soft leather chairs in here better. He has a thing for chairs."

Cloran followed the porter further down the hall, stopping at an open double-door at the very end where Len stood waiting for him. It was a dark wooden door, elaborately carved, and peering in, Cloran could see that it was a much less formal room, more like a den. Thick tapestries covered the room from wall to wall, and behind them Cloran could see that the walls were paneled with polished, red wood. There was a fireplace at the furthest end with a fire blazing within. In the middle sat a wide table with large chairs all around it, and the king sat on the farthest side talking with a man who stood before him.

Len stood at the door, and he peered through it curiously.

"Cloran, is that who I think it is?" he asked. He pointed into the room at the man that King Sakal was talking with. The man was of an average height. He wore black boots, brown woolen pants and a hooded blue cloak with white fur trim. The man was talking with Sakal and turned his head just enough for Cloran to see his face.

"Why, I believe it is. The Seer of Ketubim?"

Len nodded.

"That's who it looks like to me. What is he doing all the way out here?"

"He's here to negotiate trade between Miotes and Rogvelt," said the porter. "We have lots of sea life here, but little bread and crops, so a trade between our two cities would be a welcome one."

"He looks so young," said Cloran. "But he must be older than my father by now."

"They say he was already old at the onset of the first Nurith War," said Len quietly, staring at the man. "He'll probably be alive and kicking until he runs out of work to do."

King Sakal and the Seer of Ketubim finished their discussion. The Seer bowed to the king and left the room. Cloran and Len watched him as he walked by. He nodded at them and walked towards the stairs at the end of the hallway, disappearing from sight.

King Sakal sat talking cheerfully with a scribe that stood nearby. He was a large man and filled his big leather chair nicely. He wore white pants, white shoes and a white shirt with silver buttons. He did not wear a robe but rather a long gray coat with white fur trim, which seemed to be popular in Miotes. The porter did not enter the room but motioned for Cloran and Len to proceed. The two sailors walked into the presence of King Sakal and stopped before the table. Cloran cleared his throat.

"Greetings King Sakal, my name is—"

"Just a moment, just a moment please," said Sakal, glancing up at Cloran briefly. He turned back to his scribe. "And so the carpenter picked up the tongs, grabbed the blacksmith by the arm and said, 'Anvil? But I thought that was her name!'"

King Sakal burst into a bout of raucous laughter and his scribe chuckled politely. Sakal slapped his leg and then began to cough, but giggled when he was finished.

"Oh, I always liked that one—*Kahm! Ahm, ahm*—it's been my favorite for years. But I suppose we had best—*um, um*—get down to business."

Cloran paused for a moment and cleared his throat again.

"Greetings King Sak—"

"Bring me some roasted penguin haunches, some—*um*—walrus fins, basted in Snowglow oil, mmm…some blue fish and green fish, and maybe even some purple fish, and what is that stuff that goes with the fish? *Um, um, um*—oh yes! some pink crustaceans."

Sakal turned to Cloran and Len.

"Would you two like anything?"

Cloran glanced at Len with a cocked eyebrow, and Len quietly coughed into his fist. He turned back to the king and smiled.

"Ah, no thanks."

"You must have something. Have some—*um, um*—ale. Would you like some ale?"

"Sure."

"Three ales then!" said the king to his scribe, who quickly jotted down the list and ran off.

"There we go. It's always good to take care of some business. So then, you two are—*um, um, um*—sailors, eh?"

"Yes," said Cloran. "As I was saying, my name is—"

"Oh come, sit down, please, I don't want to look up at you, I am short enough standing—*Kahm! Ahm, ahm.*"

263

Cloran and Len obliged the king and took a seat. Cloran hesitated a moment. Sakal waited for him expectantly, wearing a big, comfortable grin, and Cloran shot another curious glance at Len before continuing.

"I am Cloran Hastings, and this is my first mate, Len," said Cloran at last, glad to get at least that far. Len nodded respectfully. He had never been in front of royalty before and didn't quite know what to say, so he decided to say nothing. King Sakal, however, seemed astounded by the names that were presented, and stood up sharply.

"Oh! Cloran Hastings! Captain of—*um, um—Wavegrazer*! Flayer of the Giddendrach and slayer of the Horned Whale! *Kahm! Ahm, ahm.*" Cloran cringed and was about to deny such a title when he paused, remembering that they had actually run into a Horned Whale.

"Hmm, I guess we did kill a Horned Whale."

"Pluck my feathers and call me an otter, I never thought I'd meet living legends! Why, we know all the songs about you here in Miotes."

"There are songs about me?" asked Cloran, mortified.

"Many! My favorite goes like this;

> *King of the waves, marine-man sailing,*
> *Master of winds, white sails flailing—*'"

"Please, stop," said Cloran abruptly. "Not that I don't appreciate it, but there's only so much a fellow can take, heh. The reason I am here is that your brother Bozin has sent me on an errand."

"Bozin! *Kahm! Ahm, ahm.* How is the old coot?"

"Fine, fine. You see, his daughter Celeste has been up here visiting for a while now, and Bozin has sent me to bring her back. I have all the papers right here."

Cloran handed Sakal a sealed letter from Bozin, but Sakal's face had changed. His smile faded and his look grew sullen. The jolly, boisterous man that had first greeted the sailors grew quiet and he furrowed his brow. He cracked the seal quickly, skimmed the note and then set it down on the table. He leaned back in his big leather chair and began to chew on his fingers.

"No, this isn't any good at all," said Sakal at last. "I have become so accustomed to her and I simply can't—*um, um, um*—send her home, not yet, not so soon. I don't have a daughter of my own and she's only been here for a few months."

"Six, actually," said Cloran.

"Aye, six, that's not very many! *Kahm! Ahm, ahm.* She should stay for a good deal longer. Why, she's charmed my entire court, and I'd dearly miss her if she left so soon."

"I understand King Sakal, but that is why I have come all this way. Your brother seemed most earnest." Sakal's eyes twinkled mischievously and he leaned forward.

"Ah, but I have you! It is too close to winter, and you can't set sail at this time of—*um, um*—year. You will stay with me for the winter, and we will treat you well, as only a legend of the sea should be treated!"

Cloran's face was lined with frustration but he tried to hide it with calm words.

"I do appreciate the offer, but I'm afraid I must decline. My orders are to bring Celeste back to Menigah before winter hits, which means I must leave as soon as possible, without any delay. Under normal circumstances I would agree with you, and would gladly stay the winter. But I must bring Celeste back to her father, and I need to leave tomorrow."

"Tomorrow! So soon! *Kahm! Ahm, ahm.* Are you sure you can make it back? As soon as the cold winds arrive, the sea will freeze over and you will be stuck."

"I am sure we can make it back, if we leave soon enough. I wouldn't attempt it if I thought we wouldn't make it."

King Sakal slouched in his chair and rubbed his face with his hands.

"Oh fine," he said. "Fine, fine, fine. It's not like I have a choice! He can have his daughter back. But tell him that she has to—*um, um*—visit me again soon. I guess I had better find a wife and have a child of my own. But that is so much work—*Kahm! Ahm, ahm.* Oh, bother it all."

"Thank you for understanding, I really do appreciate it."

"Bah, don't thank me. What are my options? Say no? *Kahm! Ahm, ahm.* The last thing I need is a fleet from Menigah—*um, um, um*—anchored off the coast, as it were. Ah well, I'm sure Celeste is tired of an old cretin like me anyhow. So you're leaving tomorrow, eh? Do you need anything for your journey south?"

"We really only need to refill on water and get some fresh foods. We have some saved from the trip here, but we may need more if the sailing south is rough."

"I'll have my—*um, um, um*—dockhands fill your ship with whatever foods we can muster for you here in Miotes. We have great seafood! It will be on the deck of your ship when you wake up in the morning. But what about you; is there anything you personally need? Clothes? Some dinner? A new hat, maybe?"

"Why? What's wrong with my hat?"

"Nothing. Well, it is a bit peculiar. That is, we Mioteans have different hats. Would you like one of those?"

Cloran laughed.

"Thank you king, but I have seen one of the Miotean hats on the captain of the *Ale Trodder*, and although they are fit for wearing up here, I think I will stick with my own hat. What I need most of all right now is sleep, so I think I will go find a bed."

Just then, a man came in with a tray full of food and another came with three tall mugs of ale. He placed the tray before the king and the mugs in front of the sailors.

"Ah, sleep," said Sakal. "All right then, if that's what you want. But drink your ale first! You must try our splendid brew— *Kahm! Ahm, ahm.*"

"Gladly!" said Cloran. He and Len lifted their tankards and drained them with a single gulp. Sakal whistled.

"I see you've had some practice!"

"We *are* sailors," said Cloran with a wink, and the king laughed.

"Indeed! Indeed. Sleep well then. I'll be sure to get some provisions ready, and I will see you in the—*um, um, um—* morning!"

With that, the sailors bowed low and left the conference room. The porter closed the large double doors and Cloran and Len found themselves alone in the long hallway. Cloran tried hard to keep his grin concealed.

"Wow," he said.

"Yep," said Len.

It was then that they saw the rest of the sailors walk up the stairs. Darrell was walking unsupported by Greaves, though he limped. They met in the middle of the hall.

"Hey! There you two are," said Richards. "We brought you some food." The sailors then offered Cloran and Len leftover tentacles, scallops, bird meat and fish. Len accepted happily but Cloran took a step back.

"Ah, no thanks boys, I think I will go find something for myself."

"It's really not that bad," said Len, munching on some tentacle, but Cloran grimaced and averted his gaze.

"How was the meeting?" asked Darrell.

"Fine. The king was pleasant enough, though it's plain that he spends far too much time in that room. We are leaving bright and early in the morning. There will be crates of food on deck that will need to be stowed before we leave. And Darrell, I see that you can walk!"

"Yeah, it seems the poison is running its course," said Darrell. "I'm not quite back to where I was, but maybe in the morning I'll be all better."

"I hope so. You boys get some sleep now; I'm off to find something to eat."

Len and the rest of the crew walked back towards their rooms talking, and Cloran walked down the stairs and out towards the city. The fires in the houses and shops burned brightly, and it seemed that most people had gone home for the evening. Cloran sighed.

"Guess I'll have dinner at breakfast," he muttered.

He saw a snow-covered hedge to the right and he slowly walked towards it. It wrapped around the capital and then opened up into a beautifully manicured garden. Short trees dotted the garden with thick, twisted trunks and bumpy stumps that poked up from the ground. They were short of leaves this time of year, but strangely enough, little blue flowers covered them, and they splayed open in the moonlight. Cloran saw many small bushes with blue leaves trimmed into fantastic shapes—there were penguins, giant turtles with long beards, human-like creatures with wide wings, and there was one bush that looked like a tusked reptilian head. Loose snow rested lightly upon the bushes, making them even more life-like in Cloran's eyes.

As he wandered the garden, he saw an old, beat up tree growing beside a wooden banister that looked southeast towards the sea. Cloran walked towards it and leaned against the banister. The full moon rose high in the sky, and it illuminated the Ring of Ice, which absorbed the moonlight and glowed a stunning blue. The sea murmured in the night and the wind blew. Cloran closed his eyes and inhaled. For as long as he could remember, it was the scent of the sea that had tightly gripped his heart, but now he could no longer smell it. At one time, he could taste the inner complexity of the ocean with one breath of air, but now that taste was bland. He opened his eyes and stared at the nearby waves, being born, riding the sea with an angry boldness, and then collapsing back into it as if they had never been. He lowered his head.

"Weird night, eh?" said a voice above him. It startled Cloran and he whipped around. He saw no one behind him, and so he looked above him. King Sakal sat in a brown wooden chair that hung in the branches of the nearby tree. He was smoking a tobacco pipe, made from some sort of white horn, and he snorted big puffs of smoke out of his nostrils.

"What are you doing up there?" asked Cloran, a little befuddled.

"Doing!" said Sakal. "Why, I'm sitting in a tree, *Kahm! Ahm, ahm.* Don't tell me that you never climbed trees as a kid."

"Oh, well yeah, I did," said Cloran, "but I never sat in them with a chair."

"How absurd!" said Sakal. "Chairs were meant for sitting, and trees were meant for climbing. If one wants to sit in a tree, it logically follows to bring a chair! *Kahm! Ahm, ahm.*"

"Hmmm. Makes sense," said Cloran. He looked back out towards the Ring of Ice and sighed again. King Sakal snorted smoke out of his nose.

"Well?" he said. "Aren't you going to answer my question?"

"What question?" asked Cloran.

"Why, I asked you if you thought this was a—*um, um*—weird night, or not."

"Oh. No, I don't think it is a weird night. It's a nice night, actually."

"Hrmph," grunted Sakal. "I'm always happy when I have a nice night. But you don't look happy at all. You look weird, so therefore, it must be a weird night for you."

"It's not that," said Cloran, gazing out to sea. "I just don't find any joy with sailing anymore. I used to, but…"

Cloran looked down and shook his head.

"You look worried," said Sakal. "I used to be worried too, but then I stopped being silly. You need to stop being silly—*Kahm! Ahm, ahm!*"

Cloran snorted.

"Silly? Why do you say that?"

"I say that because it's true!" said Sakal. "What are you worried about?"

Cloran shrugged.

"Weather, time, life—the usual."

"Exactly," said Sakal. "Silly."

Cloran was getting a little annoyed at this point and so he turned around and leaned against the banister. He cocked an eyebrow at King Sakal, who grinned at Cloran, quite pleased with himself. Cloran extended his hand forward.

"Explain," he said.

"Gladly!" said Sakal. "You are worried about weather, time and—*um, um*—life. All men worry about these things. But tell me Cloran; you've slain the Horned Whale, but can you summon the wind?"

"No," said Cloran.

"Well, what about the waves? Can you tell them to be calm, or to carry you to where you want to go?"

"Nope," said Cloran.

"Then the weather is out of your control! What use is there worrying about it?"

Cloran furrowed his brow.

"And what about time? Can you make it go faster or slower?"

Cloran shook his head.

"Well then, my lad, you can't control it either! That's two of three. What was the next one?"

"Life."

"Ah, yes, life, that's a big one," said Sakal, and he stopped to take in a big puff from his pipe. "But tell me—*um, um*—Cloran. Did you choose your mother and father? Or the place of your birth? Or the year you were born?"

"No."

"Can you tell me, with all certainty, everything that will happen to you tomorrow?"

"Well no, but—"

"There, you see?" said Sakal, and he quickly leaned forward in his chair. The chair rocked and appeared like it was about to fall, and Cloran lurched forward to catch him. King Sakal did not fall, however, and Cloran glanced up at the man. Sakal looked Cloran straight in the eyes. The tip of his pipe was in his bearded mouth, and he wore a kind smile.

"Life is like time and weather," he said. "You can manipulate your life like you can harness the wind, and you can sail through life like you sail through time, but just as no man can control the weather or reverse time, the reigns of life are not in our hands. So why worry? It is silly."

Cloran smiled.

"Sure," he said, "but it is also the nature of man to worry about such things, even if it is silly. Maybe one day I'll sit myself down and train myself never to worry. But I'll worry about that when I get home."

Cloran said good-night to the king, and he walked back towards the capital to find his room. Even though he was convinced that he could never stop worrying, his talk with the king had comforted him. Cloran slept all through the night, and he didn't dream.

Len awoke the next morning to a knock at his door. He climbed out of bed and opened it to see Cloran walking down the hall with a torch in hand, waking up the crew.

"Is it morning already?" asked Len with a yawn. Cloran knocked on the last door and spun around.

"Yes it is!" he said grinning. "It's time to get this entourage back to Menigah." The sailors were at their doors, blinking in the torchlight. "Get dressed and get downstairs. Meet at the ship, we have some loading to do before we set off."

The men mumbled and groaned but got ready. Cloran walked downstairs and through the gate to the small harbor. Many men were hauling boxes and barrels of foods and provisions onto *Wavegrazer* for her trip back home. The crew arrived at the dock a few moments later, and climbed aboard to stow away the supplies.

"Many thanks gentlemen," said Cloran to the men of Miotes who had brought them the crates. They waved and went back to their beds to sleep away the rest of the morning.

"Are you sure it's morning?" asked Turner with a yawn. "It is still so dark."

"It certainly is," said Cloran, coming aboard to help with the supplies. "I doubt we will see the sun until midday."

"What about the princess?" asked Len.

"The king will bring her down to the ship shortly. Let's have everything ready for when they get here."

King Sakal had given the sailors quite a lot of food—far more than they really needed—and it was a bit of clever engineering to find room for it all. The men filled the chambers in the bottom of the ship to capacity, and so they stacked the remaining boxes and barrels neatly in the galley. The crew went to their bunks and stowed away the things they had brought with them on land, and Cloran went to his cabin. Papers and maps littered his desk which he folded, stacked, and hid away. His clothes were strewn about, so he picked them up and threw them under his bunk. He took a thin blanket out of the room and walked into the crew's bunkroom. It was a cramped room with six bunks in two stacks, and so Cloran laid his blanket down on the floor between them.

"What's that for?" asked Mallory. He and Turner were finishing putting their things away while the others were topside waiting for the princess.

"This is for me."

"For you? What about your bed?"

"The princess will need a place to stay, and she certainly can't stay in a room full of you oafs," said Cloran with a chuckle. "I don't mind sleeping with you guys on the way back. I am hoping it will be a shorter trip anyhow."

Mallory and Turner did not like this at all.

"Take my bunk," said Turner.

"No, take my bunk," said Mallory. "You can't sleep on the floor."

"Thanks, but keep your bunks. This is my ship and I am comfortable wherever I sleep. With that barrel to comfort my head and this blanket to keep me warm, I should do just fine. But come! Let's see if the princess is here."

The three men went topside to find the rest of the crew sitting on the gunwale or dangling in the riggings, talking amongst themselves.

"Is she here?" asked Cloran but Len shook his head.

"I haven't seen her. Looks like it's just us. Wait up here Cap'n; I am sure she will be by shortly." But she was not by shortly. Cloran waited anxiously for a long while and she didn't come. If they had been someplace warmer, Cloran would have noticed a pink sky dissolve into a blue one as the sun peeked out of the sea, but he was not someplace warmer and the darkness still drenched them.

"Bah," he muttered and began to pace along the deck. Len looked at his captain worriedly.

"No sense being anxious Cap'n," he said. "She will be along anytime now, and we will make good speed going south." Cloran stopped his pacing and glanced at Len, but sighed and smiled.

"You're right. There's no need for me to fret."

He walked over towards Len, sat on the deck with his back against the gunwale, tilted his hat over his eyes and rested there.

"Have you ever met this princess, Len?" asked Darrell. He was dangling in the riggings and seemed to have fully recovered from the Man-wraith poison.

"No, I've never seen her before."

"Do you know whether she is sweet or if she is a brat?"

"I don't know."

"How old is she?"

"Look, I really don't know, your guess is as good as mine."

"I'll bet she is eight."

"What makes you think she is eight?" asked Turner.

"I'm only guessing, but it seems to me that she would still be pretty young."

"I think she is thirteen," said Jenkins. "I remember when Bozin took a wife, and the princess wasn't born much longer after that. So since he was married fourteen years ago, I think his daughter must be thirteen."

"But do you remember the actual day she was born?" asked Greaves. "Because as I recall, it was a few years after they got married before the queen ever gave birth."

"She is ten, I'm sure," said Richards. "It was three or four years after they got married before the queen gave birth."

"It doesn't sound like any of you know what you are talking about," said Len with a laugh.

"I know for sure she is eight," said Darrell earnestly. "I'll give you a wager too. If she is eight, you all have to buy me a drink when we get back to Stren, and if she isn't, I'll buy you all a drink."

"How about we make it so that whoever is closest gets the free drinks," proposed Jenkins, and they all agreed to it. In the end, Darrell was the only one that guessed eight, Jenkins and Turner guessed thirteen, Greaves and Richards guessed ten and Mallory guessed twelve. Len didn't guess, since he was too busy laughing at them all.

At length, the gate opened and out marched a handful of guards. Behind them walked a little girl and the king, escorted by even more guards. They walked right up to the ship and the guards stopped, stepped aside and made an aisle. Cloran began to snore lightly as he lay against the railing, and Len kicked him. Cloran jumped to his feet, muttering something about winter, and then turned around to see the king and the princess.

"Good morning sailors!" said King Sakal with his boisterous voice. "I hope we haven't kept you waiting. Sometimes it takes a few whips with a—*um, um, um*—pillow, as it were, to get me out of bed in the morning. This, gentlemen, is my niece, Princess Celeste."

Celeste stepped forward and curtseyed, and the sailors all bowed. She was taller than the sailors expected and reached to Sakal's shoulder. She had long brown hair, braided in the back, and she wore a blue dress with a green hem and trim. She didn't wear a crown or tiara, but rather a soft velvet strip that kept her hair out of her face. She carried a small bag in one hand, and in the other she had a small white bundle. Cloran walked down the gangway and gave a quick bow before the princess.

"It is good to finally meet you Celeste!" he said. "We have come a long way to fetch you and I hope the trip back will not be too boring for you."

"I like the water Mister Hastings sir, and I don't get bored easily," she said. "Here, I made this for you."

She motioned for Cloran to bow his head, and he did, although a bit confused. Celeste set down her bag and opened up the bundle. It was a string of white flowers tied into a necklace, and she draped it over Cloran's neck.

"I made this out of Snowglows, a pretty flower that only grows on snow. I had never seen one before, until I came here. Do you like it?" Cloran lifted his head and fingered the soft flowers.

"They are beautiful my dear," he said with a grin, "and I shall wear them every time I sail."

Celeste laughed and walked up the ramp. Len and the sailors escorted her towards the cabin to show her the ship.

"Good bye Celeste!" said Sakal on the dock, and she turned and waved at him before climbing below. Sakal sighed and shook his head.

"Now my days will be boring and dull—*Kahm! Ahm, ahm*—without her in my court."

"Don't worry too much," said Cloran with a wink. "I'm sure you'll see her again soon."

"Do you really think so?"

"Ah, well, honestly…no." King Sakal sighed and looked downcast. "But maybe he will let her visit every now and again. Work out a deal with him. He is your brother, after all."

"Yes, that is true. I'll find a way. Or maybe I will just have to sail down to Menigah every summer. Perhaps you could take me!" Cloran cringed.

"Actually, I think I may retire after this."

"Oh? And what for?" Cloran smiled and looked out to sea.

"I've got a precious Snowglow of my own waiting for me," he said.

Sakal laughed.

"Ah, you rascal! But I should have guessed. If there were anything that could keep a man away from the sea, it would be—*um, um*—love. I can see now why you want to leave so soon, and very well! Sail right away, Cloran Hastings, and sail due south. Don't make any stops, and mind the Ring of Ice! It has many tenants."

King Sakal turned and left before Cloran could ask him the meaning of his words, and the guards all left the dock with him. Cloran walked back on deck, pulled up the new gangway, which was a gift from Sakal, and approached the wheel. The dockhands cast off the ropes holding *Wavegrazer* in place, and the sailors pushed away from the dock with their wide-tipped oars. The sailors gently rowed away and Cloran aimed for the exit. Upon emerging, he saw a navy sky adorned with dim stars and a fading moon. Before him and many waves away stood the Ring of Ice, and towards it the creaking ship sailed.

CHAPTER FOURTEEN

Roundshell

Turner escorted Celeste below deck. She was excited to be on the ship and expressed interest in everything. Turner showed her to the captain's cabin, and the sailors followed close behind.

"This is where you can stay," said Turner, opening the door.

"I get this room all to myself?"

"Yes, this is your room now."

"But I am so small and you are all so big. Why do I get my own room?"

"Because you are a princess."

"But I am not a princess at sea. Here I am just another sailor like you, and Cloran is in charge. Shouldn't he get this room?" The sailors chuckled and Turner smiled.

"That makes sense," said Turner, "and while we are at sea you can be a sailor, just like us. But it is also a sailor's custom to let a lady have a room all to herself, and so that is why you get this room."

"But I don't want to be a lady. While I am here, I want to be a boy, and I want to climb the ropes and wear gray clothes and sleep in a bunk." The sailors all laughed but Celeste frowned and crossed her arms.

"I'm serious. I want to be a sailor."

"Tell you what," said Turner. "If you stay in this room, you can be a boy and eat with us and help us on deck. Deal?" Turner offered his hand and Celeste wrinkled her forehead. She put her finger to her chin and said "Hmmm," making a very serious decision, and then grasped his hand and shook it.

"Deal!"

"Celeste," said Darrell quickly. "We were all wondering…how old are you?"

"Why? How old do I look?"

"Oh, twenty!" said Darrell, and "Twenty-five!" said Richards, and "Thirty!" said Jenkins.

"Really? Ha!" she said, "that's because I'm all grown up! But I am ten, even though I don't look it."

"You all owe Greaves and I some drinks!" said Richards with a laugh, and the other sailors grumbled and went topside.

The sails were open and full, and *Wavegrazer* was making good speed. The Ring of Ice grew closer under the cloudless, dark morning sky, and spirits were high. Celeste emerged from below. She was wearing ratty pants, a worn, tucked in shirt and her hair was tied behind her head with a gray strip of cloth.

"What happened to your fancy clothes?" asked Len.

"I am a sailor now, remember? I can't get my good clothes messy. But *shhh!* Don't let my father or uncle know that I have these. 'Those aren't fit for a princess to wear,' they would say."

"Is that Celeste?" asked Cloran from behind the wheel.

"Yep!" she replied. "I've come up here to help."

Cloran blinked.

"Er, I'm not sure it's such a good idea for you to be up here. It can be pretty dangerous and you're small, so it will be easy to lose you."

Celeste lowered her eyes.

"Yes Captain Hastings sir," she said sullenly, and walked towards the door.

"Cap'n," said Turner quickly, "let her stay up here with us. I am sure she will get lonely below deck all alone, and if I were her, I wouldn't want that either."

"I can't have a kid up here getting in the way, Turner."

"I understand, but I'll keep an eye on her. Let me look after her, and I promise she won't get into any trouble." Cloran frowned for a moment but then nodded.

"All right, but watch her well! The last thing we need is a soggy and frostbitten princess." He turned to Celeste who had opened the door. "Go ahead and stick with Turner, Celeste. He will show you the ropes." Celeste brightened up right then and there, and took Turner's hand as he showed her his duties.

The sun finally rose well out of the sea and loomed to the east, warming the sailors in that cold region. The men enjoyed the light while they could and checked all the knots in the ropes, making sure everything was in order as they drew nigh the Ring of Ice. After what seemed to be a very short period of time, the sun began to fall, and soon it was wholly submerged, with the last stray

285

rays of pink sunlight fading as twilight arrived so soon in the course of the day.

"You really weren't kidding when you said we had short days and long nights," said Jenkins from atop the main mast. "I've never seen anything like it."

"Luckily, this is only in the most extreme of northerly places," said Cloran. "One day of sailing south and we should be back to regular day and night cycles."

"Are there other icy places in the world besides Miotes?"

"Not that I have ever seen. I hear the land on which Miotes rests goes even further north, ending last of all at a grand, snow-capped mountain, the largest in the world. But no water that I have ever heard of reaches that far, so I only know by rumor."

The Ring of Ice was now directly before them and stood out, almost glowing as the moon began to appear. The men lowered the sails halfway and then took to the oars. Cloran didn't want to take any risks this close to ice.

"Anyone see that channel we came in through?" asked Cloran, and the sailors scanned the ice face for the opening.

"Not me," said Jenkins. "Try heading east. The ice wall looks less smooth that way. Perhaps we can find the channel there."

Cloran ran the ship parallel to the dazzling blue and white wall of ice and the sailors rowed slowly but firmly. All except Greaves, who was below fixing lunch, and Turner, who was with Celeste at the bow of the ship showing her how to tie knots.

"This one is used for shortening a rope," Turner said. "See here how these two knots aren't tight, and you can make the rope smaller by just pulling here."

"Wow, how long did it take you to invent this knot Turner?"

"Oh, I didn't invent it," said Turner with a chuckle. "These knots are knots that have existed for as long as anyone can remember, and are essential for sailors to know. I like to go through the ropes every now and again and check to make sure they are nice, tight and even. Sometimes these sailors tie them so sloppily..."

Greaves came out onto the deck just then.

"Lunch is made, but I'm not going to deliver it to you! Come and get it now if you want any."

The sailors set down their oars and left their spots to go below with Greaves, except Cloran who still stood at the wheel.

"Come Celeste, let's get some lunch," said Turner.

"Could you bring it to me? I want to practice the knot you just showed me. I bet I can have it memorized by the time you get back!"

"All right, but don't move anywhere."

Turner left Celeste and went below deck. Celeste sat down and began working with her bit of rope, trying hard to get it right.

"No, that's not how he did it," she said to herself. She tugged at one end and it didn't slide. "Now how did it go again?" She unraveled the knots and tried again, but with the same result.

"Aww, I've forgotten already. I'll have to wait until he gets back to show me again."

Celeste stood up and walked to the starboard side of the ship. She leaned over the gunwale and stared at the dark waters. The sun had fully disappeared, leaving no trace, and the sky was now a deep, dark blue. The moon shone brightly and the stars began to sparkle. Despite the almost perpetual darkness in these northern lands, Celeste could see well, due to the ice wall. It caught the light from the moon, which magnified its pale blue glow. The light let off by the ice brightened the whole deck of the ship, and Celeste gazed across the water towards Miotes.

Though she had only been in Miotes for a number of months, she had already grown accustomed to the place. The bustle of the city kept her young mind preoccupied, and Sakal had hired many tutors to keep her busy. They taught her the short history of Miotes as well as the legends of the land, and she often went out into the woods and wild places to learn the names of the plants and animals that inhabited them. Those were her favorite times, when she could wander through the snow-covered forests, but she had always harbored a secret desire to explore the sea. Of all the places in the world, the sea was the most strange, the most uncertain and the most secret. Celeste desired to uncover these secrets, and perhaps now she would have a chance. She was furious at the captain who had taken her to Miotes, so many months before, because he never let her come above deck. She had missed so much on the trip north, but now, maybe Cloran would be able to show her things beyond her wildest imagination, and Celeste became almost giddy with anticipation for the remainder of the journey. She stared off into the darkness and inhaled the frosty air. But she was not the only one staring into the darkness.

The wind picked up and Celeste heard a soft buzzing coming from the ice. She stood up and frowned. She had never heard the wind make such a noise before. It sounded like falling trees, at first, but then it grew louder and closer, sounding much more like stones cascading down a hillside. At last she realized that it wasn't the wind at all, but something riding on the wind, or many things, things with great wings that batted the air, making a tremendous and awful racket. Shadows obscured the brilliance of the ice, and then Celeste saw the glow of a hundred eyes.

At the wheel, Cloran also heard the flapping of wings but he didn't know what to make of it. Shadowy shapes loomed before the ship, and then suddenly one of them landed on the railing. It was the size of a small child and bore a striking resemblance to a woman, only its feet were longer, had only three toes and were built for grasping. Its skin was light blue and dazzling in the moonlight, and it had white, gritty hair that reached to the back of its knees. It was clad in white trappings, weaved from this same coarse hair and Snowglows, and on its body were white markings and symbols. Its face was short and round, and it had earlobes that reached as far as its chin. It stretched out its arms and shrieked, and a fleshy membrane spread from its elbows down the side of its body. It crouched forward and spread its wings—wings that looked like butterfly wings, all blue with white splotches on them, and they grew from the spine of the creature down to its lower back. It alighted and hovered in the air, and Cloran saw two long tails dangle between its legs, each tipped with a pale, luminescent crystal. It squawked again, and dozens more landed on the railing of the ship, some in the shapes of men and others like women, and they swarmed the deck.

A scream came out from where the creatures had swarmed, and then Cloran saw Celeste borne up, grasped by her arms and lifted away from the ship. He didn't even know that she had been on deck since the sails obscured the spot where she and Turner had sat. When he saw her lifted up, his heart leapt into his throat.

"No!" he cried and left the wheel, rushing to the prow of the ship. The wheel spun, the ship jerked and the cabin door flew open.

"What's going…" started Len, but he saw the commotion on deck and rushed to assist Cloran. The sailors were right behind him, and the men dove into the swarm. Turner saw Celeste kicking amidst the winged creatures, and he grabbed her leg.

"I've got you!" he called, but the beasts around him snarled, and focused all their rage on him. They beat him with their sharp tails, ripped his clothes and cut him. They knocked Turner to the deck and he lost his hold of Celeste, but the sailors drew their swords and a sharp ring drove fear into the winged beasts. They became frantic and tried to pull away, but the sailors hacked and hewed down many of the creatures that bit and spat and swiped at them with their tails.

Celeste screamed again and Cloran spotted her, high in the air now, being borne over the waves towards the ice. She kicked and flailed her arms, knocking a few of the creatures hard in the face, but they just hissed and gripped her tighter. Soon Cloran could not see her any longer, and the creatures that were attacking them on the deck started to retreat towards the ice. The sailors swiped at them as they fled, but they were swift and agile, and shortly the men could only see dark shadows against the glowing ice. They heard one soft scream in the night, and then all was silent.

The sailors panted on the deck amidst dozens of the corpses. Cloran ran to the wheel and grasped it firmly, stopping its spinning. The men were nearly dumbfounded, each trying to figure out what had just happened. Turner stood up and ran to the gunwale.

"Celeste!" he cried, and the waves carried his voice to the Ring of Ice. It returned to him, much sadder and more pitiful, and with it came a soft chuckle from the Sea.

*   *   *

Celeste cried out in pain. Her arms were gripped tightly and she couldn't feel her hands. The flutter of thin, blue wings obscured her vision. Through the sea of wings, she caught glimpses of the ice ring, looming ever closer. She felt herself being lifted higher and higher to where the air was far colder than at sea level, and it caught her breath. She could only catch glimpses of the waves below through the rapid movement of wings, but as the creatures drew closer to the ring she could see the ice near the water; pale, rough ice that seemed magnified at that height, and then at length she saw sky, with the top of the ring below her. The creatures brought her down, all buzzing and humming together, and they landed in a large nest made from ice and flowers.

They fussed over her for a while, and Celeste held her head with her arms, terrified of the buzzing and hissing. It was so cold atop the ring, seated in the nest of ice, that Celeste began to shiver violently, her teeth chattering as she held herself to keep warm. At last the beasts left her alone, and flew off to do whatever it is that such creatures do.

With every bit of strength she had, Celeste sat up and gazed over the ledge. Below her, the ice was sheer to the water's edge. She could see a large, round chamber in the ice that led to open sea, and beyond that she could make out the shore of Miotes, but she could not see the city. She saw *Wavegrazer* running parallel to the Ring of Ice, its oars rising and falling, cutting the sea like a knife and flinging water in all directions. She called out, but her voice fell dead in the cold, windy heights. Exhausted, she lay back down in the icy nest and closed her eyes.

What seemed like hours passed in that icy numb of perpetual twilight. She stopped shivering but was still as cold as ever, and her breaths were shorter. She watched the frozen air escape her lungs and hover before drifting off the ledge, and she coughed.

All at once, a small, black shadow peered over her. She sat up with a start and scrambled to the back of the nest, but the shadow didn't move. She stared at it, and soon began to make it out.

It looked like a turtle's head attached to a long neck. It had two black eyes that blinked at her in the cold, and she could see a slight luminescence within them. It had a sharp black beak and, strangely enough, a short green beard that went from the bottom of its beak halfway down its long, scaly neck. It peered at her curiously, then blinked its eyes, turned its head, and peered at her some more.

"My, my," said a voice from the beaked head. "You don't look much like a Frostfly. You are dressed far too strangely, and you don't have wings! No, no you don't look like a Frostfly at all."

Celeste blinked at the head in the darkness.

"What is a Frostfly?" she asked weakly.

"Ah! I knew you weren't! Who ever heard of a Frostfly not knowing what a Frostfly is? Oh, I'm so good at guessing things. Frostflies live in nests like these, built atop the ice. They usually leave their young in the nests until they are old enough to fly. If you aren't a baby Frostfly, what are you doing here?"

Celeste breathed heavily and slowly. She fought off the urge to close her eyes.

"I...I was taken here by these small winged people. They took me from the deck of a ship. That one," she said, and she turned her head towards the sea, but *Wavegrazer* wasn't there. "Oh, no..." she mumbled, and closed her eyes.

"Hey, wake up girl!" said the turtle head, and it pecked her. She lurched awake and turned back towards the head.

"You can't fall asleep up here! If you do, you may not wake up. But I think I have figured out what you are; I am so clever! You must be an offering to Mister Slinky, and we must get you out of here."

"Mister Slinky?"

"Quickly, climb up onto my shell. Let's see if we can keep you from his hungry jaws."

Celeste nodded and struggled to stand up. As she did, she saw that the head did indeed belong to a large, black turtle. His shell was round, hard and black, and very cold. She leaned over the nest and dragged herself onto the turtle's shell, and the turtle helped her with his wrinkled, scaly neck.

"My name is Roundshell, and I live in the caves beneath the ice. What is your name?"

"Celeste."

"And you are a sailor on a ship?"

"Well no, I'm..." she started, but then she grinned. "Yes, I'm a sailor!"

"You're pretty small to be a sailor, but then again, the walking ones have strange customs." Roundshell started waddling across the top of the ring. "You are lucky that I found you! You see, Mister Slinky lives in that round icy room down there. We call him that because he likes to slink around and feast on Frostflies every now and again. But the Frostflies don't like to be eaten, as I am sure you can understand, and so they fly around the sea looking for seals and birds and all sorts of creatures to feed Mister Slinky in exchange for their own lives. I bet that's why they took you, see, and placed you up here to get all numb and sleepy before throwing you into Mister Slinky's lair. I'm so clever!"

Roundshell walked awkwardly around the large pieces of ice atop the ring and was making for what appeared to be a sheer drop at the edge of the ice.

"How will I get back to my ship?"

"All in good time my girl, all in good time. As I was saying, you are lucky I found you here, because I do not normally climb this far up the ice. But I was looking for worms, which sometimes manage to get frozen, and I figured I'd search around the nests to see if the Frostflies had found any. You are very fortunate indeed. Aha! a worm!"

Roundshell stopped and reached down with his long neck and started pecking at the ice. "Oh, what luck, a tasty, tasty worm." He grasped the worm with his beak and threw it into the air, catching it with his mouth and gobbling it up. He sighed in satisfaction and clucked a happy laugh.

Suddenly, Celeste heard a loud shriek and then the buzzing and flapping of wings. The Frostflies squawked and hissed behind her, and upon turning around she saw dozens of them flying her way with their fleshy feet outstretched to snag her.

"Behind us!" she said, and the turtle quickened its clumsy, waddling pace.

"Never fret my girl! They are too late, for we have made it!"

The ledge grew closer and closer, and Celeste gasped with the thought of being plunged over the side. But just as Roundshell reached the ledge, he slowed and carefully outstretched his front two legs. He pushed with his back legs and the turtle tilted over the side. Celeste could now see a well-worn trail that round its way through the ice to end at the sea below.

"Hold your breath Celeste, and hang on tight to Roundshell's round shell!"

The Frostflies cried and wailed behind them and lurched forward to snatch Celeste, but Roundshell pushed off with his feet and spread all four of his stumpy legs out. The two of them slid down the well-worn path at a great speed, and the whole while Roundshell laughed. Celeste closed her eyes as the ocean grew near, and Roundshell slid down the smooth ice until he hit the water.

The turtle plunged into the sea and the Frostflies snarled and hissed in anger at having lost their tribute. Celeste barely had a chance to take a breath before she was submerged in that icy, northern water. The coldness smote her like a thick door closing upon her face and she almost choked, but she held her breath and grasped strongly to the hard shell of the black, bearded turtle.

The wall of ice stretched a great distance below them before disappearing into the darkness. The moonlight shone through the ice and illuminated the water before them. Roundshell dove for what seemed like forever to Celeste, who was struggling to hold her breath, but it really wasn't that long before Roundshell found a large hole in the wall of ice. He swam through the hole and the small passage went up until they surfaced.

Celeste gasped for breath and clung to the shell desperately as Roundshell climbed out of the water and onto land. For land it was, not ice, that they had reached. They were in a large room seemingly chiseled out of the ice wall, and it glowed dimly. The ground was dark and soft, not frozen. To the right, the wall opened up into a narrow but deep channel of water, and it twisted on throughout the ice farther than Celeste could see. Roundshell clumsily waddled over to the center of the room and then turned around to face the water.

"P-p-please, so c-c-cold," Celeste stammered.

"Oh! What's wrong with me?" said Roundshell. "I am sorry; I forgot for a moment that you were a warm-blood. I'll warm you up, but I need to get angry first. Give me a moment..."

Roundshell closed his big black eyes and strained his neck. He clamped his beak tight and his head began to shudder.

"Cursed penguins, sneaking into my cave..." he mumbled to himself, and his shell began to tremble. "Stealing my pretty worms, ah, infernal ice penguins!" His shell began to glow, a faint black glow, until the trembling stopped and his shell dimly shone in the ice room—a sable light that reached every corner. Warmth came to Celeste's bones, and soon she stopped shivering. She stretched her body across his shell to warm every part she could, and her clothing began to dry. After a long while listening to Roundshell mutter about penguins and worms, Celeste felt much better and almost uncomfortably warm. She rolled off of Roundshell's shell and stood on the ground, examining her surroundings.

"Where are we?" she asked. Roundshell yawned, and then his beak snapped shut. He extended his long neck and looked at the princess.

"This is my home. I live here with my son and his wife."

Celeste sat on the ground near the turtle and leaned against his shell.

"Would you like some food?" he asked.

"What have you got?"

Roundshell waddled over to a corner in the room and pointed with his nose.

"Here is what we have."

Sitting in a pile sat the longest, ugliest and fattest worms that Celeste had ever seen, so cold that they could not move to escape.

"Sea worms! The tastiest things there are. We get them by blowing bubbles into the sea floor. They get caught in the air and forced out of the ground, and we snatch them up and have a tasty meal. Try one!"

"Oh, no!" said Celeste recoiling. "I can't eat that. I need real food." Roundshell blinked at her.

"But this is real food," he said, "and some of the best there is. Every turtle would love to have worms like these."

"But I am not a turtle. I am a girl."

"Right, a girl. I knew that. Are you in any terrible hurry to get back to your ship?"

"Well...I am sure the sailors—er, my shipmates, are worried and looking for me."

"We shouldn't keep them waiting then. I can swim around looking for the ship, but before we go, could you do me a favor?"

"Sure, you did save me from the Frostflies after all."

"Great!" said Roundshell eagerly, and he walked over towards the back wall, motioning for Celeste to come. He stopped in front of a small hole in the ice and pointed at it with his beak.

"I have a little granddaughter named Shorttale. She's an inquisitive turtle and runs off all the time to explore. But it is dangerous with Mister Slinky nearby, and I really want to see her back home safe. She crawled into that tunnel and hasn't come out. My son and his wife are far too big to get through that hole, and I am even bigger than they are with this infernal round shell of mine. Do you think you could crawl through and find Shorttale for me?"

"Oh, poor turtle!" said Celeste. "Of course I will look for her."

Before she could enter the hole in the ice, she heard two splashes behind her, and she spun around to see what it was.

Two large turtles emerged from the sea and shook themselves, flinging water everywhere. One had a thin shell but long body, and a short, light green beard with a green fuzzy shell. The other had a robust shell and a long neck with a fuzzy blue shell.

"Ah, my son and his wife! Hide behind me Celeste, I want to surprise them," said Roundshell, and Celeste complied. The two turtles came up to Roundshell and bowed their long necks.

"Hey dad," said one turtle. "Did you find any?"

"Only one, but I already ate it," said Roundshell.

"Well, Longneck and I found thirteen, so that should last us for a few more days. We may have to find another place to live though. The worms seem to be moving away." He shook his shell and a handful of worms fell out. The turtle next to him, who Celeste guessed was Longneck, did likewise, and there was now a nice pile of worms on the ground.

"Go ahead dad, you have the first one."

"I will, but I want to show you something first," said Roundshell. He tapped Celeste with his rear leg, and Celeste stepped out from behind his shell. The two new turtles stepped back nervously.

"Who is this?" asked Longneck.

"This is Celeste. Celeste, this is my son Thinshell and this is his wife Longneck."

"Hello," said Celeste, and she waved at them.

"I am now going to go have a worm, so you three get to know each other!"

Roundshell picked up some of the worms and brought them towards the pile in the back of the chamber. Thinshell looked at Celeste curiously with his black, blinking eyes.

"It is a pleasure to meet you," he asked, "but why are you here? And how did you get here?"

"Roundshell brought me here. He rescued me from the Frostflies."

"What was the old fellow doing up there? It's too dangerous!"

"He said he was looking for worms in the ice."

"He needs to be more careful," said Longneck. "I don't want to lose any more of my family to Mister Slinky. Why did he bring you here?"

"I lost my ship and we were going to go find it," said Celeste, "but he wants me to help him before we do. I was about to go into that hole in the ice and find Shorttale."

The two turtles glanced at each other.

"Oh...poor old turtle," said Longneck with a trembling voice, and she walked away to a corner of the room and lowered her long neck.

"Did I say something?" asked Celeste and Thinshell shook his head.

"I think I must tell you something, while you are here," he said, and he motioned with his head for Celeste to lean closer. "My wife and I had a bunch of eggs, which she laid over in that corner one day," he pointed to where Longneck stood, facing the ice wall with her head touching the ground. "Now, turtle eggs are a peculiar thing, and few of them ever hatch. This time only one egg hatched, and it turned out to be a pretty young girl turtle. We named her Shorttale."

Roundshell began humming as he plucked through the pile of worms, and every now and then he would grab one, swallow it down and laugh.

"This was many years ago, mind you. Our little Shorttale was with us one day while we were swimming around looking for worms. We all found some except her, and she was upset at being the only one not to find any. So while we were asleep that night, she snuck through a small gap in the ice to search for worms. Upon waking up and finding her missing, we were scared, but we heard her calling from the gap, saying that she was stuck. We tried to get through ourselves and rammed up against it, managing to make the gap wider, but we could never make it wide enough for us to fit through." Longneck moaned at this point and shook her head. Roundshell didn't seem to hear, and went on eating his worms.

"We were attempting to widen the gap when Shorttale started crying out loudly saying, 'Mister Slinky! Mister Slinky!' We heard a roar and some strange commotion on the other side of the

302

ice, but then all went quiet. That was the last we ever heard of her, and my poor father has never accepted the fact that she is gone."

Celeste glanced at Longneck who stood sorrowfully at her old nest, and then at Roundshell who ate his worms obliviously. She then turned towards the hole and stared at it before walking towards it.

"Be careful!" called Thinshell nervously. "We don't know what is on the other side!"

Celeste crouched down and peered into the gap. The outside of the hole was chipped and had long, horizontal grooves in it from something batting against it. It was deep and cold, but Celeste got on her hands and knees and began to crawl through. She slowly made her way to the other side, popped her head out the other end and gazed about.

She heard the lapping of water and saw that the chamber she had entered connected to the sea by a channel through the far wall. It was a large circular room and it reminded her of the one she had seen from atop the ring. A thin strip of ice stretched from the hole along the rim of the basin, widening as it went until abruptly ending, falling into the sea. She saw something on the strip of ice, and once she realized what it was, she gasped and covered her mouth. Resting at the very end of the strip and sprinkled with snow lay a small, empty turtle shell.

She almost burst into tears right there, but was startled by a sudden movement in the water. The waves had lapped calmly in that large icy basin, but were abruptly disturbed. Celeste saw what she thought was a scaly fin peek from the waters and move forward before submerging itself. Quickly but quietly, she began crawling back through the hole until she reemerged on the other side. She shuddered at the thought of what might be lurking in those waters and turned around.

Roundshell stood before Celeste, staring at her in wonder with his big round eyes. His beak slowly opened in amazement until at last he gasped with joy.

"Sh-shorttale?" he asked with a hopeful, trembling voice. Celeste looked at him, confused, and glanced at Thinshell, who glanced away and lowered his head. Celeste opened her mouth and struggled for words, not knowing what to say. Roundshell's honest face was lit up with expectation, and at last Celeste understood.

She knelt down in front of the round turtle, threw her arms around his neck and hugged him.

"Shorttale?" he asked again, but Celeste shook her head.

"No, I am not Shorttale."

"Then where is she? I miss Shorttale."

"She is gone."

Roundshell began to tremble and tried to pull away, but Celeste hugged him tight and would not let go. Celeste's presence was warm and comforting to the big turtle, and no matter how hard he tried to push the memory away, it came back to him in a flood. He finally lowered his neck, and it drooped over Celeste's shoulder. One large tear formed in the corner of his black, unblinking eye, and it fell to the ground.

"Gone," he said quietly, and he nuzzled Celeste with his beak. "My little Shorttale is gone."

*   *   *

Wavegrazer drifted slowly in the icy waters, borne by calm winds. Ice bobbed in the wake of the ship and sea birds cooed from their nests in the crevices and shelves of the ring. If anyone had seen the floating ship at that moment, he would have thought the scene serene. But on the deck, Cloran was livid. He knew that the girl should have stayed below. He was mad at the king for sending him, he was mad at the Sea for thwarting him, and he was mad at Turner for convincing him to let her stay topside. Turner said that he would look after her, and it was his responsibility to keep her safe. Cloran felt like lashing out at Turner, hitting something, venting his frustration. But Turner knelt on the deck holding his face in his hands, and they trembled.

Cloran closed his eyes and inhaled the icy air. He knew that to lose his temper and point fingers was the worst thing he could do. He needed Turner on his side, and he didn't want to alienate him. Besides, in the end it was Cloran's responsibility to keep the girl safe, no matter who he delegated the task to. It was his fault for not keeping her safety foremost on his mind, and he would be held accountable. A captain does not lose his temper, even in the direst of circumstances, and this was certainly a dire one. Who could have predicted that winged creatures would have come from nowhere to steal his precious cargo?

"I-I was only gone for a moment…" mumbled Turner under his breath.

"We don't have time to fret about it," said Cloran quickly. "We must find Celeste."

"Captain," said Turner abruptly, standing to his feet. "Let me find her. It was my job to look out for her. I must have this chance."

He looked into the eyes of his captain. Those eyes were unflinching, and he turned away quickly. He could not meet the eyes of the man who had entrusted him with this one responsibility. He had failed—failed in his duty and in doing so, thwarted their entire journey.

"All right," said Cloran calmly from the wheel. "Direct me, Turner. I will sail wherever you point."

Turner glanced up at his captain. Cloran's eyes were stern but they were also devoid of any malice. Turner realized then that he had one chance to redeem himself and make things right. He wiped his eyes and nodded his head quickly. His resolve was strengthened and he clenched his fist.

"Thank you Cap'n. I will find her."

Turner climbed the riggings and the sailors took up their oars. He had no idea where the princess was, but he was going to find her anyway, even if that meant sailing along the whole Ring of Ice. He climbed to the top of the main mast and looked towards the ice. The wall was smooth and seamless, glowing brightly in the

306

darkness, but eastward the wall was rougher and floating ice dotted the water.

"Go east," said Turner, and he pointed. "To that section of wall." Cloran spun the wheel, the sailors dipped their oars, and the ship jerked. Sailing parallel to the Ring of Ice, *Wavegrazer* soon came upon what appeared to be a weak section of the ice wall, with crumbling ice resting at its base and vertical cracks marring the surface. None of the sailors remembered seeing this when they came through the day before, but here it was.

"Look for ledges where she could have been dropped," said Turner. "There may be nests or holes or some other place where those creatures dwell." The men all looked but found nothing. The only living things beside the sailors themselves were a few birds that strutted about with their long legs.

"Look there," said Jenkins, pointing down the wall a ways. Large floating blocks of ice bobbed in the water just before them. A stretch of ice jutted out from the side of the wall, and Cloran had to sail the ship around it. On the other side, the men found themselves at the entrance to a large cove in the ice. It was a round basin that looked like it was hewn into the ring. Cloran saw a thin stretch of ice outline the chamber, and on it he saw something covered with snow, but it was too small to be Celeste. To the right he saw a crumbling channel in the wall, far too narrow for *Wavegrazer* to fit through.

What caught his attention was the crackling singing that reached his ears. Near the opening of the crumbling canal was a single point of ice, and the song was coming from atop it. Mallory raised an eyebrow when he heard the voice and then he smiled.

"No more ships to crush with my jaws,
No more gold to dress my claws.
Even though it's absurd,
I gave my word
To abide by the sailor-man's laws.

A fish is good and savory meat,
Yet none I find for me to eat.
But what's that I heard?
The sound of a bird!
It's time for Munchafish's treat!"

The giant crab stood atop the point of ice and then lunged at a long-legged bird that strode in the water nearby. The birds all around squawked and clumsily flew away, but Munchafish shrieked in delight and chomped down on his prize. The sound of the crab eating was rather unpleasant and feathers, webbed legs and a beak flew through the air. The crab did not seem to notice the ship grow near, and soon they were right behind him. Cloran ordered the anchor to be dropped and the sailors stood up from their rowing.

"Munchafish!" called Mallory. The crab cried out and spun around quickly, snapping at the air with his claws.

"What! What! Who knows Munchafish?" The size of the ship startled him and he dove into the water, only to climb out and scramble to the top of the point of ice.

"It's me, Mallory. Are you being a good crab?"

"Ah! Mallory! Don't sting me with spears. I'm being good, eating fish and munching on birds!" Mallory laughed.

"Good! I knew you would."

"Have you seen a little girl?" called down Turner from the main mast. Munchafish slapped the water with his giant claws.

"A girl! No, I have not seen a girl. I saw a turtle though, and he looked really tasty, but he was fast and was carrying something on his back."

"What was it?"

"A bundle it seemed, all gray. Maybe a pile of worms."

"Celeste was wearing gray clothes," said Darrell, and the crew all called out at once, "Where did it go?"

"Gah! Don't shout at poor Munchafish," said the crab, and he swatted the water with his claws again. "I know where he went, deep into the ice, but it is scary in there, and Munchafish doesn't want to go."

"Just lead us there," said Mallory. "We'll come with you and make sure nothing harms you. We have some Sea Lion meat for you if you help us!"

At the prospect of Sea Lion meat, the crab held still and the little claws and cutters in his mouth buzzed eagerly.

"Oh, Sea Lion meat! That is tasty flesh. Follow me then, I know the way. Do not lose Munchafish!"

The sailors lowered the dinghy and Turner climbed down into the boat.

"I'm coming too," said Mallory. "Someone needs to keep that crab in line!"

Greaves fetched some of the leftover Sea Lion meat and gave it to the two sailors. They cast off the ropes and Turner took the oars in his hands. He glanced up at Cloran and nodded firmly, then rowed away from *Wavegrazer*.

The crab leapt into the water and disappeared. He reappeared for a moment near the opening of the channel before sinking to the sea floor again. He surfaced further down the channel and then disappeared, and so Turner followed the bobbing crab.

The channel led deep into the Ring of Ice, and as far as the sailors could tell, they were passing through its length. Neither of them remembered it being very wide when they traveled through the man-made canal upon first arriving at the ring, but the path they went along never seemed to end as they followed the bobbing crab. The ice on either side of them was course and every now and then, a bit of it crumbled into the sea. Openings in the ice appeared—some wide and others narrow—and these wandered off into places the sailors would never see. The main channel they followed twisted sharply and Mallory directed Turner from the back of the boat.

At last, Munchafish led them to the end of the channel. It stopped abruptly at the entrance to a dark, blue cave. Turner rowed hard until he felt the hull of the small boat scrape against land, and then the two sailors jumped out and pulled the dinghy up out of the sea.

"Through there," said Munchafish nervously, pointing at the cave with a trembling claw. "Turtles in there with gray bundle—scary caves with sharp rocks and twists and turns—I won't go any further!"

"You did well, and thanks for leading us," said Mallory. He reached into the dinghy and threw a large bit of Sea Lion meat into the shallows.

"Ah!" the crab cried, and dove after it. "Tasty meat to be my treat!" The sailors saw lots of bubbles and heard the happy noises of the crab feasting, but then the bubbles disappeared and he never resurfaced.

"I hope we can find our way out," muttered Mallory.

"I'll worry about that after we find Celeste," said Turner.

The two sailors turned and faced the ice cave. Hesitating only a moment, they walked into the luminescent opening and were engulfed by the soft blue glow.

Turner blinked as his eyes adjusted to the dim cave. He saw a pile of worms in one corner and in another he saw two large turtles nuzzled close together, facing the wall of the cave. But in the center of the room he saw an even larger, round-shelled turtle with his neck, as it seemed to him, wrapped around Celeste, who was not moving.

"Celeste!" he cried, and both he and Mallory drew their swords, ready at that very moment to fight off any creatures that had harmed the princess. But as he called out, Celeste stood up quickly and ran to Turner, stopping him.

"Turner! Turner stop! Don't hurt Roundshell." Turner held onto Celeste who clutched his side.

"What happened? Where are those winged creatures?"

"Roundshell here saved me from them. The Frostflies took me up to the top of the ice and left me in their cold, icy nests. Roundshell found me and brought me here. We were just about to go looking for you."

"I'm sorry I didn't go looking for your ship sooner," said Roundshell quietly, and he lumbered over towards the sailors. "I asked Celeste to help me first, even though she ended up helping me in a way I did not anticipate."

A surge of emotions shot through Turner. After all the self-loathing and misery he went through when he found her gone, he wanted revenge on the creatures that had taken her. But they were not here, and he was just so glad that she was safe. He sheathed his sword and picked her up in his arms. She threw an arm around his neck and he held her, facing the turtle.

"I am so relieved that she isn't hurt! You have no idea what fears went through my mind when she was taken."

"I have a slight idea," Roundshell said quietly.

"You should have seen that nest Turner. From so far up, I could see all around, and I saw the ship! You were looking for me, but I couldn't shout loud enough."

"We had no idea where to look," said Turner. "I don't know what we would have done if we couldn't find you. I would have died before I ever stopped looking, I can assure you." He faced the large turtle that stood before him and smiled.

"Thank you so much Roundshell. Count me in your debt, and if you ever need anything, know you have friends with the sailors of *Wavegrazer*!"

"I hope I see you again Roundshell, and I am sorry for what happened. But Thinshell and Longneck love each other, so I am sure that you will once again be a grandfather, someday." The old turtle smiled and bowed his head.

"Thank you Turner, and bless you Celeste! It was good to be in the company of such a polite little girl. I have long missed it. Go now, with swift winds, and beware of Mister Slinky!"

Celeste waved good-bye and Turner carried her towards the dinghy. They climbed into the boat and Mallory pushed it into the water, leaping aboard. Both sailors were overjoyed to see Celeste safe and unharmed, but saved their many questions for later. They now faced the sea, and began the hard task of figuring out how to get out of the icy labyrinth.

CHAPTER FIFTEEN

Mister Slinky

Mallory sat at the front of the boat directing Turner through the ice. The blue cave had disappeared long ago, and the sailors had tried to retrace their steps. Celeste sat at the back of the boat watching Turner row.

"Can I help?" she asked. Turner's arms had long since grown tired but he didn't groan or complain. He slowed his pace a bit to give himself a break, but kept moving forward, eager to return to the ship.

"Sure, come here." Celeste got up and sat on Turner's knee. She grasped the end of each of the oars and moved with Turner's rowing.

"Mallory, do you know where we are going?"

"Yeah, I am almost certain... I remember this block of ice from before."

"That's what you've been saying ever since we left the cave."

"Veer left, down that passage," Mallory said, pointing. Turner (with Celeste's help) nudged the boat left and eased it down the new passage. Mallory frowned as they moved along and shook his head.

"No, this isn't right," he mumbled under his breath.

"What was that?"

"Nothing."

315

"We should be careful," said Celeste. "There are some scary things in these waters. I saw something earlier."

"What did it look like?" asked Mallory.

"Well...I don't know, really. It looked like a wing or...or a fin, with big scales all over it. It was black and green and didn't remind me of anything I have seen before."

"Maybe it was a shark."

"Could be one of the sharks we met when that Horned Whale gutted us," said Turner. But that reminded him of his permanently silver deck and he groaned.

"I don't think those sharks could manage the cold up here. I'm not sure if any shark can. Maybe it was a walrus."

"A walrus with scales?"

Mallory scratched his head.

"No, I guess not. Veer right." Turner nudged the boat right.

"What's to keep those Frostflies from finding us in here?" asked Celeste worriedly, and she eyed the ledges at the very top of the ring.

"Turner and myself," said Mallory. "We won't let them snag you. We killed a bunch of them after they made off with you, and I don't think they would like to fight us again."

"And me! I'll scare them off too. Do you have an extra sword?"

"Ah, I don't. I only have my own. Turner?"

"Nope, only have mine."

"I want one too," pouted Celeste.

"You could ask Cloran for one when we get back."

"Think he will let me have one?"

"No, not really," said Turner, and Mallory laughed.

"Aye, I don't think Cloran would be too keen on giving a ten-year-old a sharp sword."

Just then the sailors heard squawking and shrieking far above them. Shadows flitted across the ice.

"Down!" said Turner and Celeste jumped off his knee and huddled in the bottom of the boat. A group of Frostflies flew across the channel, far above them, and disappeared over the ice. Turner stopped rowing and the sailors kept as quiet as they could.

"Think they saw us?"

"Not sure," said Mallory. "I think we would know by now if they had, though." Celeste peeked over the side of the ship and looked at the sky. Turner began rowing again and Celeste jumped up.

"I want a sword so bad! That's the first thing I'll ask for when we get back."

"Good luck!" said Mallory with a chuckle.

Truthfully, Mallory had no idea where they were. He had a pretty good handle on things when they first left the cave, but by now, he wouldn't have been able to get back it if he tried. His strategy was to choose a path in the ice that seemed to be the widest, in hopes that it would eventually lead back to the sea. Then he could just follow the Ring of Ice around until he found the large round basin where *Wavegrazer* awaited them. But then again, what if he actually managed to find a way through the ring to the southern side? With Cloran on the northern side, he would have to find the original man-made channel or work his way back through the labyrinth.

While Mallory worried about such things, Celeste rowed hard with Turner. But her little arms had finally exhausted themselves and Celeste marveled how at Turner could still be rowing as steady as he was.

"I need a break," she said getting up. She leaned over the back of the boat and stared into the water as the dinghy rowed on. Despite the icy film, she could see surprisingly well, far into its depths. The sea seemed to go on forever, and she saw the sides of the channel fade into blackness. The glow of the ice underwater gave the sea an eerie appearance. It was then she noticed a dim shape appear from the darkness. She squinted curiously as it grew larger. The shape suddenly caught the glow of the ice, and Celeste realized that it was swimming straight for the surface at a great speed.

Suddenly it burst from the waves and Celeste fell back in the boat with a shriek. The sailors stood up and almost drew their swords, but the expectant attack from whatever monster had scared her never came. Celeste crouched in the boat for a long, scared moment before she slowly peered over the edge.

In the water swam a little penguin. It was dark blue with a white chest, and had light blue frills on its head that fell back over its neck, almost like hair. It had a short yellow beak and two glossy, black eyes. It cocked its head to the side and stared at Celeste curiously.

"Mek!"

"What's that?" said Mallory from the front of the boat. "I can't see it."

The penguin submerged itself and then resurfaced. It shook its head and sprayed water at Celeste.

"Mek! Brrr, mek!"

"Ugh, it got me all wet!" said Celeste, and she dried her face on her sleeve.

"Look to the sides," said Turner, rowing gently in the icy channel. The boat passed two ice shelves, one on either side. The sailors heard chattering of all kinds coming from the shelves—squawking and quacking and "Mek! Mek!" over and over again. They were covered with the blue penguins, picking at each other, splashing each other, digging in the ice and swimming.

"Noisy bunch of birds," grumbled Mallory.

"I think they're cute!" said Celeste, and she leaned over the boat again to view her new friend. The penguin scratched its chest with its beak, made a gurgling noise and then splashed Celeste with its flippers.

"Stop that!" said Celeste, wiping her face again.

"Maybe that's a sign of friendship," said Mallory with a laugh.

"Mek, mek!" said the penguin, and it submerged in the freezing water. It resurfaced at the front of the boat by Mallory, then turned and faced it. It then squawked loudly three times.

The penguins on the ice shelves immediately clattered and clucked and began scrambling towards the water. They all dove into the sea and swam under the boat, and the sailors could feel the creatures thwacking the hull of the dinghy with their flippers.

"Are they trying to tip us?" asked Turner as he worked to keep the boat steady with the oars. The penguins all resurfaced by the one that had splashed Celeste, and with a chorus of, "Mek, mek, brrr, mek!" swam away down the icy channel.

"I don't think so," said Mallory. "Row hard Turner, I think we're almost there."

Celeste hopped back onto Turner's knee and the two of them grasped the oars, rowing hard down the channel. The flock of penguins skipped across the surface of the water, making a terrible racket, and then disappeared down a path to the right.

"Right," directed Mallory, and Turner nudged the ship right. The channel widened and the water became thick and murky with bobbing ice and frozen film. The penguins still swam along at great speed, taking a turn here and there, and at each turn Mallory followed them. At last, Mallory saw an opening at the end of the channel in front of him.

"I think we're almost there!"

"It's a good—*huff!*—thing those penguins—*gasp!*—showed up, eh?" said Turner between breaths.

"I knew where I was the whole time."

"Uh-huh."

Back on board, Cloran paced the deck. He was growing impatient and worried for Mallory and Turner. They had been gone for far too long and the crew was getting restless. With every hour, Cloran knew that it would be harder and more hopeless to find Celeste well and whole, but he still had faith in Turner and was sure that if she could be found, he would find her. If not...

Just then, there was a terrible ruckus from the starboard side of the ship. Cloran leaned over to see what was going on, and to his astonishment saw dozens of penguins burst from the ice channel that Munchafish had led Mallory and Turner down. They skipped across the water and swam around the basin before scattering in all directions with squawks and "meks" a-plenty. And then a small dinghy emerged from the channel, carrying two sailors and, to Cloran's great relief, a girl.

"Look what we found!" called Mallory from the front of the boat, and the sailors on board *Wavegrazer* cheered and hooted. The rope ladder was lowered, and Turner helped Celeste up onto it. The sailors hauled the dinghy aboard and then crowded around Celeste to welcome her back. All were relieved that the worst hadn't happened to her, as many of them had feared. Cloran was particularly relieved, and he clapped Turner on the back reassuringly.

"Never doubted you for a moment! Well, not much more than a moment, anyway," he said, and Turner laughed.

"I wish I could take credit, but we probably wouldn't have had much luck finding her without a little help."

"Aye, but had you despaired when she was snatched away, you wouldn't have found her at all. And as for you!" he said to the girl. "It's time to go below, Celeste. At least until we leave these northern waters."

"Yes Cap'n," said Celeste standing straight and making a determined face. "I am a bit sleepy, after all that swimming and breath-holding. Oh! Can I have a sword?"

"A sword!" exclaimed Cloran and he chuckled, shaking his head. But Celeste frowned and wore a very serious face, and so Cloran checked himself, nodding slowly.

"Hmm. Well, the sea can be pretty dangerous, as you found out today already. I suppose it's only fitting for you to have a weapon. I'll see what I can find for you in the morning. But only if you let me teach you how to use it."

"Deal!" said Celeste, overjoyed at the prospect of getting her first sword.

"Better not let her father find out," whispered Len out of the side of his mouth.

"Who said it had to be sharp?" mumbled Cloran, and Len laughed.

Turner accompanied Celeste below and made sure she had enough blankets. When he came topside, he found the sailors at the oars, trying to turn the ship around.

"Where is the opening we came in through?" asked Cloran. "I can't see it from here."

"Right behind us. Well, to port now," said Jenkins. "Just keep turning, it will be in front of us shortly."

"Raise that anchor, let's get out of here."

The sailors struggled with the oars and the anchor, and the ship slowly turned. Cloran faced her towards the exit. Through the gap, he could see land in the distance and the very faint outline of Miotes.

Cloran rubbed his eyes and sighed. The trip had taken its toll on him, and he felt like sleeping for a year. Celeste's abduction was yet another arrow in the quiver the Sea had used against him. She was getting desperate. Cloran felt that at any moment, she would release some evil horror from her bag of tricks, and he wanted to be out of the ice before she did.

All he wanted was to get clear of the northern waters, find a strong southern wind and sail uninterrupted, straight for Stren, to be rid of the Sea forever. The only happy thought on his mind was the memory of Adaire's long auburn hair. The only thing cheerful, her face. It was she whom he longed for above all else, and he realized now that his self-imposed duty was not worth the agonizing separation from her. He questioned his wisdom. *Must I fulfill my duty, even at any cost?*

He could not think of such things now. King Sakal was right; no amount of musing and worrying would change his current situation. He had a job to finish. All he had to do was get out of the ice chamber, find the man-made channel and then sail, as fast as the winds could carry him, until he at last made it home.

Suddenly the waters trembled. A low, familiar moaning filled the chamber and shook the ship. The spray that had frozen to the sails slid off and clattered to the deck. The moan turned sharper and more piercing, and then began to creak and yawn. Then it stopped.

"That sounded like it came from beneath us..." said Jenkins nervously, climbing down from the mast. A bellow emerged from the water again, only it was louder and rose in pitch. It ricocheted off the round chamber walls and the sea within rippled.

"No," said Cloran under his breath. "She wouldn't..."

A wall of water shot up from the sea before the prow of the ship. It spiraled upward and then fell back down. The ship was drenched and the blast of water knocked the sailors over.

As the sea surged, a head appeared in the spray, and it was attached to a long, reptilian neck. The beast fully emerged from the depths and stretched. It yawned, and out of its mouth came the same creaking and moaning they had heard in the distance, the day before. It stretched and its fins touched the sides of the ice chamber, its head looming above them. Its hide was thick, black and covered with bumps and barnacles. Its snake-like neck towered above them and flexed as the beast yawned. Its head was round and long, and curling tusks broke through the upper lip of its blunt, knobby snout like fishhooks. Gray blotches covered its whole body, along with sharp ridges and scales, and its oversized eyes were round with green, narrow pupils. As it yawned, it displayed two rows of razors on its bottom jaw. The crew stood on the deck, astonished as the sea creature closed its mouth and snapped at the air.

"Giddendrach," muttered Cloran, and he closed his eyes.

The Giddendrach at last saw them and shrieked. In anger and joy, it bellowed at the ship, lifting its great spiked tail. It swung it at *Wavegrazer* with one swift motion, snapping off the main mast and flinging it against the ice wall.

"Get your spears!" cried Cloran, and the sailors ran below. The Giddendrach raged in the sea before them and smacked the water with its giant fins, drenching and rocking the ship. The sailors reemerged with spears, hooks and nets, and Celeste ran out onto the deck behind them. She took one look at the creature and screamed.

"Get her below!" Cloran ordered, and Mallory carried the wailing girl back into the bowels of the ship.

"It sure is an ugly brute," said Richards.

"It will look better after I carve it up a bit," said Darrell gripping his spear.

"My poor mast!" said Jenkins, holding a large hook on a rope. "That little worm will pay."

"I'll crack its filthy hide, just like I did the whale," growled Greaves, hefting his chisel.

"You won't be the only one," said Mallory emerging from the ship with his long spear.

"It won't make a meal out of me!" cried Turner, twirling a net, and he flung it at the Giddendrach's head with a grunt.

It stretched across the sea-monster's face and Turner pulled it tight. The Giddendrach tried to howl but it couldn't open its mouth. It thrashed its head and sent Turner flying through the air, who still clung to the end of the rope that held his net tight. Turner skimmed through the water, across the bow of the ship and high into the air.

Jenkins twirled his hook and cast it at the Giddendrach, piercing its lower jar from underneath. The hook went through its scaly skin and stuck into its jawbone. Jenkins quickly wrapped the rope around the stump of the missing mast and the sea-beast jerked. *Wavegrazer* was pulled to and fro across the water, but the Giddendrach's strength was not enough to break free.

With a mighty cry, Darrell, Greaves, Richards and Mallory leapt from the deck and onto the Giddendrach's massive body. Greaves chopped gashes into its hide, the sailors drove their spears in deep, and the Giddendrach wailed. The net around its mouth snapped, and Turner flew through the air. He fell right into the ship's remaining open sail, and then tumbled onto the deck, unconscious. The Giddendrach tried to snap at the nuisances picking at its skin, but its jaw was anchored firmly to the ship. In a mighty rage, the monster bucked like a wild horse, flinging the men on its back in all directions. They plunged into the sea with their spears still stuck in its back.

Len, spear in hand, grasped the rope that was hooked to the beast's jaw and pulled himself along it with his hands. The Giddendrach bucked and jerked, twisting Len's arms, but the first mate of *Wavegrazer* would not let go.

When he reached its head, he climbed up onto its nose and straddled its snout. Their eyes met for a brief, fierce, and hateful moment before Len thrust his long barbed spear into the right eye of the frightful dragon. The spear passed through its eye, lodging itself in the monster's brain, and a river of blood burst forth.

The Giddendrach shrieked madly. No hook or rope could hold it now. The creature thrashed about, heedless of everything. The hook cut through its jaw and released it from *Wavegrazer*, but the spear in its brain inflicted insanity.

Len fell into the water and swam towards the ship. He climbed the ropes that had been thrown over and thrust his wet and feeble body over the gunwale and onto the deck. The rest of the crew had made it back, and Turner was recovering from his fall.

"He's not dead yet, look out!" called Jenkins, and a giant tail splashed into the water right in front of them. *Wavegrazer* was tossed about like a feather in a strong wind. Its remaining mast cracked and its ropes all snapped. The dying sea-lizard squirmed and wriggled like a snake in the water, and the powerful currents it generated drew the ship towards it. The crew instinctively went for the oars and tried to row away from the writhing creature, but the currents were too strong and the oars either snapped or were lost.

"Everyone, get below!" cried Cloran from the wheel, "and do not come topside until I come for you!"

The wheel wrenched in Cloran's hands and he struggled with all his might to turn the ship around. The sailors were tired and drained, but they still had their senses. The shivering men scrambled to get below deck—all but Len. He raced over to his captain.

"Cloran!" he shouted over the din of the screeching sea-beast. "There is nothing more you can do here. If we live, we live out of luck. Come below, quickly!"

"No Len, I must not leave the wheel. If I leave the wheel, these currents will draw us under and we will drown. But I can save us! I can—"

The Giddendrach thrashed wildly and the ship lurched forward. Cloran and Len were thrown back. The ship leaned to the side and the two men slid across the deck. Cloran clung to the stump of the main mast and Len grasped hold of the railing. The wheel spun and *Wavegrazer* drew ever closer towards the flailing creature. The two men crawled with all their might back to the wheel.

"Len…" panted the exhausted Cloran, taking the wheel into his calloused hands. "Len, go below! The waves will knock you overboard if you don't get below immediately."

"I will not go without you Cloran!" said Len defiantly, standing to his feet. "If you stay out here, you will be swept away. Don't be foolish! No one can keep their feet in this torrent."

The Giddendrach was fully submerged now, its last breaths of life bubbling from its bleeding jaw. But still the body twisted and squirmed, and a whirlpool was born. The ship was drawn towards the funnel and began to circle around it, but Cloran stood firm.

"Len I order you, as your captain, to get below immediately!"

His voice was harsh and strong, and Len stood aghast, clinging to the railing in horror. The wind howled and the water lashed at the sides of the ship. *Wavegrazer* seemed to spin uncontrollably. Len looked into the eyes of his captain. Those eyes were unflinching.

"Yes Cap'n!" cried Len sorrowfully, and he clambered towards the cabin with his remaining strength. He opened the door and climbed through, but just as he did, a mighty wave hit the ship, throwing him inside. The door snapped shut behind him and he rolled down the steep stairs, crashing against a bulkhead.

Cloran struggled against the whirlpool with his maimed ship. With a mighty tug, he pulled at the wheel, and it slowly moved. The blue stones within the wheel began to glow, and lightning shot out of them, arcing from stone to stone. The lightning spread to Cloran's hands, and in an instant, engulfed his whole body. Cloran felt his hands tingle and it quickly became painful to hold the wheel, but he did not let go. He planted his feet and wrenched the wheel with all of his might, forcing the ship away from the whirlpool. The stones flashed a bright blue light and Cloran roared.

The ship trembled and tilted to its side. His arms ached and his legs wobbled. He could taste blood. But through it all, Cloran held the wheel tightly and kept a sure footing. As he forced the ship away from the center, a dragon-like head emerged from the water. A spear pierced its eye and its jaw was cut. The head wailed a loathsome wail, and sunk into the depths of the sea, never to surface again. And then the pull of the waters stopped.

"You will not take this ship!" cried Cloran, and he did not release his grasp. "You can use every weapon you have, you vile and treacherous Sea, but you will not take my crew!"

The whirlpool wobbled and failed. A spout of water in the shape of a clawed hand shot up through its center, and rose high above *Wavegrazer*. The ship spun around, but Cloran straightened her with a mighty tug of the wheel and drove her towards the opening in the ice wall, away from that terrible cove.

The spout of water fell, engulfing the deck. Cloran was swept up, his ears and mouth were filled, and all went dark.

Len awoke to a damp cloth mopping his bleeding brow. Celeste was standing over him cleaning his face. His blurry vision started to clear, and he saw that he was resting on a table in the captain's quarters. The crew sat around him wearing worried looks, and when they saw him open his eyes, they all stood and gathered close. Every muscle in his body ached. There was a ringing in his ears. And then he remembered Cloran.

"Where is he?" Len demanded, leaping off the table and staggering to his feet. Celeste looked tired and scared.

"He was topside, last I knew," she said with a trembling voice.

"The ship grew calm just a moment ago," said Richards, "and we've been fumbling around this mess, trying to find a level place to put you."

"That's a nasty bump you've got," said Turner. "You need to lie down."

Len pushed the men aside and climbed over the clutter that had been thrown around during the tempest. He ran down the narrow hallway and stumbled over barrels, crates and foodstuffs that were strewn about. He leapt up the stairs, threw open the door and disappeared outside.

"Len, wait!" called Jenkins, and he followed.

Jenkins emerged from the bowls of the ship and glanced around. The deck was a wreck. Wood, sail and rope were everywhere. The railings were busted and the masts were all gone. He looked around and saw that the Ring of Ice was far behind them. There was no Giddendrach and there were no storm clouds. The sea was as calm as ever. Cloran had managed to drive the ship out. Jenkins could see Miotes a short distance away. He turned and ran up the step towards the wheel.

Len stood quietly by the wheel. Jenkins walked up to him slowly. His face went pale but he didn't say a word. The ship creaked and a few birds circled overhead, but Jenkins fixed his vision to the wheel and covered his mouth. A moment later, he hid his face and silently went below.

Len looked at the empty place near the wheel where his captain had stood for so many years. He looked at that place where his oldest friend had cared for his life and the lives of the crew, putting them above his own. But his captain was not there.

He clenched his fists, straining to hold back tears. After a moment, he regained control, walked over to the wheel and took it into his tired hands. There were no masts, no working sails. The oars were all broken and there were no currents. *Wavegrazer* drifted listlessly in that icy water, but Len still took the wheel. Cloran wouldn't have wanted it empty.

He looked at the sky. The sun was out and the gulls were flying. The smell of the sea was powerful, and it cleared his mind. There was no storm brewing. There were no clouds on the horizon. It was a beautiful day.

Len stood motionless at the wheel as the ship drifted slowly towards land.

* * *

Adaire set down some beer for the men at the table. She collected the empty glasses, endured their flirtatious remarks, and then turned to go back into the kitchen.

Just then, a sailor entered the room. He wore a blue bandanna, a faded blue shirt, ratty blue pants and a grave face.

She ran up to Len eagerly, but Len did not speak. She looked into his eyes and became afraid. He drew her near and hugged her. Then he whispered something into her ear.

Adaire took three shaky steps back, dropped her tray and collapsed to the floor.

CHAPTER SIXTEEN
An Oral History

Ashdun stood outside the Jade Unicorn. It was night, but the lights inside were warm and comforting. He was tired and hungry, but here he could alleviate both. He was a traveling poet, and happened to be one of the most skilled in all of Menigah. He knew every song and every rhyme, and had performed his craft in the greatest of halls. Tonight, however, he was not at a great hall. He was at a simple pub and suffering from traveler's fatigue, and if he could find a meal and a moment's rest by sharing his finely honed art, he would.

He entered and was greeted by the boisterous talking of half-drunk sailors and businessmen, but Ashdun was not daunted. He strode to the very center of the large, cluttered room, took a chair and stood upon it.

"Good evening friends!" he said loudly, and the busy chattering of the patrons ceased while all eyes turned to him. "My name is Ashdun and I am a traveling poet. I know every song and every rhyme, and if any of you would be so kind as to provide me with a meal and a stiff drink, I will gladly share my craft with you all, right here, atop this chair."

The patrons all howled and clapped and slammed their tankards on the tables. "I'll buy you a drink!" called some, "Have a meal on me!" called others and, "Sit at our table!" called even more. Ashdun smiled and cleared his throat.

"Many thanks my good friends, and now, what would you like to hear?" The men all muttered amongst each other, trying to think of a good song when someone shouted out, "Old Roper!" and the rest of the patrons all laughed and clapped and said, "Yes, Old Roper, recite Old Roper!"

Ashdun hummed and tapped his chin.

"That is a good one! But I think I have a better one. I know a sad tale, one that I sang to King Bozin himself not many nights ago, and it left the king and his daughter weeping. It is called The Tale of Cloran Hastings, and happens to be my specialty."

The men in the pub quieted down and glanced at each other. They were familiar with the tale, if only because it hit so close to home.

"Sing, good poet," called one man as he raised his tankard, and the patrons all nodded and raised theirs as well. Ashdun cleared his throat and hummed. He then looked up and his face was drawn, his back was strait and his chest puffed out. When he opened his mouth, low, beautiful notes emerged; slow at first and very soft. His voice graced every ear, and every eye was drawn to the man on the chair as the melody drifted through the room, touching the pity, love and sorrow of every man.

"Wavegrazer was the finest ship
To ever graze the waves,
And yet she hadn't seen the land,
For many blustery days.

Her captain was a mighty man;
Hastings was his name;
He was the finest of the sea,
And was a man of fame.

But in the end his fame, it came
To be his greatest doom;
His fate arrived upon swift hooves,
In early afternoon.

'Cloran Hastings, man of the sea,
Hearken to your king;
You must do a job for me;
My daughter, you must bring.'

The message came at Cloran's rest
After months at sea;
Who is he that hates me so,
To have told the king of me?

But I am bound by duty's call
To do whatever he asks,
To fetch his daughter from the north,
And bear this daunting task.'

Adaire was his ladylove
For whom he forsook the sea,
But fate arrived to claim her prize,
And so she made this plea:

'Promise me,' said Adaire,
'That you will soon return.
For I have waited long for you,
And for your love I yearn.'

'To make this promise would be rash,
For no one knows his fate;
But promise I shall, to ease your mind;
You won't have long to wait.'

Giddendrach did fight the ship,
The sailors fought back bravely;
The men were beat, the masts all broke,
But Cloran fought on gravely.

He took the wheel into hands,
Atop that watery frost.
The Sea—alas!—fought angrily,
And Cloran Hastings was lost.

The crew searched for days on end,

Throughout the Ring of Ice,
But with no sign, the sailors knew,
He'd paid the highest price.

O, Cloran! You hapless soul,
You broke your solemn oath;
Never again will you see she
To whom you were betrothed.

O, Adaire! Your gentle nature
Is reduced to tears,
For the Sea has claimed the man
That you have loved for years.

And you, who listen to this tale,
Take this one thought home:
Never tempt the jealous sea,
Or else you'll die alone."

*   *   *

Far away, in a land unknown to the men of Stren, a woman with red hair pulled a senseless sailor from the sea.

<u>APPENDIX</u>

I. On Naming Conventions

The names of all the characters are in an unknown language, for naturally, if they spoke a language that we do not, they must have given each other names that are unfamiliar to us. I have retained many of these original names, such as Cloran, Bozin, Mundin, Sakal and numerous others. I changed some of them due to their complexity or awkwardness, and replaced them with names not found within the world in order to make the text more readable. Thus, some of the characters have explicitly English names, like Adaire and Percy.

Additionally, I changed Cloran's last name and the proper names of all his crew members due to the unique language conventions of their world. Each profession has its own suffix that is tacked on to the name of a man who works in that profession. The suffix for a sailor is "-ais", and therefore the real surname of every sailor on board *Wavegrazer* ends in "-ais". For example, Greaves' real last name is Graveosais (note the professional suffix). While this made perfect sense to the people in that world, it would have become confusing and distracting to those unfamiliar with their naming customs, and so I changed their names in order to simplify the narrative. The same is true for certain place-names, such as the Reef of Many Graves, though the originals were kept whenever possible (Stren, Rogvelt, etc.).

I made these changes only to help with the flow of the story, and I chose names that closely resembled the originals. The reader must bear this in mind so that he does not think that there is discontinuity within the world in which this tale takes place.

II. On the Nature of the World

This story takes place in a world called Ænurin. Nurin created the Kalani and gave them all names: Jarnok, Goondagk, Sarvest, Justarn, Kerast and Talitar. He also made a bride for himself, whom he named Ænurin (which means "of Nurin").

Ænurin rebelled against Nurin. Her consciousness separated from her physical being, and she split her consciousness into twelve pieces. These twelve pieces became the first twelve humans and gave birth to the six races of humanity. They all lived upon the physical part of Ænurin, which consisted of land, air, and sea.

The Kalani also erred and were sent to guide humanity, but Talitar, the second-born, rebelled against Nurin and corrupted a race of humans. He renamed himself Nurik, and one of his first evil deeds was to dip his hand into the Pendant of Kindlings, which Ænurin herself used to create all plant and animal life when she was still whole, and he cast the evil Noths into existence. Many other tales recount the horrors he did to humanity and his fellow Kalani in full. These tales, as well as a complete account of the foundations of existence, can be read in a separate work entitled simply *Ænurin.*

    The Tale of Cloran Hastings takes place upon this world called Ænurin, only many ages after its foundation. The races of men have changed over time and the Kalani no longer have direct influence over men. Mankind now has a dim recollection of its own history. They believe the Kalani are merely stars or constellations, as Richards demonstrated when he spoke with Esmer, and they hold many other inaccuracies to be true.

III. On the Nurith Wars

The Nurith Wars are referenced a number of times throughout this narrative. A comprehensive history of the Nurith Wars is far too complicated to relate here, but there are a few details that the reader might like to know:

    A) **The First Nurith War** – Nurik sent his Noths to wreak death and destruction, for he hated all things living. There was an island continent that was divided into two halves, one half called Macerios and the other called Pintheo. The Noths seduced a number of men from Pintheo into doing their bidding. These men became known as the Nurith. The Nurith corrupted the governance of Pintheo and convinced them to declare war on Macerios, since relations between the two powers had already been on shaky ground.

Gyrlon, along with a number of other elders from Macerios such as Natalph and Kaedmon, did not know that the Nurith were behind the aggressive Pintheans, and so they defended themselves with force.

B) The Second Nurith War – Gyrlon's son, Rone, continued the fight of his father against the Pintheans. With the help of Natalph, he discovered that the Nurith were the cause of the war, and so he sought to free Pintheo from the evil hand of the Nurith.

C) The Third Nurith War – After the first two Nurith Wars, Macerios and Pintheo merged to become the country called Rogvelt. But Rone and his followers received news that the Noths had infested the lands of Menigah, a landmass far south of them, and were using it as a base of attack against Rogvelt.

This was indeed true. While the first two Nurith Wars were being waged, one powerful Noth named Sheth devised a plan to take control of Menigah. King Linus of Menigah died, and upon his death, the barons quarreled amongst themselves, each wanting to become his successor. One baron named Bozin sought out Sheth and asked for his assistance. Sheth agreed and possessed

Bozin's body, and used him to defeat the other barons and gain control of Menigah. Bozin became king, but Sheth would not leave his body. Instead, he began to build his forces of Noths and Nurith, hoping to take all of Rogvelt.

Therefore, Rone, Natalph, the Seer of Ketubim and many others journeyed to Menigah to fight the Noths and free Bozin from Sheth's possession.

D) The Aftermath – The three Nurith Wars were hard on Menigah, and especially the sailing profession. It wasn't until after the war was over that the economy rekindled and sailors became necessary again for trade. This narrative takes place a number of years after the three Nurith Wars, but not so long after that the memory of the wars was forgotten.

IV. On the Talking Beasts

All beasts that have the powers of speech are descended from a certain group of creatures that were once human. The details can be found in *Ænurin*, but simply, one of the ancient races of mankind became cursed, and their curse was that they and their offspring would forever appear in the shape of beasts.

These men took on the guises of a myriad of different creatures. At first, they resisted their new animal instincts and tried to maintain the dignity of mankind, but as the years went on, each succeeding generation became more beastly, until at length they began to eat, live and kill like beasts. Some of them were able to retain a spark of their humanity and, though they lived as beasts, they treated each other and especially other humans with respect, dignity and kindness. The majority of them, however, fell prey to their animal nature and the only human aspect they retained was their ability to speak. None of them now know that they descend from a race that used to be human, for the practice of record-keeping disappeared within their first few generations.

Most of the beasts in this narrative are actual animal-kind, though a few, such as Munchafish and Roundshell, descend from these ancient cursed men. Care must be taken that they are not confused with monsters, such as the Giddendrach and the Frostflies, for not only do monsters differ from beasts in that they have an innate hatred of humanity, they also differ from the talking-beasts in that they cannot communicate in a sophisticated manner, except amongst each other.

GLOSSARY

Æ

ÆNURIN: Nurin's mate. She rebelled against Nurin and split her consciousness into twelve parts. These parts became humanity. The physical part of her is the world on which humanity resides.

A

ADAIRE: A hostess at the Jade Unicorn. She and Cloran have been in love for many years, but the sea has kept them apart.

ASHDUN: A traveling poet.

ALE TRODDER: A patrol ship of Miotes.

ARCHEEN: Ruler of the Archineans.

ARCHINEANS: Underwater creatures ruled by Archeen who follow a deity named Nodde. They can change between fish and man shape.

B

BALLAD SEA, The: The sea west of Rogvelt.

BLUE BANE: Percy's ship. It has one large blue sail.

BOF: Percy's first mate.

BOZIN, King: The king of the continent of Menigah. His daughter, Princess Celeste, went to visit King Bozin's brother, and she has not yet returned.

C

CELESTE, Princess: The daughter of King Bozin. She left Menigah to visit her uncle.

CLORAN HASTINGS, Captain: Known by many as the best sailor in the world; the Flayer of the Giddendrach and the Slayer of the Horned Whale. These titles really annoy him.

COCKEYED ERNST: A marauder captain.

D

DARRELL: One of Cloran's six sailors. Darrell is a hothead and loves a good fight.

E

ESMER: Richard's love. They met on an enchanted island in the middle of the Sea of Dirges.

F

FROSTFLIES: Human-like winged creatures that live atop the Ring of Ice.

G

GERBALD: A Sea Horse with thick, flowing mane. He is Staghorn's pet and is very strong. He likes tormenting Mallory and spitting water at people.

GIDDENDRACH: An ancient sea creature that appears in the guise of a dragon or serpent. Few have ever seen one and even fewer have lived through the encounter.

GOLDENHÆM: A tree that was ripped from the soil and made golden by Justarn the Gold. It was turned into a dwelling and there Justarn resided.

GOONDAGK: Goondagk the Silver is one of the six Kalani.

GREAVES: One of Cloran's six sailors. Greaves is a strong man and a fierce fighter. He is also the ship's cook, and is a good one, despite Richard's complaints.

GYRLON: One of the four Elders from the Nurith Wars. He was instrumental during the first Nurith War.

H

HORNED WHALE: An ancient sea creature that appears in the guise of a giant whale with a fierce horn jutting from its head. It is said that the whale is hostile and can sink a ship with one strike.

J

JADE UNICORN, The: A pub near the shore in the port town of Stren.

JARNOK: Jarnok the Grey is one of the six Kalani.

JAZOK: Seneschal of King Bozin. A longtime friend of Bozin.

JENKINS: One of Cloran's six sailors. Jenkins is the ship's lookout and spends much of his time at the top of the main mast.

JESSIE: Mallory's wife.

JUSTARN: Justarn the Gold is one of the six Kalani.

K

KAEDMON: One of the Elders from the Nurith Wars. He was instrumental during the first and second Nurith Wars.

KALANI: Beings created by Nurin to glimmer in the night sky. There are six in all.

KERAST: Kerast the Green is one of the six Kalani.

KRACKAMAN: A large, gold-hoarding crab that likes rings, spears and other shiny objects. He is also a poet.

L

LADY WITH THE RED HAIR, The: A woman who walks every day to a fountain in the center of a lake in order to fetch some water.

LANALEE: A mystical woman who taught Old Roper how to make a sail. She married him and lives with him at the bottom of the sea.

LEN, First Mate: The first mate of *Wavegrazer*. He is Cloran's oldest and closest friend, and they take turns sailing the ship.

LINUS, King: The king of Menigah. When he died, the barons struggled amongst themselves for the kingship. Bozin won with the help of the Noth-lord Sheth.

LONGNECK: A female turtle. Wife of Thinshell.

M

MACEREANS: The people of Macerios.

MACERIOS: Before the end of the Nurith Wars, this was the name given to the southern and western lands of the current continent of Rogvelt.

MALLORY: One of Cloran's six sailors. He regrets being away from his wife Jessie and loathes anything that might keep him from her permanently.

MAN-WRAITH: A very pale creature made from a fibrous substance.

MAN-WRAITH CASTLE: A castle that is rumored to be floating in the middle of the Sea of Dirges.

MARV: A Man-wraith. He guards a certain hallway.

MENIGAH: The continent ruled by King Bozin. The heroes of Rogvelt and the Macerean Knights recently freed it from Noth oppression.

MENIGANS: The people of Menigah.

MERCOS: A tailor who lives in Stren.

MERCOS' EMBROIDERY: A tailor shop in Stren. Run by Mercos.

MIOTEANS: The people of Miotes.

MIOTES: An island continent in the far northern regions of the world. King Sakal, the brother of King Bozin, rules over this land.

MUNCHAFISH: A large crab that has given up the life of a thief and leaves men alone, only hunting animals. He is still a poet.

MUNDIN, King: King of the Man-wraiths.

N

NATALPH: One of the four Elders from the Nurith Wars. Little is known about the man, but he always arrives in time of trouble. He hasn't been seen in years. He was instrumental during the first two Nurith Wars.

NURIN: Creator of all.

NURIK: The name Talitar gave himself.

NURITH: Men whom the Noths have corrupted.

NODDE: The deity of the Archineans.

NOTHS: Evil beings brought into the world by Talitar.

O

OGGRANK: A sea-giant that fought against Sarvest the Blue during the earliest age.

OLD ROPER: A nautical hero. It is said that he gave knowledge of the sail to mankind. He is a giant and resides at the bottom of the ocean with his wife Lanalee, and welcomes the spirits of those who die at sea.

P

PENDANT OF KINDLINGS, The: When Ænurin was complete, she formed the Pendant of Kindlings and used it to create all vegetable and animal life. Talitar used it to create the Noths.

PERAN: Mercos' errand boy.

PERCY: One of Cloran and Len's old shipmates under Old Captain Reuben. He captains *Blue Bane*.

PHIL: A Man-wraith. He guards the harbor to the Man-wraith Castle. He likes to thwack large fish with bricks.

PINTHEANS: The people of Pintheo.

PINTHEO: Before the end of the Nurith Wars, this was the name given to the northern lands of the current continent of Rogvelt.

R

REEF OF MANY GRAVES, The: A reef a few days' sail north of Stren. It is a treacherous place.

RICHARDS: One of Cloran's six sailors. He loves to crack a joke, and while his jokes are not malicious, he does get on the crew's nerves at times. He is the youngest member of the crew.

RING OF ICE, The: A large ice ring that separates Miotes from the rest of the sea.

ROGVELT: The unified countries of Macerios and Pintheo. The continent lies far north of the continent of Menigah.

RONE: Gyrlon's son. He was instrumental during the second and third Nurith Wars. He is one of the elders of Rogvelt.

ROUGH WATERS: A marauding vessel.

ROUNDSHELL: An old turtle with a short green beard.

REUBEN, Old Captain: The original captain of *Wavegrazer*. He was Cloran, Len and Percy's old captain.

S

SAKAL, King: Brother of King Bozin. King Sakal rules the continent of Miotes, far in the northern waters of the Sea of Dirges. He has a speech impediment.

SARVEST: Sarvest the Blue is one of the six Kalani.

SEA: A venomous and jealous entity. She destroys at a whim. Once she chooses an object of destruction, she never relents. She cannot stand for her men to be loved by another.

SEA LIONS: Sea animals with the bodies of seals and the heads of lions. They are covered in thick hair and they have long, flowing mane. They make great coats.

SEA OF DIRGES, The: The sea east of Rogvelt and north of Menigah.

SEER OF KETUBIM, The: One of the four Elders from the first Nurith War. He was important to the success of the all three Nurith Wars. He lives on the floating island of Ketubim, which lies near the south-eastern shores of Rogvelt and is a large port city.

SHETH, Noth-lord: Leader of the evil Noths, second only to Nurik. Sheth possessed King Bozin during the Nurith Wars, but he was defeated by Rone and the Macerean Knights.

STAGHORN: A strange man-like creature who collects spears and sits on a little rock island. Plants grow on him. Mermaids throw coral rings at him.

SHORTTAIL: A small, girl turtle. Daughter of Thinshell and Roundneck.

SNOWGLOW: A type of flower that only grows on snow.

STREN: A large port town on the northern tip of Menigah. It is Cloran's hometown and is the capitol city of Menigah.

T

TALITAR: Talitar the Red is one of the six Kalani. He rebelled against Nurin.

THINSHELL: A small, thin turtle with a green beard. Son of Roundshell.

TIMSON: A stranded sailor.

TOSH THE BARKEEP: The barkeep of the Jade Unicorn.

TURNER: One of Cloran's six sailors. He is obsessed with cleanliness and is always getting on the crew for being messy.

W

WAVEGRAZER: Cloran Hastings's ship. Former ship of Old Captain Reuben.

WELLARD: A stranded sailor.

Made in the USA
Lexington, KY
14 December 2012